DAY WITHOUT END

A novel of World War Two

VAN VAN PRAAG

Foreword by Steve W. Chadde

TO DINA

Day Without End
A novel of World War Two

Van Van Praag
with a new Foreword by Steve W. Chadde

Foreword copyright © 2014 by Steve W. Chadde
Printed in the United States of America.

ISBN: 978-1088155936

Day Without End, by Van Van Praag, was first published in 1949 by William Sloane Associates, Inc., New York. The book was reissued in 1951 under the title *Combat.* The original book is now in the public domain.

TYPEFACE: Athelas 10.5/13

FOREWORD

DAY WITHOUT END is a fictional account of a U.S. Army platoon fighting in the difficult hedgerow country of Normandy, France, several weeks after the D-Day landings. The book follows the battle-weary infantrymen, led by Lieutenant Paul Roth, during the course of a single, gut-wrenching day near St. Lô. Their relief, promised for many days, has not come, and except for a handful of green replacements, all of the men are approaching an acute state of battle fatigue. From a pre-dawn patrol to a terrible twilight, Roth's platoon is followed through every protracted moment of a day that seems to have been diverted from the normal course of time and to run on forever.

The brutalization, indignity, and degradation of war are well-portrayed by Van Praag. He records the infantryman's rage at the stupidities and callousness of those higher-up in the chain of command. The Colonel, for example, insists that an impregnable position be taken against impossible odds, or that an untenable and strategically meaningless post be held. The men are strafed and bombed by American planes, and shelled by their own rear-line artillery. Finally, the cumulative effects of 59 days of combat take their toll on the weary Paul Roth, as his burden of leadership responsibility and fatigue lead to his sad collapse.

Little is known abut author Van Praag. The inside cover of the original edition of *Day Without End* states that "he led an informal life. Born in New York City in 1920, he has been a truck salesman, a World's Fair lecturer, a tentative and temporary hobo, and a soldier. Mr. Van Praag spent five years in the army. After enlisting he was promoted through the ranks until he was commissioned a 2nd Lieutenant. He fought in France as a platoon leader, was wounded and returned home a casualty."

The book was the basis for the movie *Men in War* (1951), but the setting was changed to a single day of action in 1950 in the Korean conflict. The Pentagon refused any cooperation with the producer and condemned the film for its depiction of an undisciplined U.S. Army unit.

Day Without End remains a minor classic in the genre of combat accounts of the Normandy campaign following D-Day. Although fictional, the book is realistic in its portrayal of the danger, daily struggles, and boredom experienced by the enlisted men and junior officers fighting at the front lines.

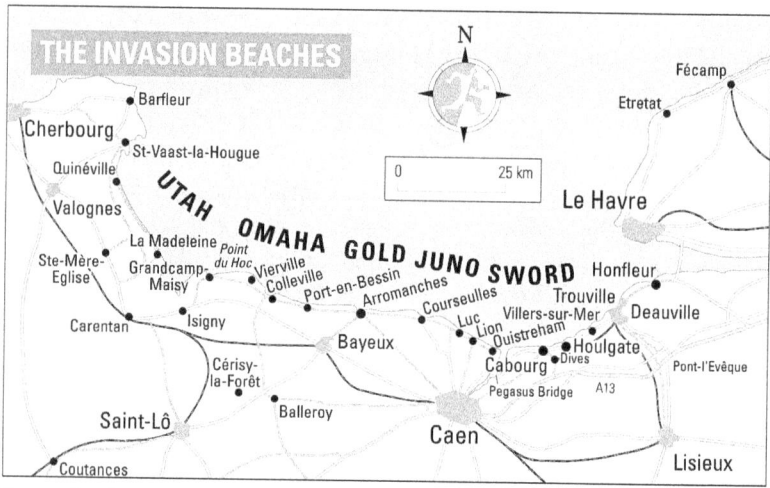

Generalized setting of *Day Without End* in Normandy, France.

DAY WITHOUT END

U.S. GI's rest outside an épicerie (grocery store) in Sainte-Mère-Église, Normandy, France, June 1944.

Chapter One

Through the ground mist dawn began to light the battered fields. Shafts of gray appeared between the leaves of the gnarled trees, and night shadows faded.

Some miles to the south, scattered flashes tore open the hovering day, baring the skies in brief nakedness. Following the flashes came solemn rumbles which echoed from hill to hill, bounded off house and barn and shed doors, and reached down into holes in the ground with mournful promise.

In the east, a flight of planes moaned in the retreat home from a mission over Germany. Antiaircraft batteries from the German side opened up in spasms, their steel fountains spraying up and after the path of the bomber flight.

On the ground, in the fields, cows continued the sad lowing which had been constant throughout the night. They chomped their cuds in frothy cadence, apparently unaware of the sounds of gunfire and planes.

This was Normandy, fifty-eight days after the invasion of France, and the First Platoon of B Company of an infantry regiment held down a position somewhere on that beaten soil, somewhere near a village called St. Mère du Prée.

Paul Roth, the platoon leader, grunted and stirred in his sleep. The vision was more vivid than reality. She was with him again, her breasts, her round arms, lips. . . . He shivered and opened his eyes. He squirmed, alive to the stabs of the sharp roots and rocks lining his foxhole. He twisted and turned to evade the painful edges, but it did no good. He fell back peevishly. His head throbbed, and his eyes burned. There was a warning pulse tapping at his piles.

Men of the platoon, on duty at the hedgerow, nodded, the damp dawn bringing new aches, new necessity for sleep. They rubbed their eyes, scratched their unwashed bodies, and yanked their beards. They blearily squinted toward the enemy position.

A soldier left his post on the embankment, leaned over a foxhole, and impatiently waved his arms, shouting at the sleeping occupant. The sleeping man opened his eyes. He argued, cursed, screamed at the disturber of his sleep, but finally scrambled up out of the hole and stumbled to the hedgerow.

The impatient soldier ran to the weeds behind the littered area of the front line. He tore open the first layer of impregnated twill uniform, the next of khaki, the last of long woolen drawers, then urinated with a relieved sigh.

A series of blasts cracked the silence, and the earth rocked with nauseating vibrations. The impatient soldier slammed himself face down into the muddy pool.

It was the German greeting of the dawn, seven rounds from an eighty-eight. Many hundred yards away, in the Third Battalion's sector, a man's voice raised and lowered in a series of shrieks, crying out in question, fear, agony, loss. He shrieked until there were no shrieks left, then it was silent again along the line.

Paul Roth moved again, and this time he sat up, sure that he could hear his joints creaking, his muscles snapping. He thought ruefully of the dream. It was a nasty way to begin the day.

He lit a cigarette and gazed at the area around him, at the foxholes dug into the hedgerow, at the litter of empty ration cases, water cans, castoff cotton socks, cigarette butts, all the discard that a fighting unit drops when it has stopped for any time.

He smoked and shivered. Two days had gone by since they had been in that position. The first few hours, even the first day, had been welcome relief from constant fighting, but then monotony had taken hold, creating new effects. Nerves tightened. Lying in a hole at night sweating out barrages, screaming-meemies, and strafing was, in one sense, worse than movement and action, the steady pace when a man has very little chance to think.

Roth struggled out of his hole, keeping his back bowed, his head below the thorny top of the hedgerow. He scanned the position, wondering what duty he would first perform. He yawned and scratched himself, remembering dimly the last bath he had had two months before. A bath—he wondered how one would feel now, what it would do for his spirit, his aches, the itching?

He yawned again and glanced down at Verne Potter, the platoon runner, sleeping in the foxhole next to his. Potter lay curled in a tight ball, his right arm locked securely about his rifle, his head resting on his pack. The kid was nineteen, but asleep he looked no more than fourteen.

Roth suddenly threw himself to the ground. A whispering, whishing, shirring flutter burned the air overhead, vibrating louder with each split second until it hit crescendo directly above him. It finally passed and died with a sick hiss in the distance. He picked himself up off the ground and grinned nervously; it was one of their own, a one-fifty-five feeling out a distant enemy installation. He listened until he heard the shell explode with a dull rumble in the far-off hills.

Clutching his carbine, he began to walk down the line of his platoon's position. He moved to the right, toward the sentry posts near the country road. Ten men were stationed along the hedgerow, and the others, the remainder of the platoon's original strength of forty, were asleep in their foxholes. Twenty men should have outposted the position at night, but due to casualties which had not been replaced, only the barest minimum was used. Luck and hope filled the gaps.

Roth stopped about twenty yards from the right corner of his line and leaned over a deep foxhole.

Sergeant Jamborsky, the leader of the second squad, the unit defending the area near the road, lay in the hole. His helmet was pulled down over his brow, and his legs were doubled beneath him. He sat up, startled for a second, as Roth spoke to him.

"How are your men doing?" Roth asked.

"I guess they're okay," the Sergeant said.

"Why aren't you out checking on them now? And why weren't you out last night making your rounds?" Roth snapped.

"I wuz out a coupla times last night, Lieutenant!"

Roth hesitated for a moment before he spoke again. "I made four rounds last night, and each time I passed you were snoring here as though you were back in garrison! What's going on?"

For the past week, whenever he spoke, Jamborsky's lips had quivered. "Gee, I wuz out last night . . . you can ask any of the guys! Christ, ask Schmidt, ask Reubens, ask Saunders! Sure I wuz out! Whaddya take me for anyway, Lieutenant!" he whined.

"Well, stay on your toes, and keep after your squad," Roth said less harshly. "We're all tired, but we can't take any chances on a breakthrough. Remember what happened in the Third Battalion the other night when a couple of men on post fell asleep!"

Roth walked on. He knew there wasn't much he could say to Jamborsky; the man was about finished. He once had been a good squad leader, but when the days had stretched into weeks and the going got tougher, he had lost his spark.

Jamborsky crawled out of his hole and caught up to Roth. He ambled crookedly, his back bowed, his heavy arms reaching to his knees. His round face had become unhealthily puffy, spotted red, and his eyes were swollen.

"When're they gonna relieve us, Lieutenant? When're they gonna relieve us? Geez, we've been in the line for two months!" the Sergeant said, trying unsuccessfully to bare his teeth in a smile.

Roth turned, ill at ease. "We hope next week, maybe sooner. They're still waiting for replacements to come in from the beach."

"Christ, they oughta relieve us! Christ, what in hell do they think we're made of? I heard the other outfits're gettin' relieved every week! Christ, it wuzn't like this in the last war!"

Roth tried to be cheerful, but joy had been lost some weeks past. "That was the last war. Don't worry about it, Jamborsky . . . they'll relieve us when they're ready."

"I hope so! Geez, I hope so!"

The Sergeant's lips were wet, and a bubble of spittle ran down his chin. He mumbled something to himself, turned, and went back to his foxhole. As he walked, his head bobbed as though he were ducking shells. His fingers opened and closed spasmodically, and his shoulders twitched.

Roth knew the Sergeant would either have to be broken to a private, or sent back to the exhaustion center. The man was becoming a danger.

"Anything doing, Schmidt?" Roth said, stopping at the juncture of the hedgerow and the road.

"Haven't seen anything, Lieutenant. Maybe they pulled out," said

Schmidt, a slender, redheaded soldier.

"I don't think so," Roth said. "They'll keep quiet for a few hours... let us think they're asleep... then all hell'll break loose. Say, have you been relieved?"

"I just came on an hour ago. I took Reubens' place," Schmidt said, pointing to a foxhole where a man lay snoring.

"Keep your eyes open... the Jerries are starting to send through a tank at a time as a feeler. In case anything happens, do you think you know enough now about the bazooka?" Schmidt's face brightened. "That's just what I wanted to speak to you about, Lieutenant," he said breathlessly. "I never had much training in the line... do you think there'd be a chance for me to get a truck again? You know, that's what I did most of the time I was in the army."

"Yes, I know... but what can we do? You were sent to us as a rifleman, and I needed you on the bazooka. Maybe if we ever get to a rest area, I'll see what can be done."

"It isn't that I'm afraid to be up here in the line, Lieutenant. It's... you know what I mean... it's that I feel better driving a truck because that's what I was trained for, and I can do a better job."

"We'll see. Anyway, how about the bazooka?"

"I'm no expert, but I guess I can handle it okay. Only I hope I don't have to handle it!"

Roth smiled. "You'll do all right. If anything happens, Reubens will be right along with you. He's had lots of experience."

"When... when're we going to be relieved, Lieutenant?" the young soldier asked shyly.

Roth slowly shook his head. "That I don't know... I don't know," he said, looking to the front, to the too quiet fields. It was the same old question, the main topic of discussion, the subject of prayers, from private on up to colonel.

Roth turned again to Schmidt. "Anything doing in the Second Platoon?" he asked.

"There was a little shooting during the night. Might've been a patrol... sounded like it," Schmidt said.

"Maybe I'll take a look," Roth mused. He hadn't seen Hartley, the Second's leader, since the previous day, and he wondered how he was making out.

Roth turned away from the soldier and looked out across the land. The sun had risen, a low ball on the horizon, and the day had grown somewhat warmer since dawn. There were distant rumblings, and thin wisps of smoke trickled into the sky from behind the distant hills.

The distance, the sun and the sky, and the rising smoke seemed unreal, and even the rumblings, at that moment, were not too threatening. It was the distance, the future, that Paul Roth thought of, hoped for. The entire two months of action had been a dream, a nightmare of fever sweats, of horrors chasing him over the width and breadth of France, and it was only the end of the dream that held any importance. The end of the war, he thought, but even that end might be the one he didn't want, the death from which he tried to shut his eyes, trembled at during dark nights....

"Lieutenant!"

Roth was startled. His head snapped back, and he almost lost his helmet. "Wh... huh?" he stuttered dumbly.

"I just got a call on the 536!"

It was Verne Potter, his runner, still blinking the sleep from his eyes, but looking a lot more alive than when he slept.

"Who was it?" Roth asked.

The runner breathed hard and rested his rifle butt on the ground. "Company Commander, sir. He wants you right away."

"I wonder what's up now?" Roth mumbled, half to himself.

"It... it looks like a patrol. At least, it sounded like it over the radio," Potter offered, his eyes widening in expectation.

"It would be! Christ, they don't even give us a chance to take a morning crap in this outfit!" Roth said peevishly. "All right, come on, let's go."

Potter lifted his rifle, and the two moved off to the rear.

As they walked, Roth angrily kicked at empty cans and ration cartons. He was getting to be the prize sucker, he felt. Since the three other original platoon leaders of the outfit had become casualties, the brunt of patrol missions had fallen on his shoulders. The replacement officers had been with the outfit long enough to take out a patrol! One day in combat was all a man needed to know about being shot at and shooting....

The B Company command post was about four hundred yards behind the front. It stood in a pleasant, parklike area rimmed by ancient oak trees and encircled by a thick, moss-padded stone wall. The command jeep and three jeeps from the Weapons Platoon were dispersed under the trees, hidden from above by the foliage. Some fifty-caliber machine guns, sloppily camouflaged with already dead branches and crumbling leaves, were set up along the periphery of the area as antiaircraft defense. Men on duty at the guns slept near them.

The headquarters group, the runners, drivers, communications men, and mail orderly, had their foxholes dug in a semicircle around the command post. The CP itself was a deep wide pit, braced above with logs, a roofing of tin, and a blanket of earth on top.

Leaving Potter outside, Roth climbed down into the half-dark dugout.

Kaplan, the communications sergeant, was listening in at his field telephone. He nodded to Roth.

Hannegan, the wiry first sergeant from Texas, lay sprawled in a corner wheezily snoring through his open mouth.

Lieutenant Andrew Dougall, the company commander, squatted on the ground, a map spread between his chunky legs. One hand held a red pencil and in his other was a half-chewed K-ration chocolate bar. Dougall was a tall, blond, beefy, powerfully framed man who, before the war, had studied for the opera. He had liked to sing at any time, any place, but for weeks now nobody had heard him sing at all. Much of his beef seemed to have melted away, and his ruddy, handsome face was gaunt with worry and fatigue.

"What's up, Andy?" Roth said.

"You're just the man I want," Dougall said, his mouth filled with chocolate.

"Yeah? What's it this time?" Roth said, knowing already.

"You'll have to take out a patrol," Dougall said.

"Am I the only platoon leader in this lousy outfit?" Roth said, anger rising. "I've been on patrol every single day for two goddam weeks, and I'm sick and tired of it! How long do you expect me to last?"

"You're the only experienced man I've got," Dougall said.

"How about John Hartley?" Roth said, feeling sorry the moment he mentioned his friend's name, and also sorry that he hadn't been able to see him that morning.

"He was on patrol last night. You can't expect him to go out again?"

"Well... no. No, I guess I can't," Roth grumbled.

Dougall gulped down the rest of the chocolate, then stood up and lit a cigarette. He kept his head lowered to avoid the logs bracing the dugout. He spoke quietly. "Hell, do you think I want to keep sending you out day after day? I don't like this any more than you. But this is an order from battalion headquarters . . . they want the most experienced man to go on this patrol."

Tears of rage and impotence started to Roth's eyes. "The hell with battalion! If those bastards are so goddamned smart, why aren't they up here doing the fighting, instead of sitting on their asses thinking up a patrol every time they don't have what to do!"

Dougall nodded his head. "I agree with you . . . but what can I do? Orders are orders."

"If you'd only let me get on the phone, I'd tell Wormsley a thing or two!" Roth shouted. "That bastard is supposed to be the S-2, and we're doing all his lousy patrol work for him!"

"Don't get excited. You know bitching won't do any good," Dougall said.

Roth laughed hoarsely. "I've learned that enough times. Well, what's it going to be today?" he said, rubbing his eyes with his knuckles.

Dougall clapped Roth on the shoulder. "Good! They want you to get around the left flank of St. Mère du Prée, and see what's doing," he said.

Dougall picked up the map from the floor and showed Roth the sections he had marked in with pencil. "You're to move down this draw until you come to the sunken road. Cross the sunken road and move along this line of trees until you come to the road at the right of the village. Colonel Nielsen wants you to engage in a fire fight and see what they've got in the town."

"How many men do I take along?"

"Ten."

"How many casualties does he want me to take?" Roth asked.

"None . . . if you can help it. Set up a base of fire, and keep in constant contact with us. You're to hold the position until you're given orders to withdraw."

"Sounds like a good deal . . . me and ten men against the whole German Army! Maybe they'd like us to move on to Berlin, after we've cleaned out this place?"

"I'm sorry, Paul, but it's all we can spare. You'll have to do your best."

Dougall handed Roth the map and set his watch with the platoon leader's. "Move out at nine," he stated with finality.

Roth looked at his watch again. "That gives me about an hour. How about artillery?" he asked.

"You don't get any. Everything is tied up for some other mission."
"Daniel Boone and his ten boy scouts, huh?"
Dougall smiled.
Roth smiled faintly and climbed out of the dugout.

Chapter Two

FIRST BATTALION HEADQUARTERS was dispersed in and about a small farmyard five hundred yards to the left and in front of a strategic crossroads. Dugouts and foxholes had been dug in the yard, far enough from the stone farmhouse to be clear of collapsing walls in the event of shellfire. Drivers lounged around their jeeps and trucks, smoking and lazily chatting. The Intelligence Platoon lay sleeping in their foxholes. The night before they had been out on a patrol in maintenance of contact with the Third Battalion on the right.

Lieutenant Colonel Nielsen, Lieutenant Wormsley, an enlisted man, and a German prisoner stood near the entrance to the command dugout.

Nielsen was attempting to question the prisoner. "What outfit are you from?" he demanded for the tenth time.

The prisoner, a short stocky blond man, smiled. "Gerhard Spausler, 625492," he repeated in nearly perfect English.

Nielsen removed his helmet from his bald, sweating skull. "Goddamit, man! Tell me what outfit you're from, or well really show you how tough we can get!"

"Gerhard Spausler, 625492." The German looked with contempt at the Battalion Commander.

"Let me try him, sir," requested Wormsley.

"Go ahead." The Colonel gestured impatiently with his hand.

"What's the 4th SS Regiment doing now?" asked Wormsley in a friendly tone. "Are you still being held in reserve?"

The German prisoner continued to smile. His teeth were yellow, and there was a black gap in front, where one tooth was missing.

Nielsen wanted to place a handkerchief under his nose. The German gave off a sour, unwashed odor.

Wormsley continued to try friendliness. "We know you're from the 4th, but all we want is verification for our records. You give us the information we want, and nobody will be the wiser. We'll send you back to a prisoner-of-war camp, and the war'll be over for you."

The German still smiled arrogantly.

"You'll have more to eat than you've had the last ten years," the Battalion Intelligence Officer went on. "And you only work eight hours a day. Anything you want to do ... you have your choice."

The prisoner laughed.

The Colonel's face became red with anger. "That's enough, Wormsley! We'll try the other cure! Show him that we're not as softhearted as he's been taught!"

Wormsley liked the smooth approach. He felt that he was born to be a diplomat. "I believe I can get what we want from him, sir, if you'll only give me a little more time."

"You've had enough time," said the Colonel. "You've worked on him all morning, and see how far you've got!"

The enlisted man, a tall powerfully built sergeant, glanced expectantly at the Battalion Commander. He ran his tongue over his lips as though they had suddenly gone dry, and his hand squeezed the barrel of his rifle until the knuckles became white.

The Colonel turned to the prisoner. "Corporal, are you going to give us the information? This is the last time I'll ask you."

The prisoner spat in the dust.

Colonel Nielsen's lips trembled slightly. "Sergeant, exercise this man!" He beckoned to Lieutenant Wormsley, and the two climbed down into the dugout.

The Sergeant lifted his rifle, attached his bayonet to the stud on the barrel, and held it at high port. He smiled coldly. "My name is Wishnewsky," he said to the prisoner. "Does the name mean anything to you?"

"Why should it?" said the German.

"It's a Polish name," said the Sergeant.

"There are many Polish names," said the prisoner dryly. "Even some of us Germans have Polish names."

"Not this boy," said Wishnewsky. "I was born in Warsaw." The prisoner shrugged his shoulders.

"Achtung! March! Start marching!" ordered the Sergeant. The German moved off at a slow pace.

"Faster!" said the Sergeant. "March in a circle!"

The prisoner picked up the pace.

Wishnewsky lightly pricked the point of his bayonet against the prisoner's buttocks, and the German's body snapped forward in a jerking motion. He looked behind at his tormenter. "The Geneva rules ...!"

"There ain't no Geneva here!" snarled Wishnewsky. "And there wasn't no Geneva in Warsaw! Double time!"

The German began to trot, with the Sergeant behind him. The prisoner's knees were trembling as he ran.

"Faster, you German Hitler son of a bitch!" the Sergeant shouted; he jammed the point of the bayonet brutally into the prisoner's buttocks.

The German turned his head for a moment; the expression of arrogance had disappeared from his face.

"Remember Warsaw!" taunted Wishnewsky. "You blew my father's head off, and whipped my mother to death!" He inverted his rifle and clubbed the butt against the upper part of the prisoner's back.

The prisoner fell to his knees and began to plead, but the words would not come out of his mouth.

"Get up, you friggin' son of a bitch!" The Sergeant swung the full force of his combat shoe between the German's legs, catching him under the testicles.

In a clawing, swimming contortion the prisoner struggled to his feet and again began to run with his body doubled over.

"Remember Warsaw!" the Sergeant screamed. His helmet had fallen off, and his black hair blew wildly in the breeze. "Remember Warsaw! You took my sisters to your slave camps! Run, you dirty stinking bastard! Keep running until you're ready to talk!"

The prisoner ran, and gagging sobs tore from his chest Again he stumbled to the ground; he cried in terrified shrieks. "Please ... please ... please, I can't run ... my breath ...!" Spittle ran down his chin.

Wishnewsky bent over, grabbed the prisoner by the hair and yanked him to his feet. A handful of hair ripped out and stuck to his hand. He again swung his foot, missed the German's buttocks, but caught him on the calf of his leg. "Run until you're ready to talk!" He prodded him with the bayonet. A small blob of blood shone on the pointed tip.

The German ran a few more paces and fell to the ground. He groveled in the dust, his hands clenched up to the Sergeant in an attitude of prayer. Huge sobs shook his body, and his mouth was covered with foam as though he had half completed a shaving ritual. "I'll give you information!" he moaned. "Please... no more... I'll talk...!"

Wishnewsky's fingers curled as he controlled the impulse to finish the job. He aimed one last kick at the prisoner and caught him in the ribs. He walked over to the dark entrance of the dugout and called down: "He's ready, sir. Easier than I expected, too." He smiled.

Toward the German lines, in a thicket, an American soldier lay wounded, dying. The fields were a green pain, the skies a blurring gray of torture, and the trees swayed to the tune of his flesh pounding, tearing impotently, and all was covered by a searing red of high sun's fire. The soldier's clotted face contorted, as if by this effort the torn dead body could move slightly and frighten away the feeding flies and maggots. One cluster fed on his leg, and a crawling mass of fat grubby creatures squirmed over the wide bloody emptiness where his stomach had been.

He turned his eyes away, back to the fields and the skies. Sometimes it was easy to forget when the arms and the legs were throbbing, but this moment all was numbness, a death, save for the feeding on his living portions.

A day. Two. Three. How many days for complete death, instead of this foul half state, the soul already gone and the body screaming for release? His head was in a hole; the pressure bore through the ground and knives pressed into the soft bones of his skull.

They would never come for him. Dead. All was dead. The company wiped out. The war over. Why didn't they come and bury him?

Foul stink; it dried under him caked into scales clinging to his flesh. Putrefaction blown on the wind. Enemy flesh. Too strong. His rotting flesh burning under his nostrils. No more puke left to puke. He moaned and closed his eyes and prayed for a shell to finish the death.

The hand of mother coming in out of the night, soothing and

healing his fever, and a cup of tea with lemon. Dancing nightmare in a day too long, the night everlasting. He couldn't die. Immortal as the saints in the book. Crap on all the gods! Holy Mary Mother of God!

He willed himself to death and it would not come; he was corruption without release. Maggots crawling, and the grave not dug. No shovels, no earth, no coffin. No death. A shell exploded in the distance, a thousand miles in the distance, and no death. The maggots crawled and grew fat and laughed, their bellies filled with rotting blood. He willed death. Holy Mary!

Paul Roth leaned his back against the hedgerow and removed his helmet. He took out the fiber liner and poured three inches of water from his canteen into the metal section. He found a steel mirror at the bottom of his pack and examined his face. Exhaustion showed in his bloodshot eyes, and the reddish beard, which made him look fifteen years older than his twenty-five, was encrusted with dirt. He wondered what friends, the people back home, might think if they could see him now.

A shave might help his spirits, but there wasn't enough water for a shave, and besides he'd probably yank off half his skin in the attempt. He dipped his hands into the rancid water, cupped his palms, and splashed his face.

Rodriguez, the Mexican-Indian platoon sergeant from Arizona, lay on his back near Roth. He was a slender, delicately shaped man of thirty.

"Yes, sir," the Sergeant was saying, mostly to himself, "the old army really was tough! I'll never forget, back in thirty-eight, when we hiked from Fort Benning to Fort Jackson. A hundred and twenty in the sun, and carrying full field equipment!" He shook his head reminiscently.

Roth turned from the mirror. "I suppose this isn't tough?" he said, smiling.

"I ain't saying this isn't tough. Only in the old days they had soldiers! Now these draftees . . . they just don't have the stuff."

"Where are all your old regular army men . . . now?"

Rodriguez yanked reflectively at his ear. "It beats me, sir. Maybe they're all generals now. You know, I can remember when Colonel Nielsen was just a shavetail . . . all proud and shined up in his new pinks, and couldn't get out of his own way!"

"He manages to get in our way pretty often," Roth said.

"Yes, sir. I guess he's changed lots since he had a platoon."

Roth again held the mirror to his face. He removed a dusty comb from his back pocket and ran it through his hair, but the scrubby knots, formed by the pressure of his helmet, merely sprang back into place. He put the comb in his pocket, replaced the mirror in his pack, and stretched out on the ground.

Roth glanced at his platoon sergeant. "Let me know when fifteen minutes are up, Rodriguez. I want to see if I can catch a nap before the patrol."

Rodriguez stood up and scratched his behind. "I'll check on the men meanwhile . . . see if they're getting ready."

Roth closed his eyes. "Okay," he murmured.

Carlos Motoya squirted a thin stream of tobacco juice at an empty ration box. "Ho! You think this is war! A few shells at night, a mortar shell. . . a night patrol? Just you wait!" He stretched languidly and shifted his body to a more comfortable position against the hedgerow.

Jamborsky's body was half in his foxhole, his head sunk low between his shoulders. "Whaddya wanta do, discourage the guy? He's new, give him time . . . he'll learn!" His eyes blinked, and his head jerked slightly.

"I realize it's rough, no pink tea," said McCrea, a clean-cut man in his middle thirties. "I asked for it . . . and here I am."

"Ah, some guys are crazy!" exclaimed Reubens, puffing out his round cheeks contemptuously. "I'm here because I gotta be. A personal letter from the President, they give me a gun, tell me to salute all officers. . . so here I am." He gestured expansively with his arms. "The next lecture will be on military courtesy and discipline!"

The four men, recently awakened by Sergeant Rodriguez, were sprawled about Sergeant Jamborsky's foxhole. They yawned and belched and flatulated, and had been grousing about the impending patrol. McCrea, a new replacement, was excited. He had joined the outfit two days before, and it was to be his first action.

Motoya continued in the same mood. "I'm sick and tired of waiting! Why don't we move? We're getting slow . . . some night we'll relax. We do it now. They'll sneak in behind us.

Then . . . whoosh! It's the knife or bayonet!" He made a slicing motion with his hand across his throat.

"Baloney, there's nobody gonna sneak in!" said Jamborsky, the tic on his face becoming more pronounced.

"No?" said Motoya. "That's what you think! They ain't so dumb!"

"So what!" said Reubens. "So they'll cut our throats. That'll be *some* relief!" He laughed hoarsely, not knowing what his laughter was about.

"Cut it out!" said Jamborsky. "Whaddya trying to do, scare McCrea?"

Motoya laughed sarcastically and slapped the dusty earth with his hands. "You ain't worried about no one but yourself! Whatsa matter, Sarge, losin' your nerve?"

"Who's losin' whose nerve?" bellowed Jamborsky aggressively, half rising out of his hole.

"Sit down and shut up!" said Motoya. "You don't fool me!"

"Who's losin' whose nerve?" Jamborsky repeated and sank back into his hole.

Motoya waved his arm in a gesture of dismissal. He didn't want to push old "Jam" too far. The poor bastard was cracking, it was easy to see that. More than anything else, he felt sorry for him.

With shaking hands Jamborsky lit a cigarette and tried to appear unconcerned about the last accusation. He noticed that the men knew he was going. But he couldn't help it. He wasn't made for fifty-eight days in the line. A week or two weeks was okay, but not fifty-eight solid, backbreaking days. He had to go, one way or the other. There was no way out; he was caught in between.

McCrea saw the knowing looks cross each man's face, and he felt embarrassed. "I . . . I heard the Lieutenant say they're straightening out the lines," he spoke, trying to appear cheerful. "When they've done that, then we're supposed to move."

"They're always straightening out lines, or reorganizing!" said Reubens. "Whenever we're stuck, they have some excuse ready! I don't think the bastards running this show know what in the hell they're doing!"

"I wish I was a general," said Motoya. "Nothing to do all day but walk around in fresh pinks, and lay the French broads. That's the life for me! I should have stayed over the hill!"

"I wouldn't want the responsibility," said Reubens. "The layin' part's okay, but not the responsibility."

"Christ, what kind of responsibility is there to sending a bunch of jerks out to be killed?" said Motoya.

"You'd be surprised . . . you'd be surprised," said Reubens.

"I saw Eisenhower when we were coming through the replacement depot," offered McCrea. "Boy, he's a swell guy!"

"That's just the racket!" said Motoya. "They act nice to your face, and they always got the knife ready!"

"Not Eisenhower," said Reubens. "From what I hear, he's a pretty good guy. Got the welfare of his men first."

"You can shove 'em all!" said Motoya. "I should've stayed in London!"

"They would've caught up with you," said Reubens.

"Not this guy," said Motoya, thumping his chest in boast. "Where I was shacked up, they'd of never got me!"

"Then why did you come back?" asked Reubens.

"I don't know," said Motoya. "Maybe . . . maybe I was homesick, or something."

A sharp crack, as if a large limb had broken, interrupted the conversation of the four men, and as a unit they hit the ground. Jamborsky shrank into his hole, his head between his legs and his hands grasping his ankles.

McCrea, Motoya, and Reubens lifted their faces anxiously from the dust. "Who's shootin'?" screamed Motoya.

"Sniper!" called a voice from the hedgerow.

"Where is he?" shouted Motoya.

"I can't see the son of a bitch!" called Hugo Schlenk from his post on the hedgerow.

Motoya spat into the dust, cradled his rifle in his arms, and began to crawl towards the hedgerow.

"Where in the hell you goin'?" hissed Reubens.

"I'm gonna see if I can get the bastard!" muttered Motoya. He wanted to kill, couldn't stand the idea of Germans and snipers, and him being out there. He wanted to kill, the more the better.

A chorus of voices were shouting from all along the hedgerow: "Where is the son of a bitch?" "Watch the dirty bastard!" "He's up in that tree!" "No, he's in those bushes!" "He's in the tree!"

A second shot snapped out. A short scream came from the left, hesitated in mid-air, and cut off as suddenly as it was uttered. "Help! Hel . . ." it died in space.

Motoya crawled to the hedgerow and cautiously raised himself up beside Hugo Schlenk. He rested his rifle on top of the earthen parapet and whispered to Schlenk. "Can you see him?"

"I ain't sure, but I think he's in that tree over there!" Schlenk said, pointing to a heavily foliaged apple tree standing about three hundred yards to their front. The approach to the tree was a hedge affording excellent cover which extended directly back to the enemy position.

Motoya scanned the field of tall grass, his eyes resting when they reached the tree, but he saw no discernible movement.

He cursed under his breath and again began to search the field, taking exceptional care to cover every inch of ground leading to the tree.

Some wild shots came from the hedgerow. The newer men were getting trigger-happy; they would fire until they had used up all their ammunition. Motoya again cursed.

His eyes stopped short at a clump of grass that seemed to be moving minutely away from the direction of the wind. He closed his left eye, adjusted the sight on his M-1, and took a deep breath. The grass stopped moving. A certain thickness could be seen near the top blades.

Motoya let out half his breath and slowly squeezed the trigger. The heavy force of the recoil was a satisfying power. He took another breath, let half out, and squeezed the trigger a second time.

A scream of shocked surprise came from the tall clump of grass, and a figure stumbled out, hands partly raised in surrender. It swayed drunkenly.

Motoya's arms stiffened, and for an instant he was about to lower his rifle. Instead, he again aimed and squeezed, and the stumbling figure stopped short, spun in a half circle, and fell forward. Its legs twitched and then became still.

Motoya spat in the dust and lowered himself from the hedge. One less for the books. They were less than scum, lower than animals, and if he were allowed to he'd kill every goddamned one.

Sergeant Rodriguez walked over and grasped Motoya gently by the arm. He spoke in his usually quiet voice. "Why didn't you let him give up?"

"How do I know he wanted to give up?" said Motoya.

"He had his hands raised," said Rodriguez almost in a whisper.

"I didn't see it," muttered Motoya. "I can't watch everything!"

"Be careful next time," said Rodriguez. "You know they want every prisoner we can take."

"When a bastard's shootin' at me, I can't worry about prisoners," said Motoya, jerking his arm back from the Sergeant's light grip. He walked away.

Rodriguez shrugged his shoulders. The kid was a killer, but there was nothing he could do about it except try to carry out orders as they were given. And he was no angel himself. Not after the time back near the beach when he got trigger-happy and mowed down the Jerries coming out of that farmhouse with their hands raised.

Jamborsky was still huddled in his hole, his hands cupped tightly over his ears when he was aroused by Reubens. "What? Whatsa . . . whatsa matter?" he exclaimed fearfully when the chubby man shook him brusquely.

"It's all over," said Reubens. "You can get up now."

"What's over? I was only sleeping." Jamborsky yawned heavily to give the impression that he had just been awakened.

"You sure were," said Reubens, shaking his head.

Paul Roth rolled over on his side and tried to keep his eyes closed. Snipers during the day and shellfire at night, all tricks to tear the soul from a man, he thought. He couldn't remember when he had had a decent night's rest, a night without any clashing, rattling, rumbling to gnaw the roots of his mind. His head hurt as though his pulse were beating there, and his heart was a frightened animal biting through the lining of his chest.

But it was what he wanted. He was an infantryman, a man with hair on his chest, fighting muscles. When he had put in for OCS he had specifically requested Infantry School. Why? What made him want to prove to the world that he was a man among men? Did he still retain his childhood fears? No, he had completely changed, and except for a few doubts now and then he was no longer a creature of the dreamworld of frightening shadows, terrible forms. But was it so? Fear was universal, buried in all men's souls.

Roth bit his lip; he was there and nothing much he could do about it, no way out. He had made his bed, or foxhole, and was lying in it. . .

Would Ellen forget? Probably. Couldn't expect someone to wait for years. Strange that he couldn't remember ever having loved her. He tried to recapture some feeling, some sense of longing or loss, but all sentiment seemed to have dried within him. He knew he had loved her, and would love her again when he came back. . . .

All that existed now was the will to survive, to eat and sleep and scratch, to empty one's bladder and bowels. No really decent emotion could be felt, with home a hazy place from some dream long gone. War was a sponge that dehydrated a man, sucked his heart and soul and mind until the only thing left was a black scab.

But he was a fool, Roth knew. If he really wanted to be in the infantry, he would have been much better off had he remained a private in the line. Then he'd have had only himself to look after, and not the lives of forty men. The smart uniform and the privileges of an officer's life in garrison was not such a hard pill to take, but in combat it had become a minus quantity. Playing father-confessor, nursemaid, tactician, leader for forty men over the width and breadth of France was a hell of a bargain. He was no leader; the past weeks had convinced him.

There was no way out, no way except to be killed or wounded or to blow his top. There had been many nights when he almost hoped for the blessed relief of tearing steel to solve his problems. But steel could kill, and death still was not fashionable. For the Japs, yes. The Germans, possibly. But life was the American style.

Even losing a leg was not so bad. When Pauker had written back to the outfit from the hospital, he had seemed to be quite cheerful about the price he had paid for getting out of the war.

He turned over on his back and cursed aloud. Too many thoughts going through his mind. He still had responsibility, a platoon to lead. Think the way he was thinking, and there were many things worse than combat fatigue. There were paths with no way back....

Night patrols were the toughest. His night blindness was growing worse, and he never knew where he was going to step next. Some night when it was cloudy, with no moon to light the way, might mean the finish, the end he didn't want.

Roth sat erect and shook his head from side to side. His mind was becoming too cluttered. He picked up his carbine, field-stripped it, and began to clean the weapon. He looked over at Verne Potter, his runner.

"Are you about set?" the Lieutenant asked.

Potter again looked worried, as though he were about due for another tearful spell. "Yes... yes, sir. When do we move out?" he asked.

Roth glanced at his watch. "Another few minutes," he said.

"Do... do you really need me?" stuttered Potter.

"I guess I do," said Roth. "I wish I didn't have to take you on this one, but you're the only man in the platoon who knows anything about wire."

"Reubens does," offered Potter.

"Not enough. He can't splice," said Roth.

"Yes, sir." Potter lowered his eyes.

Colonel Nielsen had his ear glued to the field telephone in the battalion dugout. "Yes, sir. They're going out in another few minutes!" he said into the speaker. "Right! Yes, sir!" He hung the phone on the hook and turned to Lieutenant Wormsley. "That was the Regimental Commander. Did B Company's patrol go out yet?"

"Do you still want them to go out?" asked Wormsley. "I thought we had enough information from the prisoner?"

"The old man wants a patrol," said the Colonel crisply. "Besides, who knows whether the prisoner is telling the truth?"

"He should be after that treatment," said the Intelligence Officer.

"Well, I don't trust them," said Nielsen. "They'd steal from their own dead mothers. Get Dougall on the phone."

Wormsley turned the hand crank on the field phone. "Star One, calling Charley One.... Star One, calling Charley One.... Let me speak to Lieutenant Dougall. Hello, Andy?... Wormsley... did your men leave?... Yeah.... Yeah!" His voice assumed a conciliatory tone. "Still and all they have to go out... that's orders from Regiment... yes, yes... okay, Andy."

Wormsley replaced the phone on the leather box.

"Is he beefing again?" asked Nielsen.

"The same as usual," said Wormsley.

"I don't know what I'm going to do with that man," said Nielsen. "The strain is telling on him. Are they moving out?"

"Yes, sir. In a couple of minutes."

Chapter Three

Paul Roth adjusted his cartridge belt, loaded and locked his carbine, and set his steel helmet squarely on his head. He checked the time, patted the map folded in his breast pocket, and walked towards the center of the perimeter defense area. "Rodriguez!" he called. "Get the men together!"

Sergeant Rodriguez walked along the hedgerow, shouting as he went for the chosen men. Some came up from foxholes where they had curled up for a few final minutes of rest; others appeared from various attitudes of relaxation, adjustment of field equipment, and the performances of natural functions.

As the men of the patrol began to appear, Roth squatted on the ground, opened his map, and removed the compass from the canvas carrier on his cartridge belt.

"Keep spread out," Roth told the assembling men as they crowded around him. "Take some distance."

Grumbling, the men put space between themselves and squatted on the earth. Some still adjusted their cartridge belts, a few nervously locked and unlocked their pieces, and one or two bit into white lips.

"You fellows all set?" asked Roth.

A mumbled chorus of assent was uttered.

"Sergeant Rodriguez."

"Here, sir."

"Sergeant Warner."

"Here."

"Motoya."
"Yoh!"
"Reubens."
"Here, sir."
"Schlenk."
"Here."
"Colucci."
"Here."
"Greenberg."
"Here, sir."
"Reilly."
"Here."
"McCrea."
"Huh . . . here, sir."
"Potter."
"Here, sir."

Roth cleared his dry throat. "For a change we're going out on patrol," he said.

"Will they serve tea?" queried Motoya.

"Any dancing?" said Reubens.

"Cold showers and a rubdown?" said Colucci.

Roth laughed and held up his hand. "All right, that's enough! We don't have much time. Here's your order: The enemy is about a thousand yards to the front holding the village of St. Mère du Prée. We don't know exactly how many men they've got. There may be only a company, or there may be a battalion or a regiment.

"Our mission is to get around the right flank of that village and see what they've got. To do that, we're going to have to get into a fire fight."

The Lieutenant pointed to his map and beckoned the men to move in closer. He continued the five-paragraph field order. "We move down this wooded draw until we come to the sunken road, which we cross. Then we move down this line of trees until we come to the outposts of the enemy lines. From there on out, we have our troubles.

"You all know where the aid station is." He waved his hand. "It's two hundred yards behind Battalion Headquarters in the woods. I'll use arm and hand signals, or the whistle, for most orders. Potter, your wire okay?"

The platoon runner nodded his head.

"Are there any questions?" asked Roth.

"Yeah, when do we get relieved?" smirked Reubens.

"Cut the crap!" said Roth. "Any questions about the patrol?"

"How about the wounded?" asked Greenberg.

"The same as always," said Roth. "We leave them. If they can get back under their own power, fine. If not . . ." He held out his open palms. "Reilly and Greenberg, scouts. I'll be right behind you."

"Gosh, suh, I've been a scout on ever' gol-danged patrol!" rebelled Reilly in his soft Texas drawl.

"Well, that's what you are," said Roth. "You've been trained as one. Rodriguez, take up the rear. Reubens, left flank, Schlenk, right flank. Potter, stay with Rodriguez and be careful with the wire. Whenever I signal, get the phone up to me as fast as you can."

"Yes sir," gulped Potter, trailing his fingers over the large spool hanging from a strap around his neck.

Roth checked his watch. Two minutes to nine. His throat was parched and his stomach was tied in knots. If he had eaten any substantial food, he would be nauseated. He had urinated a few minutes before, but his bladder again felt as if it were filled to the bursting point.

He raised his compass and squinted through the eyepiece until the needle rested near the direction he wanted. He did not need an exact azimuth; he had traveled practically the same route on other patrols. This time he used the instrument as a ritual.

As he stood there, Roth felt the old fears return in increasing proportions and again began to offer up wild prayers that some last minute eventuality would remove him from the leadership of the patrol. His confidence completely disappeared. It was always the same before a patrol or an attack; but each time it grew worse.

God, for a sniper's bullet to tear through his flesh and wound him enough to be sent to the rear where he could finish out the war in a limited-service capacity. He was no hero, and he knew it. A month ago he had thought differently, but the stinking ovens of war had burned out all desire for glory.

He could let one shot go from his carbine at his foot, inadvertently of course, just as they moved over the hedgerow. Nobody would see it. They, too, had their minds on other things and wouldn't think about or care whether a shooting were accidental or premeditated.

He didn't want to die. No, no one wants to die. But a wound would be the saving factor, heaven-sent release from the constant horror of fight and move, and dig and fight, and rest, to fight and move again. There was no end. No end except death or madness.

"Let's move out!" Roth shouted. He raised his arm high in the air and brought it slowly down toward the ground.

The two scouts, Reilly first, followed by Greenberg, took the lead. The patrol moved along the hedgerow until they arrived at the far left corner of the platoon's perimeter.

Reilly cautiously lifted his head over the top and peered into the distance. He hesitated and squirmed his body around, contorting as though he were suffering from a bad case of lice. He adjusted his cartridge belt, squinted through the sights of his rifle, and scratched himself between his buttocks.

The sun was high in the sky. Chained circles of smoke formed a lacy haze over the horizon. Under the rumble of artillery the atmosphere shimmered and danced like a plucked guitar string. Leading down from the hedgerow was the draw, surrounded on both sides by scrubby trees and thickly growing, thorny bushes. The bottom of the draw was damp and sticky from puddles that had failed to evaporate after the heavy rains of July.

"Get going!" Roth tensely ordered.

"I... I think I see something," stuttered Reilly.

"Where?" asked Roth, moving close to the Texan.

Reilly pointed down the draw.

The Lieutenant squinted into the shadowed haze. "I don't see a thing," he said. "Let's go!"

Reilly hurriedly threw himself over the hedgerow, landing clumsily on his stomach on the other side. He raised his head in fearful expectation and scanned the terrain to the front. All was quiet. He slowly arose to his feet, paused for a moment, and began to move forward.

Greenberg clambered over the parapet, landed on his feet, and followed the lead scout. Roth climbed over and was followed in turn by the others.

Reilly chewed his tobacco rapidly and forgot to spit out the accumulated brown juice. His grip on his rifle tightened until the steel and wood cut into his hands. As he walked, he searched the brush and the trees with his eyes. The rustle of the breeze against the foliage and the flutterings of frightened birds created a tense cacophony. Every noise contained another within itself, each one mysterious and each hiding an enemy.

Roth's heart thumped in cadence with his moving feet. The draw and the distance, and the fight to come, were delicate tortures, with the anticipation being a hundred times worse than the final realization. During an action a man had no time to think.

He turned his head. "Spread out . . . five yards!" No matter how many times the men were told, they kept bunching up. Targets for one shell.

Roth again turned his head. "Goddamit! Five yards!" he shouted. When the mission was over, his voice would almost be gone. Three years of training, fifty-eight days in the line, and men still didn't have the sense to stay apart.

"What's he beefin' about?" Colucci muttered to Schlenk.

"Dispersion," said Schlenk, as though quoting from a manual. "Five yards in close country, and ten to fifteen in the open fields. You know, what they taught you in basic training."

"This ain't basic!" groused Colucci. "What's he think we are, boy scouts?"

"It's for your own good," said Schlenk. "Whaddya think'd happen if a shell landed, and we were all stuck together?"

"Ah, who cares!" said Colucci despondently.

Schlenk tried to keep alert. He wanted to get another sniper. He'd show these guys, all the time back in training calling him Dutch, and Heinie, and Hitler. So what if he was born in Germany? He was as good an American as any one of them. Better,

maybe. He had more snipers to his credit than any of the guys, except maybe Motoya or Saunders. Snipers were okay . . . what he didn't like was shells and strafing at night.

Colucci kept his eyes on the ground. He didn't want to see. It was better that way. When he didn't look up, he didn't worry so much. He learned that one day off the beach. Keep your eyes on the ground and don't worry. When the payoff came, he was right in there shooting with the rest of them, but on a patrol he liked to keep his eyes on the ground. He didn't like what he couldn't see, and when he tried to see what was hidden, fear clawed around his heart.

Think of other things all the time. Force yourself to think different, and a guy'll be okay. Think of a piece of tail, of the "Whorehouse of All Nations" on Fourth Street in the "Village," and beer and hamburgers after. But the cops cleaned up on all the whores since the war, and a guy coming home on furlough couldn't even find himself a decent piece of ass anymore . . . and the other broads were getting too smart. They wanted you to spend ten or fifteen bucks on them, and fill them full of food and booze before they'd even let you get a muzzle, but who wants to get a stoneache? Better a guy should jerk off.

If he ever got back with ribbons and medals, and maybe some stripes on his arm, he'd show the bastards. He'd get back. Sure he'd get back. Even when he was a little kid he knew that nothing real bad could ever happen to him. It might happen to someone else, but never to him. Even when he played hooky, more times than anyone in the school, they never got wise to him. Nothing could happen. He fingered the St. Christopher's medal which dangled outside his denim shirt.

Reilly stopped suddenly, and Roth held up his hand in signal for a halt.

"What's up?" asked the Lieutenant.

Reilly signaled for caution and hit the ground. The men following needed no signal. Automatically they smashed their bodies to the earth, but their eyes stayed fixed on the first scout.

The Texan wet his lips with his tongue. He could have sworn he heard something moving behind a tree which lay directly ahead. He raised his rifle, aimed through the sights, and began to squeeze the trigger. Before the hammer fell he released the pressure and turned his head back to the platoon leader. He had a sickly smile on his face. "I thought I heard something," he said, and rose to his feet.

Roth signaled the men to rise and move on. "Watch what you're doing," he warned the scout. "You'll have us jumping at every sound."

Reilly tried to smile, but the result was a stiff grin. He moved out, and the patrol followed.

Roth glanced at his watch. "Step it up, Reilly," he called.

"Gosh, this is rough country, suh!" Reilly called back. "If I go any faster, I won't be able to see what's goin' on!"

"I know," said Roth. "But we don't have too much time. Try anyway, huh?"

Reilly stiffened his lips and walked faster. He tripped on a root that stuck out of the ground, and cursed. He gripped his rifle tighter.

Faster, faster, faster, thought Roth. Everything faster in the army. Hurry up and wait. Sit around for days doing nothing, and then when you move it's always hurry.

"Slow it down there! Goddamit!" an angry voice called from the rear.

Roth turned his head.

"Slow it down!" the voice came again. "You're losing us back here!" It was Rodriguez.

The Lieutenant shook his head defeatedly. "Slow it down, Reilly," he called. "Same pace as before." Impossible to satisfy everyone in the world, yet it was true that too fast a pace at the front could force men in the rear practically to run.

Reilly laughed. He spat a slippery blob of tobacco juice at the base of a tree which stood beside the draw. It was a direct hit and splattered in a growing circle which formed a fantastic pattern such as an ink blot will make when squeezed between the folds of a sheet of paper.

The Texan didn't mind the infantry, except for the combat part. Back in garrison it wasn't so bad. Plenty of fresh air and exercise to keep a man from growing soft. But this combat business got on a man's nerves. Here, they shot for keeps. He'd just as soon be driving a truck, now, a good distance behind the lines, where he could get his fresh air without someone wanting to shoot him up all the time. Or even it wouldn't be a bad job to be pounding a typewriter in the chairborne infantry, if he could type, if he could write.

Cooks didn't have a bad job. All the chow a man could eat, and plenty of time off between shifts to sleep, or to roam around the countryside and get a good looksee at what kind of crops they growed in this part of the world. Their cattle looked pretty peaked, and Lord, their pigs didn't have nary a pound of fat on their bones. Miserable creatures.

Lord, back home he'd bet the old man was doing plenty of hog-killing, what with the war and prices going up, and everything so scarce just the way the old man said in the letter he had his old teacher write him.

Another couple of months and he would have gotten deferred to do farm work. The old man was getting pretty stiff around the joints, and nary a man worth a damn could be found to help, but just like the army they seen fit to send him over before the release come through.

Danged combat wasn't worth one bit of a damn, not one bit. No sir, he didn't mind hunting, but not when the other guy was doing the hunting at him. He ought to be back home feeding the troops so that they could fight better. Instead, he was up here just like the other poor bastards, and hoping and praying that the Jerry's hunting wasn't going to be good . . . not when he was holding down the front of the point.

Roth looked at his watch and raised his arm. The men uttered expressions of relief and lowered themselves to the ground.

"Keep your eyes opened!" shouted Roth. "This is no goddamned siesta!" He walked towards the rear, and felt a cold chill in having his back turned to the enemy side.

"What's eating his ass?" Greenberg asked Reilly.

"I guess he doesn't like the huntin' season," said Reilly.

"I never saw him lose his temper until lately," said Greenberg. "Do you think he's blowin' his top?"

"Not him!" said Reilly. "He's the best goldanged platoon leader in the regiment!"

"Oh, I don't know," said Greenberg. "I don't think he's so hot. I never saw him do so damned much."

"He stays up in the front all the time, and he wouldn't let you do what he won't do first," said Reilly.

"So what? He's getting paid for it."

"How about the time he cleaned out that houseful of snipers? And when he stood up alone with a whole Jerry squad and threw grenades with 'em?"

Greenberg shook his head. "I don't remember that."

"You wouldn't. You weren't with us then."

"Yeah . . . yeah, that's right," agreed Greenberg. "I suppose I was still in the replacement depot." His nose itched, and he placed his index finger into one nostril and began to pry loose some collected soot.

Roth squatted beside Potter. The young soldier looked worried, and his lower lip drooped despondently. "How's the wire?" asked the Lieutenant.

"No trouble," said Potter. "Only it's getting awfully heavy. I wish someone else could help me."

"Try sticking it out a while longer," said Roth. "We don't have much farther to go."

"They should give us more men," said Rodriguez, taking up his usual cudgel. "They can't keep men in the line for so long, and then expect them to do a good job . . ."

"I know, I know," said Roth abruptly. "But you can't fight city hall. We've got a job to do, and that's all there is to it." He turned again to Potter. "Ring the CP."

Potter lifted the receiver off the hook, and revolved the crank handle. He listened for a moment, and handed the phone to Lieutenant Roth.

"Charley Two, calling Charley One," repeated Roth. "Charley Two to Charley One.... Andy?... yeah, Roth speaking.... That's right.... No, for Christ sake! What do they think we've got, bicycles?... Hurry? How in the hell can we hurry?... still in the draw.... If that bastard thinks he can do better, send him down here!... I don't give a goddam whether he is listening! We're not supermen!... Okay.... I'll do the best I can. Out."

Roth rudely handed the phone to Potter and threw up his hands in angry desperation. "How do you like that? The son of a bitch wants us to speed it up!"

"Nielsen?" said Rodriguez.

"Who else?" said Roth.

"It wasn't that way in the old army," said Rodriguez reminiscently. "Officers were taught to think of their men first."

"Well, this isn't the old army!" said Roth brusquely. Sergeant Warner, leader of the first squad, came over to the three men. He was a very small man, no more than five feet three, and built like a jockey. His shriveled, prematurely aged face was excessively pale. "I think I found O'Connor, sir," he said to Roth.

"O'Connor?" questioned Roth. "Who's he?"

"That replacement we lost on patrol down near here about a week ago," said Warner.

"O'Connor.... O'Connor?" wondered Roth. "Was he the fellow who went on that patrol with Saunders?"

Warner looked ill. "That's the man. I think I found him."

"Where?" asked Roth.

"In the bushes down there," said Warner, pointing.

Roth was silent for a moment. "Maybe... maybe I'd better take a look myself. Want to show me where he is?"

"I... I don't want to see him again," said Warner. "But if you...."

"Oh come on!" said Roth feigning cheerfulness. "You've been around long enough not to let bodies bother you. Come on, show me where it is!"

Warner shook his head rebelliously, but started towards the center of the draw. Roth followed.

"Watch that water, Colucci," the Lieutenant warned as he passed the muscular Italian-American. "You don't want a dose of cramps, now."

Colucci removed his lips from the neck of his canteen and nodded his head. He was thirsty and had been sucking voraciously at the warm, rust-tasting water.

"How's it going, Hugo?" Roth greeted the slender blond soldier.

Schlenk smiled. "Pretty good, sir." The Lieutenant wasn't such a bad guy.

"This way," said Warner. He led the Lieutenant to the left of the draw, into an area of high thick bushes and dense weeds.

A rotting sweetish odor hung heavily about the thicket. Roth stifled an impulse to turn on his heels and run until he could find some place where a fresh northern gale was blowing. He removed a handkerchief from his pocket and held it over his mouth and nose.

Warner pointed downwards. He had grown paler, and his larynx moved up and down in spasmodic cadence.

Two clotted legs of meat, purplish with rot, lay limp under a low hanging blanket of leaves. Yellowish bones, snapped at thigh and calf, showed jagged edges through the dark coagulation. What appeared as a single living black entity, upon second examination, proved to be a mass of thousands of flies feeding upon the dead putrefaction. White, fat-bellied, squirming grubs maneuvered for position in conflict with the winged scavengers.

A gaping cavern had been the stomach and it was alive, writhing with the crawling things moving in and out in a constant, never-ending chain.

The eyes of the thing were staring dumbly, questioningly at the sky coming through the spaces between the overhanging leaves. Its mouth was open in an attitude of expectancy.

Roth bent over, held his breath, and, when his fingers touched the chain around the body's neck, closed his eyes and hastily removed the identification tags and religious medal. He clenched them tightly in his hand, stood erect, turned on his heels in a quick about-face, and opened his eyes. He retained one tag and threw the other one, with the religious medal, over his shoulder. They landed on the body.

Warner crossed himself and suddenly stumbled into the bushes on his left. Roth heard a thick splashing on the grass.

Roth slowly walked away. He gagged and felt the pain of bile rising. He squeezed his stomach with his hands, and his throat knotted and twisted, and his intestines tightened painfully, but nothing came up. He increased the pressure on his stomach, but all that came out was a mouthful of sourish saliva. He walked toward his men, his head pounding and his guts lying rotten and unsatisfied.

When he reached the draw, he opened his closed fist and read the dog tag: Emmett O'Connor, 33444065, C, T1945.

When the lines passed the draw, Service Company would shovel up the thing, dump it into a mattress cover, and remove it to the rear where it would be picked up by a Graves Registration outfit. The Catholic Chaplain would give it the correct prayer, it would get a white cross in the flat field overlooking the English Channel, its family would receive a two-star telegram, and they would have a Mass said. Periodically, candles would be lighted.

Warner came out a short while after Roth. He wiped his mouth with his sleeve. Holy Mary! he cried to himself. Jesus, Jesus, Jesus, is this the way to die, to rot a stinking scab on the foul scurvy earth, food for creatures from the lower depths! Mother of God!

"Whatsa matter, Warner?" asked Colucci, lounging on his side and smoking a cigarette.

Warner motioned with his head. "O'Connor," he said.

"What about him?" asked Colucci.

"We just found him," said Warner.

"No kiddin'! Dead, huh?"

"Yeah."

"Holy Christ!" exclaimed Colucci. "Musta been there for a week!" What a way to die. Nothing but the goddam nature. Trees and bushes, and nothing else. Better not think. Keep your eyes on the ground and remember the whores, and the beer joints, and a big hot steaming pizza on a cold night after a big time.

Chapter Four

REILLY LAY ON HIS STOMACH, his rifle butt pressed into his shoulder, and searched the draw to the front and to the flanks. Greenberg squatted five yards behind, his M-1 cradled in his lap.

"They finally found O'Connor," said Greenberg.

"Yeah, I heard 'em talkin' about it," said Reilly. "He must of really been ripe!"

"Smells it," said Greenberg, his nostrils wrinkling and twitching.

"Worse'n a goddam hog!" said Reilly in wonder.

"Worse than the Gowanus Canal," said Greenberg.

"What's that?"

"A canal in Greenpoint, Brooklyn."

"Why's it stink?"

"When you get to Brooklyn you'll see. They empty garbage in it."

"Oh."

Greenberg lit a cigarette and blew the smoke up towards his face, letting the vapors circle thickly about his nose. *Allav a sholem....*

"On your feet!" ordered Lieutenant Roth, walking towards the head of the column. "On your feet, and for Christ's sake keep your distance!"

Adjusting their belts and securing their weapons, the men stood erect.

Reilly moved out on the platoon leader's signal.

Warner ran up and down the line of the patrol, checking on the progress of the men. "Open it up!" he called. "Keep your eyes open!

Watch those flanks!" His short legs churned like pistons as he trotted back and forth.

"Don't get your balls in an uproar, shorty!" Motoya taunted.

"Worry about your own balls, you big spic!" Warner returned as he passed Motoya.

Motoya laughed. The little guy had more guts than anybody in the platoon. That's why he liked to kid him.

"How much further do we have to go?" asked McCrea.

"What's your hurry?" said Motoya. "You'll get plenty of action, and sooner than you expect."

"It's not that. I was just wondering, that's all," said McCrea. His sandy hair hung shaggily out of the sides of his helmet. His mouth was gritted.

"About another fifteen minutes," said Motoya.

McCrea tightened his grip on the rifle. He was determined to do a good job. He wasn't afraid. He couldn't be, or otherwise he would never have given up his deferment and volunteered for the infantry. But it was unfortunate that he had missed the opportunity to go to Officer Candidate School. Alice would have liked that, and besides the extra money would have come in handy. Clothing for the kids had gone sky high, and the price of food was way up. And an allotment didn't solve too many problems. Lucky that he put away some money the year before. How long could it last?

The ground opened up in front of the patrol, and roared and rocked and vibrated in deafening, chilling thunder. As one man they hit the earth, smashing their bodies brutally down. They buried their faces between their arms and held their breaths.

Another series of blasts saturated space, each one lifting the men inches off the ground and at completion dropping them back with unleashed fury. Ribs ached, felt crushed, and insides swelled and twisted with concussion.

The center of impact was in a small clearing directly ahead, with the dispersion landing on both sides of the gully.

Roth's head shook with ague. His lips trembled and tears of fright came to his eyes. Quiet for an instant, and then another series of horrifying, promising blasts. His long nails clawed into the earth, and his toes beat an uncontrollable tattoo.

At each blast Reilly's eyes blinked. He raised his head for a second, but could see nothing beyond the geysers of earth and brush spraying up in front of him and the impenetrable brown cloud which followed. He wanted to run to the rear and keep on running until there was no more breath left in his body.

Oi vay'es mir.... Gott zol mir helfen, Greenberg moaned. He wanted to get out of there. He wanted to die, to be hit and become unconscious, anything to get away from the bursting fear, searing, ripping, tearing the heart from his being. He was frozen, he couldn't move, could do nothing but wait for the next blasts to come and make his blood ice. Paralyzed and sick and torn inside... waiting... *vay'es mir*... goddamnedfuckingnogoodgoddamned war!

Potter lay across the spool of wire, and hopeless tears wet the earth. His silhouette was too high across the wire but he couldn't move. His body jerked with sobs. Mother, mother, mother, where are you? He placed his hands over his ears, but the blasts became louder. He bit into his lips until the blood ran down his tongue.

Motoya felt the red urge to kill, kill, kill. It was sterility... not being able to get it up anymore. He couldn't move but he wanted to get his hands around a German's throat and rip it to shreds and watch the thick blood flow, and stick a knife in his stomach and tear out his stinking guts. He wanted to kill and murder and destroy, and keep on killing and murdering until there was one long trail of blood and guts from there to Berlin. But he couldn't move. Christ, he couldn't move and he wanted to get his hands into live flesh. Christ, he was scared! He didn't want to die!

"Rat sons of bitches!" Motoya screamed out unheard. "Come out and fight, you miserable stinking no good sons of rat bitches! Fight, you bastards! Fight... Fight... Fight!" His voice rose to a falsetto scream.

They'd have to get through the open space, thought Rodriguez. It was concentration fire; the Lieutenant should know that. The book clearly stated that open spaces of approach routes were usually heavily targeted-in by artillery fire. The book said to double-time through a shelled area. The Lieutenant should know that. Christ, he studied the book! Christ, the noise was loud! He wiped the sweat from his face.

Another instant of quiet hovered. Roth raised his head. The shelled area was a hollow bowl about thirty square yards and devoid of vegetation. "We're going to run for it!" he screamed to his men, and instantly was sorry for the decision. They could get killed running across... but also could get killed if they remained as they were. "One at a time! Reilly... get moving!"

The Texan turned his head toward his leader, and his eyes pleaded. He looked back toward the front, but remained frozen.

"Get going, Reilly!" screamed Roth in high pitch.

Reilly again turned his head towards the Lieutenant. His lips moved, but no sound came out.

Roth snaked his way on his belly to where Reilly lay. "Get up and run for it!" he ordered.

Drops of spittle had caked on Reilly's lips. He tried to speak, to rationalize to the crazy man, but the sounds were stuck deep inside.

Roth grabbed him by the shoulder and roughly shook him. "Goddamit, get moving!"

Reilly rose to his knees, jerked to his feet, and suddenly started across the shelled ground. Another series of blasts roared, and huge clouds of smoke and dust poured into the air.

The man stumbled, and for a split second Roth could not see him through the thick brown fog. But when the earth settled, the man had cleared the concentration area and hurled himself in a sliding dive into the brush on the other side. He crawled about twenty more yards into the brush and buried his face between his arms.

"Okay, Greenberg! Let's go!" Roth ordered.

Greenberg scrambled to his feet and zig-zagged across like a drunken ballet dancer. He twisted and turned, his knees lifted high as though he were treading with bare feet upon broken glass. He reached the other side and fell beside Reilly.

Roth beckoned to the other men. McCrea was next and he cleared the field, running upright and swift without hesitation.

Reubens followed. He ran clumsily, and as he reached the center of the bowl another series of blasts pounded the earth. He paused and almost stopped, and seemed to flounder confusedly.

"Keep going!" Roth screamed. "Keep going, you goddamned fool!"

Reubens turned his head right and left, his round cheeks chalky with fear. He dug his heels into the ground and made the other side without being hit. He slid to the earth and patted it lovingly with his hand.

The blasts continued to come in spaced bursts. Five landed, followed by hesitant silence, and then five more.

The rest of the men stopped at the edge of the clearing, waited for the silence to come, and then sped across during the vacuum of momentary respite.

Schlenk followed Reubens, and after him came Motoya. Motoya screamed incoherent imprecations at the fates and forces that had brought him to the land of destruction.

Warner came next, his short legs moving so fast that each separate step could barely be discerned.

Colucci followed Warner, his eyes still aimed at the ground and his wide shoulders bunched up as though he were in the semifinals of the Golden Gloves at Madison Square Garden.

"Give me that wire," said Rodriguez.

"I can make it, Sergeant," said Potter.

"I'll carry it across. You can take it from there," said Rodriguez.

Potter did not insist. He removed the reel of wire from around his neck and handed it to the Platoon Sergeant. He sprinted across the clearing, his arms working back and forth in a rowing motion. The tears had begun to dry on his face, and light streaks showed where the salt liquid had washed away the caked dirt.

"You're next," called Roth.

"I can wait, Lieutenant," said Rodriguez.

"Move out," Roth ordered.

The Sergeant slung his rifle over his back, raised the reel of wire so that it wouldn't bounce against his chest, and trotted across the clearing. He appeared calm and impassive.

Roth raised his carbine, took a large gulp of air into his lungs, and hurled himself across the brown patch of earth. It was the first time he took the high dive at the pool and his heart climbed up to his mouth... his eyes sightless. A roar behind almost threw him to the ground, but he recovered his footing, clawed forward with his arms clutching the upraised weapon, and landed in the brush on the other side. The blasts went on, but with no break between. They probably just made it. As he swallowed air, his throat made hoarse grating sounds.

"You all right?" asked Rodriguez, lying next to the Lieutenant.

Roth panted trying to find the words. "Sure... sure... how are the men?"

"All here," said Rodriguez. "Lucky too... listen to that!"

The explosions behind them grew louder and more intensive. From their position it seemed as if an entire battalion of artillery were concentrated upon that one small segment of earth.

"We'd better go ... and quick," said Roth, rising to his feet but keeping his silhouette low. "They'll start searching and traversing in a minute!"

Rodriguez blew a shrill blast on his whistle. "Get up!" he called. "On the double!"

The men rose to their feet, rubbing the dust from their eyes and spitting it from their mouths.

Reilly started walking, followed by the others.

"Double time!" shouted Rodriguez. "Move your ass! They'll be zeroing in here in a second!"

They moved off at a slow trot, and panted and wheezed and cursed at one another.

"Get off my heels, you dumb bastard!" Motoya screamed to Warner.

"Stir your ass and I won't step all over you!" panted Warner.

Roth ran towards the front. "Pick it up!" he shouted. "You're like a bunch of old men!" Pounding, beating into the ground, fear directly behind them like a mad insane animal thirsting for blood. He felt the bile coming up and it choked him and made it almost impossible to get fresh breath into his lungs. Every step was the last. One more and he would fall to the ground and let it take him. Death would come as welcome as the tender hand of mother. One more step and he'd fall, and the shells would land on him and tear his body asunder, and rip the final spark from his huge pounding heart. On and on, up the hills, and down the hills, and over the hills ... through the forests and over the hedges. Running without breath in his body.

"Why the hell don't he slow down!" cried Colucci. "Slow down, for Jesus' sake!" he screamed.

"Shut up!" called Warner. "Wanta get your ass shot off?"

"Lieutenant, you're losing the men!" Rodriguez called down from the rear of the column.

Unhearing, Roth continued to run behind the two scouts.

Rodriguez forced himself to run faster and tried to reach the head of the column. The Lieutenant was going mad. How did he expect the men to keep up?

Roth suddenly slowed down to a fast walk. He held up his hand, and the rest of the patrol followed suit. Schlenk stumbled and almost fell, but Rodriguez, coming up behind him, grasped him by the collar and helped him regain his balance.

Rodriguez continued to run until he came up beside Roth. The Lieutenant's breath wheezed.

"That . . . that was a little too fast for the men in the rear," offered Rodriguez.

"We had to get out . . . shellfire!" panted Roth.

"Yeah, but you're losing the men," said Rodriguez.

"You don't want them to get killed!" spat Roth. "This isn't maneuvers, you know!"

"I know sir, but . . ." Rodriguez held out his hands in a querulous gesture. He turned and walked back to the rear. The Lieutenant did run too fast. He should have taken up a more even pace. The men would last longer that way.

"Is this the way it always is?" McCrea asked when he had caught his breath.

"This is nothing!" grinned Reubens on the left flank. "Wait'll we have a real attack! Then you'll see something!"

"It ain't much worse," called Schlenk from his position on the right. "Only a hundred times more artillery fire and machine guns and rifles and mortars and tanks. Not much worse, though."

"Are *you* trying to be funny?" said Reubens.

"No. This ain't the time for jokes," said Schlenk.

Reubens waved his hand contemptuously. "What a dumb Dutch bastard! A hundred times more artillery, and it ain't much worse!"

"I didn't say it wasn't worse. That ain't what I meant."

"Ah, you heinies are all alike!" said Reubens. "Don't know your ass from a hole in the wall!"

"A lot smarter than you, you sheeny bastard!" returned Schlenk.

"You're jealous, that's the trouble!" said Reubens, his face reddening.

"Jealous of you, hah!" Schlenk laughed coldly.

The two men became quiet, each lost in his own discomfort.

The column plodded on. The shell-bursts from behind became a dull rumble, but their presence remained like the few points of fever after the crisis of an illness has been passed. It was the knowledge that there would be more relapses, and very serious ones, before the illness was finally cured.

The draw became deeper as they moved along, and the foliage was thicker. Heavy roots projecting above ground made movement more treacherous. The men walked slowly, their nerves taut. They fearfully peered through the dark foliage, imagining an enemy in every shadow, behind each bush, and strapped into the upper branches of all the trees. Faces twitched, and heads jerked at every sound of nature: of leaves blowing in the slight breeze, twigs crackling under their feet, and the frightened flutter of birds in the damp air.

The soldiers drew upon their graveyard courage, and tried to whistle under their breaths. A few hummed snatches of popular songs, but stopped abruptly in the middle as memory of the words and tunes failed. All knowledge was of the present; the past and the future had no existence save in the knowledge of death and maiming, and songs could not be brought back.

A staccato rattle came out of the dark, and little circles appeared in a growing, smoking chain along the ground. The patrol fell to the earth and began to fire their weapons in the general direction of the shots.

"Where's it coming from?" shouted Roth.

Reilly and Greenberg anxiously searched the underbrush. "I think it's coming from there!" said Greenberg, and pointed to the right front.

Roth tried to pierce the thick foliage, but he could not pick up a clue to the shooting.

Sergeant Rodriguez infiltrated to the front by running a few short steps and falling to the ground, to rise again and run some more steps. "Can you see anything?" he whispered to Roth.

"Nothing," said Roth. "They must be dug in someplace."

"I think it's a burp-gun," said Rodriguez.

Another rapid burst sprayed the ground a few inches from the platoon leader and the Sergeant. The two froze and tried to shrink their bodies. The dust that kicked up blew into their eyes and momentarily blinded them. Rodriguez blew his nose on his sleeve.

Roth aimed his carbine to the right and emptied a clip of eight rounds. Another burst opened up as if in contempt for Roth's shooting.

"I see him!" Rodriguez whispered. He rolled over on his side, reached into the deep pocket of his denim trousers, and removed a grenade. He held the explosive along the four fingers of his right hand, guided it from the rear with his thumb, and carefully aimed it to the right. He rose to one knee, pulled the pin with his left hand, counted seconds, then hurled the missile with all his strength. The air hung still, as though time had stopped, until the quiet was drummed by a dull explosion. Rodriguez uttered a satisfied sigh, reached into his pocket again, went through the same quick, careful actions, and threw another grenade.

Roth rapidly inserted another clip in his carbine and let eight more shots go in the direction of the grenade explosions.

They waited . . . thirty . . . forty . . . fifty seconds. The silence grew and became a penetrating force. Rodriguez jumped to his feet and ran towards the bushes. He kicked apart the shrubbery and beckoned to Roth.

The platoon leader joined the Sergeant. A figure clad in dusty blue-gray was rigid behind the bush. It still stood supported on one knee, the Schmeisser machine pistol smoking on the ground between its legs. An expression of stunned surprise was on its face.

Rodriguez swung his foot at the dead figure. It hesitated limply for an instant and rolled over with a dull thud.

"Good work!" said Roth.

"I thought I had the bastard spotted!" said the Sergeant triumphantly. It was a rare thrill to see the result of his handicraft. In combat a man usually doesn't see how he kills, except for an occasional sniper twisting down from a tree or spinning out of a church steeple.

Roth felt happiness for the first time that day. It was a relief to see your enemy, and to know that he was human, and bled and hurt and died the same; and was not a supernatural being lurking in the shadows. The action of the past minute was an orgasm of emotion; his body loosened and relaxed.

Roth lifted his arm and signaled the men to move forward. "Stir your asses!" he called. He could almost sing, and wanted to run and shout and do a little dance. If all combat was as easy as this one, it wouldn't be so bad. Almost fun; shooting ducks in a gallery at Coney Island. To meet your enemy face to face and match your skill with his, with the best man to win. Wars should be made with rules and regulations like a sporting match. Give each opposing army a section of land, load them up with all the ammunition they could carry, and let them shoot it out. No artillery, no strafing, no screaming-meemies, no phosphorus bombs, no disemboweled bodies, no limbs lost, no combat fatigue. No, only small clean holes with life pouring out, and the cold clean friendly hand of death to receive the loser. Then, death might be more fashionable. Death itself could not be so bad; not the objective kind. The living death, the fear of the unknown and the darkness, the shadows and the stinging vines, and the stink, and the legs and arms flying in the air, was the horror.

They moved onward. The ground dried as the morning grew warmer. The draw gradually began to thin out, and the sun and open patches could be seen through the foliage hundreds of yards in the distance.

The two scouts became more alert. The draw was dangerous and could hide unforeseen things, but a newer element, another type of terrain, always contained other dangers that had to be looked for carefully. One of the major commandments during training had been to be doubly vigilant when coming from a wooded area into the clear. Anything could happen.

The temperature mounted, but the air became cleaner. A dry breeze blew, dispelling the odor of dampness that had been following them ever since they had left the perimeter defense. It helped to refresh sore lungs and brought new blood into tired bodies. Spirits lifted as they smelled the apple wine carried on the breeze from some orchard outside the draw and sensed the warmth the sun would bring.

Chapter Five

As they marched the two scouts surveyed the widening foliage for signs of movement, but they saw nothing except the green of the rolling fields beyond the draw.

Roth's spirits continued to mount. The wonder of time came back, and he marveled over the vagaries of each circling of the small hand on his watch. Each minute in combat was a separate existence. One lived a complete emotional life in a single revolution of the second hand on a military wrist watch.

The patrol finally left the draw and came into the open. After marching a few hundred yards more, they arrived at the sunken road. There they halted. Reilly and Greenberg made a visual reconnaissance of the deep cut and of the ground on the other side. They lowered themselves and started over.

The sunken road was a narrow gorge seven feet deep and eight feet wide, muddy on the bottom, and walled with heavy stinging-nettle vines. The lands of Normandy were crisscrossed by many such roads, and battles had often been fought to secure them. That day the dark cut was silent, and the patrol passed it safely.

When they all had climbed to the other side, Roth let the men rest for a few minutes. He scanned the line of trees and the field they would have to cross in order to approach the town.

Except for the trees the terrain was fairly open, and they could move with greater speed than before. The countryside consisted of gently rolling pastures which dipped and billowed onward to the hills in the distance. From his map, Roth saw that the town lay just before the beginning of the hills and to the right of the line of trees that they would have as a guide.

Cows impassively munched the green grass of the pastures, and birds lazily swooped and circled on the warm breeze. It was a scene of peace without an element to indicate that a war was being fought or that the enemy might be lying in wait behind any one of the numerous crevices, hollows, and bushes of the pasture land. Thousands of them could be holed up, camouflaged, and in readiness.

"Let's move out!" ordered the Lieutenant. "And open up! Take ten yards!"

The two scouts started. Roth waited until they were well out and then took up his position.

Rodriguez walked up to Roth. His pipe was inclined at the usual angle in the corner of his mouth, and blue-bordered smoke rings twisted upward. "Do you think I ought to stay nearer you?" he asked.

"I don't see why," said Roth.

"I figured you might need me up here . . . just in case we run into any trouble."

"I'll tell you what. Stay closer to the middle. Then you can come up when I want you, and we won't be taking any chances of one shell getting the both of us. Maybe I will need you for a flanking movement. . . ."

"Sure," said Rodriguez. "Warner can take care of the rear and keep them from straggling."

"Okay," said Roth. "But every once in a while try to keep your eyes open there."

Rodriguez walked toward the center of the column. "Warner, take my place at the rear," he said to the short squad leader.

"What's up?" asked Warner.

"I'm taking your place here, to be near the Lieutenant," said Rodriguez.

"What's the matter, you taking over the platoon?" Rodriguez' lips angrily stiffened over his pipe stem. "Don't be a jerk! Roth's the best man they've got in the outfit! Get to the back, and watch out for stragglers!"

Warner turned and ran to the end of the column. He took a place near Potter, who struggled along under the heavy weight of the reel of telephone wire. The thin strand trailed out behind, a snaking black line over the route traveled.

It wasn't a bad idea after all to be away from the front, Warner felt. In the rear a man could breathe easier, and have more time to protect himself in case of any sudden attack from the front. Of course, there always remained the chance of sneak attacks from the flanks or rear, but that could be overlooked for the present. If a man worries about every single possibility, his mind won't last long.

The patrol spread out across the fields in an extended, staggered column. They moved faster than they had in the draw. They guided on the straight line of trees bordering the fields, keeping their eyes and ears alert to hidden things in the woods. It was a favorite trick of the Germans to strap themselves in the branches of a tree, camouflaged by green-spotted sniper suits and pieces of natural foliage, and pick off men as they passed on patrol.

A low hum suddenly came from the horizon, a hum that grew louder with each second. Lieutenant Roth blew three blasts on his whistle, and brought his arm down in signal, but the men needed neither the signal nor the whistle. They hit the ground and cradled their heads between their arms, the old fears returning the instant their ears caught the dread sound of an approaching plane.

The hum became a blazing roar shooting a few feet above the earth and coming directly at the patrol. A blasting, tinny rattle shattered their eardrums, and the earth, torn up by flaming tracer bullets, sprayed over them. The roar diminished as the plane passed.

The men anxiously raised their heads and followed the plane's progress. It pulled up, seemed to climb vertically into the blue sky, twisted over with an inverted, pancaking convolution, and dived back at them. They heard the wild screaming of the wind against its wings, and the metallic whine of its wide-open engine. The machine guns clacked again in a spitting roar. Straining each muscle and fiber, the men prayed and cursed in prayer, and hoped in prayer, and willed that the bullets were not meant for them.

Roth dug his nails into the ground until they became painfully filled with rough gravel. He held his breath and forced it against the walls of his lungs.

Reilly closed his eyes tightly until he could feel the tears break loose under the pressure of his lids. He willed himself back in Texas with the throat of a hog under the killing knife, and the blood pouring into the pail for blood pudding, and the last soprano shriek of the animal as its breath plunged from its body.

Greenberg prayed for the first time since he had been bar mitzvahed and called upon God to bring him back, and, with his fingers in his ears, tried to shut out the roar of the bursting bullets; but the sounds came louder and he felt the touch of death.

McCrea kept his eyes wide open. He didn't want to miss a thing... but it did bring cold fear into a man's blood and he wanted to get back, had to get back, because Alice wasn't too strong after the second one came. And they all needed him at home, and he was a fool to have ever volunteered for the infantry, or even the army. He had a deferment, and his moral responsibility was back with them, not up here with death one second away. He closed his eyes.

Reubens shook his head like a wetted dog, in a straining attempt to eliminate the blasts from his splitting eardrums. He wanted to get up and run into the woods, to get away from the strafing. He knew that if he could get into the woods the plane couldn't follow, but he just lay there, unable to move except for the agitated twitchings of his neck.

Schlenk clenched his fists and cursed the fact that a German race had ever been created by some mistake of God, and that he had been born a member of that race through no fault of his own, and he knew that if he killed one German for every round of ammunition issued to him the curse of his blood would be wiped out, because Germans would no longer exist. He'd change his name to Brown, or Smith, or Jones, and be an American and forever forget that twenty years ago he had been born in Frankfort. He hated his parents for having allowed him to be born there. When the plane swooped and fired again his teeth bit against his teeth, and his tongue felt the grit of chipped enamel.

Motoya screamed at the top of his voice. "Kill! Kill! Kill the friggin' sons of bitches!" The vision of his knife tearing into their guts and creasing across their stinking throats was almost a physical feeling, better than a sexual feeling, and if he could just get a few he'd never want to have a woman again. It was so good to get a knife in. His hands opened and closed savagely, and he called upon his patron saint to give him strength and to burn the fear from his body so that he wouldn't have to lie on the ground tasting his own impotence.

Rodriguez still gripped his pipe, his clenched teeth forming new marks on the bit of the stem. The plane's racket almost had him unnerved. He'd much rather be under an artillery concentration, or shooting it out with a sniper. If he had a machine gun he would be up on one knee, swinging the weapon on a free traverse, fighting it out with the plane. This way he could do nothing but hope for the best.

Colucci's eyes were closed. He couldn't bring himself back to the Village, or Fourth Street, or anything else. Nothing existed but the gigantic presence of the plane's engine, the spitting machine guns, and him holding on for life. His body trembled.

Warner sang a stream of vehement profanity. Whenever they were strafed, none of their own ships ever appeared to fight off the enemy. They'd lie there like crippled children until the German either got tired or ran out of ammunition.

Potter cried. He cried for home and the safe bed, and knew it would not be much longer that he'd be able to stand being shelled and strafed and fired at by a thousand different kinds of weapons. His body trembled, and he dug his fists into his eyes to block the tears.

The plane came back for the last time, fired a few short parting bursts, and gradually disappeared into the sky.

The men stiffly, and still cautiously, rose to their feet. They cursed in the direction of the fading plane.

Still shaking, Roth gave the signal for the patrol to form and move out. He was about to start following his scouts when there was a call from behind.

"Hold up, Lieutenant!" Warner shouted. "I think they got Colucci!"

Roth shouted to the two scouts to halt and walked to the rear. Colucci lay face down, the position he had been in during the strafing. He was motionless. Warner turned him over on his back.

The soldier was dead. His eyes were closed, and the tired lines had disappeared from his cheeks. He appeared to be at peace.

Roth removed one of the dog tags. He now had two to return to Service Company. Two more sets of affidavits that he'd have to sign, and swear and attest to, in order that two more men could be declared officially dead. He jingled the two metal tags in his pocket and wondered how many more would be clanging together by the time the day was over.

"Move out!" he called, and trotted back to his position behind the scouts.

Reilly and Greenberg stepped out. They held their rifles at high port and scanned the skies now, as well as the front and flanks.

"Do we just leave him like that?" asked McCrea.

"We don't carry him with us," said Reubens.

"Doesn't anybody come to pick him up?"

Reubens shrugged his shoulders. "Maybe in a week, maybe in a month... if the lines ever get up this far. Man, will he be ripe by then!"

"Can't something be done...?"

"Would you want us to carry along the stiff with us?" said Reubens.

"No, but I only thought..." McCrea's voice trailed off.

The woods directly ahead of the scouts abruptly cut off at a square corner. Roth signaled a right turn and ordered the patrol to fix bayonets. They were nearing the flank of St. Mère du Prée.

The scouts proceeded cautiously. As they made the right turn they could see the distant gray stones of the small village.

Directly ahead was a stone wall, and beyond the wall a flat green field extending four hundred yards to the outskirts of St. Mère du Prée. The village consisted of twenty small houses built around a road junction. Skirting the houses were scattered trees, a few barns, and at the left a church and graveyard.

The patrol halted, and Roth stationed them along the wall, with fifteen yards between each man. He removed his field glasses from the case on his back, adjusted them for sight, and began to survey the village. He took house by house, carefully stopping at each darkened window and moving on to the next. He saw nothing. From where he stood, the village seemed deserted. He continued his sweep, searching the church, the steeple tower, the graveyard, and the barns.

"Rodriguez! Come on over here!" Roth called.

The Platoon Sergeant came up to the Lieutenant. "Yes sir?"

"Can you see anything in there?" said Roth.

The Sergeant adjusted his own glasses, and traversed the buildings and surrounding terrain. He worked slowly, taking care not to miss an inch of space. "I can't see a thing," he said, finally lowering the binoculars.

"What do you think?" queried Roth.

The Sergeant scratched his chin. "There must be troops there. Otherwise, why would they send us out on this patrol?"

"You think they might've pulled out during the night?"

"There was plenty of firing coming from there all last night," said the Sergeant.

"Yeah... yeah, that's right," Roth said.

"I'll bet they're there," Rodriguez said, "it may be a trap!"

"I think so too," said Roth. "Well, we'll see. You keep control on the left, and I'll take the right." He again peered through his glasses, charted the information he wanted in his mind, and returned the instrument to the case on his back.

The platoon leader shoved a fresh clip of carbine ammunition into his weapon and called to the patrol. "Range: four hundred! Front! Reilly, Greenberg, McCrea, Reubens, take the left flank! Schlenk, Motoya, Warner, take the right! Sixteen rounds, medium!"

They rested their rifles on top of the wall, set the sights to the correct range, and turned their heads to watch the actions of the Lieutenant.

Roth brought his hand down in choppy motions, and the quiet was rent by the staccato explosions of nine rifles firing simultaneously.

Roth began to fire his carbine at different sections of the village. The recoil was a powerful consciousness that eliminated all suspense. He was aware only of the sharp crack of his weapon, the resultant kickback to his shoulder, and the hope of an enemy falling each time a round sped from the chamber to a darkened window in the village. He squeezed the trigger sensuously and felt the power run through the muscles of his arms, shoulders, and back.

The rapidity of the firing slowly decreased, until only a few scattered shots resounded. Then they stopped. The men looked towards their leader.

Roth rested his carbine against the wall and again searched the village with his glasses, but still saw no evidence of movement. He replaced the binoculars, secured his weapon, and gave the order to fire another sixteen rounds.

The men fired faster. Anger, coupled with relief, was felt at the lack of activity in the village. They wanted to return to the comparative safety of the perimeter defense in the rear, but they also craved the knowledge of their steel tearing into the flesh of the enemy.

"Potter, bring up the phone!" Roth shouted, after the second round had been completed.

The runner dashed over with the spool of wire and handed the phone to the Lieutenant; he stayed close and listened avidly to what followed. Roth revolved the crank handle and signaled into the speaker: "Charley Two to Charley One.... Charley Two to Charley One.... Hello, Andy?... Yeah, this is Roth.... That's right.... It seems deserted... maybe they pulled out?... No, they're not giving us any action.... Yeah, we're at the stone wall.... Look on your map.... How about us coming in?... No, there's nothing going on.... Go into it? Maybe it's a trap.... I know, I know.... Is he there?... Is he listening? ... Well, I hope he drops dead!... Okay, okay... we'll try it...."

Roth handed the phone to Potter. "Saddle up!" he ordered his men. "We're going over the wall! I don't know what's going on there, so infiltrate over... one at a time!"

Grasping his rifle in one hand and hurdling the wall with the other, Reilly was the first over. He sprinted fifteen paces, hit the ground, examined the terrain to the front, sprang to his feet, and sprinted another few paces and again hit the ground.

The others followed. Swiftly they jumped the wall, ran, and hit the ground, and ran and hit the ground. Potter was the last man over. He lay close to the wall behind the others.

The patrol sprawled on their stomachs in an extended V-formation pointed by the scouts in front. "Hit it again!" ordered Roth, after he saw that they were all safely over.

Reilly and Greenberg stood erect and began sprinting. Abruptly machine-gun cross fire from the village blazed across the field. The two men dug earth, and the guns became silent.

The scouts again raised themselves and tried to run, and the machine guns, supported by the fire of numerous rifles, again opened up. The scouts clawed for the earth.

"Open fire!" Roth screamed from his prone position.

The men squinted through their sights and tried to get their bearings on the machine guns and rifle fire, but the distance was confusing. They fired some wild shots at the village, and the machine guns blasted back in return. The Germans seemed to be well dug in and camouflaged, and to be using smokeless powder.

Roth stared until his eyes burned, but he received no clear impression from the gray walls.

Another burst opened up. Flaming tracer tails poured in a red-hosed stream three feet above their heads. The men dropped to the earth.

"Second house from the well on the left!" called Roth to his section of the line. The men fumbled with their weapons, aimed hastily, and fired a hail of bullets into a small thatched-roofed house. Chinks of stone and sparks from the impact of the rounds scattered in all directions from the target. There was a second's pause, then the machine guns and rifles from the enemy side again tore loose. Their aim remained high, and the bullets streamed safely overhead.

"They're shooting high, Lieutenant!" shouted Rodriguez above the clamor. "I don't think they're in the houses at all . . . may be beyond, behind the road junction!"

"It can't be coming from there!" Roth shouted back. "How can they see us?"

"Harassing fire! They must have observation!"

Roth was puzzled, but the Sergeant's appraisal could be correct. "We're moving forward!" he called to the patrol. "Infiltrate! Short jumps!"

The two scouts jumped to their feet, and, zig-zagging like frightened jack rabbits, ran ten paces and hit the ground in a cloud of dust.

Roth, McCrea, Reubens, and Schlenk followed. As Schlenk was about to hit the ground after his short dash, the enemy guns again blazed open. Schlenk stopped short as though he had collided with a brick wall. He stiffened, slowly sank to the ground, and rolled over on his side, holding his left arm tightly with his right hand.

"Help! Help!" he called in a frightened voice.

"Where're you hit?" shouted Roth.

"In the arm! In the arm!" cried Schlenk. "Oh, it hurts!"

"Any place else?" asked Roth.

"I . . . I don't think so!" moaned Schlenk. "Oh, somebody help me!"

"Can you make it back?" asked Roth.

"I don't know! I don't know!" whimpered Schlenk.

"Try and get back," said Roth. "You know the way, don't you?"

Schlenk nodded his head dumbly. He rose to his feet, clutching the arm with the opposite hand, and began to stagger toward the rear. The enemy's weapons again rattled, and the young soldier drunkenly sprawled to the ground. When the shots stopped, he regained his feet and staggered on. Every time he ran, the enemy teased him with their bullets. Struggling, panting, lurching like a sinking ship in a storm at sea, he finally reached the stone wall. Using his good arm as leverage, he clumsily vaulted the wall and landed on his hip and shoulder on the other side. A spatter of earth sprayed the section of wall that he had climbed. He picked himself up and continued to run wildly to the rear.

Roth sighed when Schlenk disappeared around the juncture of the trees and the meadow. "I want every section of the village covered this time!" he shouted. "Don't miss an inch! Fire when ready, and take your time!"

The men, each choosing his own target carefully, began to space rounds at the buildings ahead. They paid specific attention to the windows, doors, and misty shadows at the corners of the houses. Gravel, chipped stone, dry thatch, and steaming clouds of dust exploded volcanically, covering the small village with a translucent fog that became harder to penetrate with each minute of firing.

They sweated under the heat of the morning sun, and the rough woolen underwear tops clung irritatingly to their backs. They fired eight rounds each, reloaded and fired again, the process continuing in a flat roar. Some of the shots went wild and threw up clods of earth many yards in front of the village, and others arched over the houses to become lost in the fields beyond.

"Cease fire! Cease fire!" shouted Roth, laying his hot weapon on the ground in front of him. The men continued to fire, hypnotized by the power of their rifles and the blindness of their desire to reach out and see a tangible result accomplished by their lethal skill.

"Cease fire!" Roth called again, but the men continued to aim and squeeze. He stuck his whistle between his lips and applied the full force of his lungs to the aperture. He blew until the pressure of his blood pounded in his head. The firing gradually stopped; a few scattered shots still resounded, and then complete silence.

The Lieutenant cupped his hands to his mouth and was about to shout another order, when bedlam from the other side tore apart the silence. Twelve streams of crisscrossing tracers burned the air above, supported by what sounded like hundreds of rifles. The tracers were lower, as if the elevating mechanisms on the enemy machine guns had been dropped a few mils in order to finally get on the target. And mortars started to blast. Dull roars added heavy overtones to the tenor of the tracers, and thirty yards to the front six small craters miraculously appeared.

"Back over the wall!" Roth ordered. "Start moving...one at a time!"

Potter was the first. He ran, both arms pumping madly, the swinging spool of wire on his chest forgotten. He hurdled the wall in a frightened speedy leap, barely using his arms as leverage. When he was over he crouched, his head below the top and hidden from sight.

A steady blanket of tracers smoked through the air, and the light sixty-millimeter mortars began to decorate the field with craters. The pattern pinpointed and spread like delicate crochet work, each new hole adding to a never-ending, widening circle of holes.

The men ran wildly back, failing to infiltrate and forgetting every basic element of orderly withdrawal. As they went over the wall they bruised their legs and stomachs and crunched the bones of their knees against the rough stone surface. They crouched in trembling anticipation, awaiting with dread the next trick of the hidden enemy.

Roth raised his head and looked at the men huddled along the wall. "Spread out!" he cried. Reluctantly they added distance between themselves.

The mortars moved in, narrowing the distance between the field and the wall. One landed on the wall, a few yards to the right of the patrol, and two more exploded behind them, scattering whizzing, circling fragments of steel in all directions.

"Potter! Potter!" called the platoon leader. "Bring over the wire!"

With his back bent over double, Verne Potter scurried up to Roth. The spool of wire hung a few inches off the ground.

Frantically, Roth spun the crank handle. When he heard Dougall's voice, he shouted into the phone. "We're pulling back! They had us pinned down and we had to withdraw behind the wall!"

"Did you get any information?" asked Dougall.

"About two companies there," said Roth. "Reinforced with machine guns and mortars! Only they're not in the town! They're behind . . . probably dug in!"

"Can't you get into the town?" asked Dougall.

"Are you crazy? Ten men against almost a battalion!"

There was a pause from the other end, as if Dougall had his hand over the phone and was speaking to someone at his side. "Colonel Nielsen wants you to try again," Dougall's voice returned. "He wants you to get as close to the town as possible and see what's in there."

"We can't get near it!" Roth argued. "We were pinned down! What's he want us to do, commit suicide?"

There was another pause before Dougall again spoke. "He wants to know why you don't try rushing the place?"

Roth exploded. "Why doesn't he come down here and rush it if he's so goddamned smart? I'm not taking my men into that field again!"

The meadow behind the wall rocked with huge eruptions. The Germans had their artillery trained on the small grid square and were measuring out the terrain in carefully blocked steps.

"They got their artillery on us now!" Roth shouted. "We can't stay much longer!"

Another pause. Roth lay on the ground with the phone under his chest, and his head between his arms. "Colonel Nielsen wants you to stay where you are for a while, and see what further information you can get," said Dougall, his voice almost lost in the blasting sounds.

"Fuck Colonel Nielsen!" screamed Roth, tears of rage and fear rolling down his cheeks. "Tell the son of a bitch he's not going to be a hero with our lives! We're coming in!" He whimpered and released the switch on the phone handle. He wanted to kill the Battalion Commander, to get his hands around his throat and tear out his life.

"We're going back!" shouted Roth to the patrol. "Double time . . . take the edge of the field away from the shelling!" A heavy concentration was falling. The explosions crept in toward the wall, and in a few seconds the blasts would fall directly on it.

The men sprang to their feet and ran wildly to the right, veering in a wide semicircle toward the rear and the dark draw behind.

Chapter Six

His face glowing with anger, Lieutenant Colonel Nielsen turned to Lieutenant Dougall. "I heard his last remarks and I'm going to have him court-martialed for it! You're my witness!"

"What remarks, sir?" asked Dougall.

"The remarks he made about me!" fumed the Colonel. Dougall scratched his chest. "I don't remember any remarks about you, sir. Unless you mean about having to pull back because he was pinned down?"

"That isn't what I meant!" the Battalion Commander shouted. "I'm going to have that fool court-martialed if it's the last thing I do! This isn't the first time he's been insubordinate! And for backing him up, I'm withdrawing your promotion to captain! The recommendation was made out this morning, but I can tear it up!" He bit his short blackened fingernails, glared scornfully at the massive officer, and walked away.

Dougall laughed. He opened his mouth and the full power of his bass voice rocked against the damp earth walls of the dugout. He held his hands over his stomach and his body rocked, and his eyes grew wet with magic tears of relief. He smashed his fists against the walls and laughed louder, straining with all his being to bring up every unpleasantness experienced since the invasion. No emotion remained but the bursting of his wild joy, and he wanted to howl to everyone to join him.

Bruce Hannegan, the wiry first sergeant, stared with disbelief at the Company Commander. It was the first time that he had really seen the "old man" laugh since they embarked at Bournemouth. He stared first with amazement, then with wonder, and finally he too began to smile. His teeth parted and he chuckled. The mood expanded, and a loud laugh broke from his throat. He cackled, and a hoarse roar tore loose from his chest, and he rocked in rhythm with the Company Commander. His laugh rose up to a falsetto pitch and tears rolled freely down his face.

"Did you hear that?" shouted Dougall. "He's not going to put me in for promotion! Why, the man's a humorist!" He continued to laugh.

"I heard him! Yes sir, I heard the fat bastard!" roared the Sergeant.

"He's going to court-martial Roth, and without a witness!" added Dougall. "What's he expect to do, manufacture one?"

"He should get a medal for coming down to our CP!" said Hannegan. "Should we put him in for the D.S.C. this time?"

"No, he's far more worthy! The Congressional Medal for this act of bravery! Lieutenant Colonel Nielsen, for conspicuous gallantry above and beyond the call of duty. He this day risked his life by personally appearing only four hundred yards behind the front lines to inform one company commander that he is tearing up his promotion, and will court-martial one poor harassed first lieutenant who didn't particularly feel in the mood to commit suicide!"

"The Colonel bravely risked his precious fat neck by walking upright through a hail of mosquitoes, lice, and stinging nettles to personally deliver the ultimatum!" the First Sergeant elaborated.

The two men laughed until their strength was drained. Still smiling they sank to the floor, their bodies quivering from the uncommon effort.

"Seriously though, do you think he can do anything about Roth?" Hannegan asked.

Dougall waved his hand contemptuously. "There isn't much he can do if he has no witnesses."

"What about us?"

"Did you hear anything out of the ordinary?"

Hannegan smiled. "I get you, sir."

"Boy, I'd like to see that bastard around here during an attack!" hoped Dougall reflectively. "If one of his officers wouldn't get him, you can be sure one of the men would!"

"You won't see him within a thousand yards of the front!" said Hannegan. "He'll be so deep in his hole, you'd need an elevator to get down to see him!"

"Why, *he's* in for the Silver Star!" said Dougall cynically. "Is that right? Who recommended him for this one?"

"Wormsley again."

"That jerk! They'd better get someone else to do the recommending," said Hannegan. "A few more and headquarters'll get wise."

"They don't mind! They're all doing it. It seems to be the policy to have the battalion staffs well decorated."

"The alumni association of West Point again, huh?"

"That's the size of it," said Dougall. "Colonel Ainsley, the regimental exec., got the D.S.C. for crossing a road when he was warned by the man guarding it not to. The road was zeroed in, Ainsley got shot in the ass, and a nice medal for his stupidity."

"All we can get here are Bronze Stars," said Hannegan. "Four per cent per command a week. I hear the Wacs are getting them, too. One for each mission under a major or higher, and an oak-leaf cluster for every special job."

"No, it's five missions," stated Dougall. "Christ, Hannegan, are you trying to cheapen the medal? One mission . . . !"

Hannegan lounged against the wall of the dugout and rolled a cigarette. The paper they were sending down was pretty thin stuff. He shook his head solemnly. The strain was telling on everyone. He was glad that Dougall had laughed. . . do the boy good. He was the conscientious type who carried the troubles of the world on his shoulders, and if he didn't have the company to worry about, he surer than hell would find something else.

Dougall absently made marks in pencil on his map and softly hummed the melody of the quartet from Rigoletto. From the opera in Frisco to the smoke of Normandy was quite a jump . . . from the delicate shadings of music to the timpani of combat in three short years. But he had a feeling that he would never sing again. There were twinges of intuition that came to him out of the night which told him the narrow confines of the opera stage would never again be able to hold him. He wanted to sing, yet he felt that that life was done with, a part of the past that would remain only in memory.

Fate could play funny tricks, like the trick of the war and his becoming a combat soldier. The twinge on dark nights told him that he was forever to roam. There was an element greater than the music, and the stage, and the orchestra tuning up before a performance, that whispered to him and told him that he would have to seek and find before he'd ever come to rest.

And now it was so far away. The Hill and the lessons, and the practicing every day for years, ever since he discovered he could sing in the college glee club. But the voice was harsh and burned from too many cigarettes, and from shouting orders and commands, and screaming at his men to take cover during a heavy bombardment, and quarts of cognac whenever they liberated a wine cellar.

He could come back... a few months of practice was all he needed ... but he knew he'd never return. The past was a closed book.

He loved music, the swaying of the violins and cellos, and the rumble of the percussion pieces, and his voice coming out clear and strong... but it no longer was enough. He had no idea where he was to go or what he'd find when he got there, but the journey itself was evident. He had to go.

There was a lull after the last harassing barrage, and the men of the first platoon who had been left at the perimeter defense came up from their holes to take advantage of the rare warm sun. Coombs, Hohmeyer, and Sanchez were on the hedgerow, and the others sprawled about on the ground in various attitudes of repose. Their weapons were near them, locked and ready.

"How come you get away from Federal agents?" asked Ernest Groggins. His innocent face was wide open, eagerly awaiting another chapter of Staff Sergeant Saunders' adventurous career.

Saunders munched on his cud reflectively, spat a blob of brown juice into the grass a short distance away, and twanged nasally: "Wal, them Federal guys has to work with local authorities to git any inf'rmation. And if them little boys wander alone up in the hills, they're liable to git lost. Mebbe a BAR'll git 'em ... mebbe they'll fall down a hole and never no more return. If you don't know hill country, it's purty rough to wander 'round in. So, they gotta contac' the sheriff and ask him if anybody's been manufactur'n round them parts. If the sheriff wants to, he kin give 'em the inf'rmation."

The Sergeant's mouth filled up, and he leaned over and let fly another stream of tobacco juice along the path of the wind. It flew straight and spattered stickily against the base of a tree stump. He paused a moment, made sure of his audience's attention, and then continued.

"Wal, the sheriff's my third cousin once removed, and he has a powerful thirst. I supply him a gallon or so a week, the Federal men don't git no inf'rmation, and I kin run my business honest and respectable."

"Boy, that's all right!" exclaimed Groggins. "What a racket! That's what I'm gonna do when this is over!"

"Tell us about Leavenworth," requested Schmidt, the redheaded soldier. "Was it tough?"

"Nah," said Saunders serenely. "I had 'em eatin' out my hand!"

"Say, how did you get caught if you had the law wised up?" asked Jamborsky.

"It's a long story," yawned the Sergeant. "Woman trouble . . . the same ole thing."

The breeze blew stronger from the west, and the men began to wrinkle up their persecuted nostrils.

"What a stink!" exclaimed Sergeant Olivet, the third squad leader. "Christ, what an abortion!"

"What stink? I don't smell nothing," said Groggins. He had had a cold since they landed.

"Now I'm sure you're not human!" said Olivet in disgust. "The stink of dead horses, and cows, and lousy Jerries!"

"I can't smell nothing," insisted Groggins.

"How about our own guys?" said Jamborsky. "Christ, I can smell 'em in my sleep . . . and recognize each one!"

"If there wuzn't that stink blowin' all the time, I think I'd git lonesome," said Saunders.

"It's worse than the shelling," said Schmidt.

"Nothing's worse than that," said Jamborsky. "Only this goddam smell keeps reminding . . . keeps reminding you that maybe you're next . . . !"

"It ain't so bad," said Saunders. "No worse'n a hog pen back home. Lord, I even think the hogs smell worse!"

"I never smelled a hog in my life, and I never intend to in the future!" Olivet said flatly. "When I get back I'm going to stick to the city

"... the smokier the better ... and I don't want to see another green thing as long as I live!"

"Well, I like the country, and farmin' ain't so bad," said Groggins. "Grow your own stuff, and never have no worry about where your next meal's comin' from."

"It ain't the way I heard it!" said Olivet. "You farmers are always bellyaching that you're not getting prices for your crops, or that they're not growing, or that you're always starving because of this or that administration!"

"I ain't never bellyached," said Groggins. "I get more to eat home than I can put in my stomach!" He slapped his hard belly.

"Then why are you farmers always bitching?" insisted Olivet.

"I don't know," said Groggins. "I ain't never heard any of em."

"Watch it!" screamed Jamborsky, flattening himself on the ground.

A whispering, whishing flutter vibrated overhead and exploded in the field behind the men. They hurled themselves to the ground, with a few managing to make it to their foxholes.

The whispering promises continued to come in groups of three. Shells burst in front of the hedgerow, in the field behind, and directly on the platoon area.

Jamborsky rolled for one of the holes. He landed on top of Groggins who had his face buried in his hands and his knees drawn up under his chin.

The shells slithered over, roaring, blasting, and searing the air with shattering sirening jagged-edged fragments. The shrapnel, whining like an approaching police siren, could be heard moaning closer and closer.

Jamborsky's body shook spasmodically. Sweat streamed from his pores, saturating his clothing and the tight earth surrounding him. At each blast his teeth chattered and a gagging moan came up from his stomach. He jammed his hands over his ears, and the long nails drew blood from the sensitive, dirty skin. Dry sobs rolled off his lips, and he started to scream. He laughed and screamed in turn, not knowing why the laughter poured out, or from what depths came the strange screams. They tore out of his bowels, and he no longer could hear the blasting of the artillery. He beat his head upon Groggins' back and kicked the sides of the foxhole with his feet.

With a tremendous effort Groggins raised up his body and struggled loose from the writhing weight of the Sergeant. He ran from the hole as fast as he could in order to get away from the sound of the terrible laughter.

Jamborsky sobbed and shrieked and moaned, and lumps of sour vomit trickled down his chin to fall upon the dark earth of the hole. He rolled his face in the mess, and the sticky compound smeared his nose and forehead.

The concentration ended. Saunders and Olivet dashed over to the screaming hole. It was a struggle to lift Jamborsky to his feet, and when they got him back to daylight he suddenly jerked loose and raced wildly about the platoon area. His breath came in hoarse grating paroxysms, his laughter shrieking like the dying whinnies of a torn horse.

He kept his head down as he circled the area and screamed and shouted and laughed at the ground beneath him. White froth bubbled from his mouth; his helmet had fallen off behind him; and he shambled like a crazed ape. The screams grew higher until the sounds were almost lost in the upper pitches.

Saunders hurled himself at the broken man, tackled him below the knees, and brought him to the ground.

Olivet came up behind, fell to the earth beside Saunders, and helped him to pin the man's arms and legs.

"Let's go! Some more of you men!" shouted Saunders as he struggled with the screaming Jamborsky.

A few of the men rushed over to help subdue the Sergeant. Jamborsky rolled and twisted and snapped his body, his strength prodigious under the pressure of all the bodies. His screams died down but the laughter continued in a sobbing jerky fashion, hoarse as a child in a croupy spasm.

With the help of the other men, Saunders and Olivet raised the Sergeant to his feet and dragged him to the rear.

"We'll take him to the aid station," said Saunders. "Give him some 'blue eighty-eights.' " He laughed humorlessly, and tried to think of something else.

"Holy Jesus Christ!" muttered Private Hohmeyer, as he saw what happened from the hedgerow. "Holy good Jesus Christ!"

Chapter Seven

QUIETLY AND WEARILY, the patrol plodded through the draw. The sun, hot and high in the sky, lighted many of the formerly dark shadows of the heavily foliaged route. The ground steamed under the rays of the sun, its odor carrying the overpowering musk of decay.

The men panted and muttered profanities under their breaths, and constantly raised their hands to wipe the stinging sweat from their faces. Their feet squashed and sucked in the black dampness beneath.

They were nearing the perimeter defense. Through the trees and underbrush they could see the familiar hedgerow running at right angles to the draw; and the few black blobs of heads along the parapet became more distinct. Without an order the pace increased, and they struggled and floundered to hasten the moment when they would fall to the ground under the large protection of the wall of earth, brush, and thorns.

The men again began to talk. Home was any place familiar: a piece of ground where they would not have to move or feel the presence of the unknown; where they could rest and become lost in sleep.

Finally they reached the confines of the hedgerow and with voluble expressions of relief climbed to the other side. The strain was over, the patrol completed. There was nothing to do now but forget . . . forget what was past, or what might happen in the coming minutes or hours.

"Disperse the men and see that they get some rest/' said Roth to his Sergeant.

"Yes, sir," said Rodriguez. "How about rations?"

"See Saunders. If none came in, tell him to get hold of the Battalion S-4."

Roth slung his carbine over his shoulder and walked towards the Company CP. He thrust his hands in his pockets and shuffled slowly across the field. He heard a hushed whishing overhead, but he did not pause. Let them come.

When he reached the company command post, he climbed down the fire-step into the dugout and took a seat, his back resting against the earth wall. He lit a cigarette and sucked in refreshing gulps of blue smoke.

Dougall sat on a raised plank, studying a set of maps. He glanced up when the Lieutenant entered and motioned that he would be with him shortly.

Hannegan was puzzling over the morning report, the long black leather pad opened on his crossed knees. His brow was wrinkled as he added a column of figures on a piece of scrap paper. He bit the tip of his pencil and mumbled a series of long drawn-out sons of bitches, cursing the unknown powers which had ordained that a first sergeant do clerical work.

Lieutenant Dougall completed his examination of the maps and looked up at Roth. "It didn't go so hot, did it?" he said sympathetically.

"It never does," said Roth, his eyes searching the ground.

"How many men did you lose?" asked Dougall.

"Two. Colucci killed, and Schlenk hit."

"I saw Schlenk. He came in a while ago," said Dougall. "Was he hurt bad?" asked Roth.

"Bones in his wrist broken . . . he'll be all right. Too bad about Colucci, though."

"He went quick . . . the easy way."

"You lost Jamborsky, also," said Dougall.

Roth raised his head. "Yeah? What happened to him?"

"He blew his top. They dragged him to the aid station a while ago," said Dougall.

"Good. . . he was ready for it," said Roth.

Dougall pondered for a moment. "Are you certain there's about two companies at St. Mere?" he finally asked.

"There could be more . . . maybe three at the most," said Roth.

"The Battalion Commander is plenty sore at you," offered Dougall slowly.

Roth did not look up. "So what," he murmured.

"I think he heard what you said over the phone," said Dougall quietly. "He's talking court-martial."

Roth shook his head slightly.

Dougall uttered a short laugh. "He doesn't like being called a son of a bitch. He's sensitive that way."

"He's a bastard," Roth stated flatly.

Dougall stood up and came over to Roth. He placed his hand gently on the Lieutenant's shoulder. "You'll have to get hold of yourself, Paul. You just can't go around blowing your top at battalion commanders. You know they can court-martial you . . . have you broken for insubordination at the front." Roth looked up with tears in his eyes. "I don't give a damn any more!"

"I know how you feel. But we're still here to carry out orders, regardless of how senseless we may think them to be."

"This patrol was unnecessary!" said Roth, his voice rising. "They have all the information they need! Why in the hell did they have to send us out and get one man killed and another wounded?"

"Information has to be kept fresh . . . has to be renewed constantly."

"It's the same old goddamned story! Without knowing their ass from a hole in the ground they send ten men out, against maybe three hundred, to get slaughtered! That lousy Wormsley . . . who's supposed to do most of the patrolling . . . gets a bug up his ass every time he thinks he should make noises like an intelligence officer."

"Orders for *this* patrol came from Regimental Headquarters," said Dougall.

"They don't know what they're doing either!" said Roth. "Why don't they give orders to fight, instead of hanging around with their thumbs up their asses?"

"We're attacking this afternoon," stated Dougall.

"It's about time," said Roth. "When?"

"About one o'clock. I'll send a runner down when the order is ready."

Roth lit another cigarette on the butt of the old one and stared at the ground.

Dougall tried to think of words, something to lessen Roth's despair. The motif had been the same recently, when any of the officers returned from patrol. They shouted and bitched, and raised their voices high to the unhearing heavens over the futility of patrolling through the black nights and misty days. And it couldn't be helped. Their nerves were strained to the breaking point. Another few days in the line and he wouldn't be able to vouch for the minds of anyone in the outfit.

"Why don't you go back to your platoon and get some rest?" suggested Dougall.

"Maybe I will," said Roth listlessly. He stood up and started to leave the dugout. "See you later." He climbed out of the hole in the earth and walked across the fields towards his men.

The First Platoon area was quiet. The men on day duty rested against the hedgerow and stared across the blowing grass of the fields to the front. The men who had come off patrol were curled up asleep in their foxholes, their dirty, bearded faces tightened even in repose. A few other men sprawled on the ground around some heating coffee and conversed in monotonous tones, keeping their minds off reality until the stimulant was hot enough to drink. Sergeant Olivet crouched, stripped to the waist, and shaved. Even in combat he remained scrupulously clean and managed to shave once a week.

Sergeant Saunders walked up to Roth. "The Third Battalion had tank trouble this morning. Do you think I oughta put an extra bazooka along the road?"

"Whatever you think best," said Roth without looking at the Sergeant and moving on towards his foxhole.

The Sergeant gazed after the Lieutenant. The boy sure must have been done in from that patrol. He turned around and called for some men.

Roth sank into his hole, removed the cartridge belt and slung it over the edge, near his hand where it could be grasped in a hurry, rested the carbine beside him, and tipped his helmet back on the ground as a pillow. He closed his eyes and tried to sleep, twisting and turning to fit his body to the contour of the protecting depth.

His eyelids started to grow heavy. Suddenly he squirmed and sat up. Something was biting him. He searched with his hand at the small of his back and angrily dug his nails into the thin skin over his spine. The itch relieved, he again lay back and closed his eyes.

There was a pattering staccato rattle coming from the distance, miles away. Some outfit, German or American or British, pulling off some rapid-fire. Then he could hear the round luscious plop of mortar firing pins being set off as they dropped into the shiny belly of a sixty or eighty-one millimeter weapon. He counted the seconds. One .. two .. three .. four .. five .. six .. seven ... and the dull thuds as they exploded in some other sector. Poor bastards ... mortars could really be aimed.

He shifted and rolled over on his other side. Planes came from the direction of the Channel. American. The British were flying most of the night missions. Someone was shouting ... probably screaming ... behind another hill. It came as a wail, almost a whisper, but the earth of the foxhole was a sound shell, and he could hear it clearly. It stopped in space, seemed to float like a glider on a windless day, and then continued on, quivering and vibrating up to a higher key until the sound was lost. But he knew that it still issued from the stranger's throat.

The cows in the fields lowed monotonously. He had almost forgotten them, yet their presence was as usual as the constant sigh of the wind humming through the trees. They were up there on four legs, and some on shattered knee bones, chomping away as they always had done, dumb both to pain and peace. Shells could pass clean through their bodies, he thought, but they probably would continue to chomp their cuds until the last red flow of life streamed from their veins to the grass beneath them. Did they feel pain? He often wondered. If he possessed such impassivity, he would have made a great soldier. The great ones had it. But he had not been born a soldier, and no amount of indoctrination could make him into one. Perhaps the ability to soldier was an attribute of birth, present in every throb of a man's being. . . an appendage like his arms and legs. . . .

The breeze rustled through the trees, and trickled through the grass, and whispered like the voice of his conscience. What conscience? He had no conscience but for the preservation of his own life, limbs, and sanity: preservation so that he could ultimately get home and pick up life from where he had left off. Life? Life? He hadn't even known what it was all about, this life that had been talked of, and so much written about, and spouted redundantly by poets throughout the ages. He had been a miserable suckling, an adolescent with hair on his face. This life that he hadn't yet lived and knew even less about. That's why he wanted to live.

He rolled over again. The distant noises became more annoying. His ears had become more sharply tuned to the sounds of nature and man, and it was like knowing a new language. He could gather together each sound, or group of sounds, and by the pitch tell exactly what was taking place. The clanging of truck doors behind the lines told him that they were moving up supplies and ammunition for the coming attack; the roaring motors disappearing over the horizon was proof that they were empty and returning to the rear for new loads. The occasional shirring overhead, with the solemn distant blasts on the enemy positions, told him the field artillery was preparing fire data for future concentrations, probably to be used in support of their attack. The rattling of the small observation plane overhead, shaking like a rusty washing machine, was evidence that additional pin-point targets were being surveyed. And the man who screamed in the distance most likely had been wounded, or cried out his last defiance at a life that betrayed him, or had lost his conscious equilibrium and returned to other levels. Or he might have been screaming with the sheer joy of living.

Roth twisted and squirmed, but his eyeballs did not acquire the necessary heavy feeling. One leg began to itch and he kicked at it with the opposite foot until the crawling thing disappeared. He rolled some gravel between his thumb and forefinger and tried to think of women's breasts. But his imagination lay fallow, unseeded and parched. Only the present existed, and that was far worse than all the evils that the fancy could conceive. He felt a pulse beating on his temples, a tiny vein that twisted and jumped. Another attack, one leading into the next with no respite . . . only the white-boned presence of reality. He had had it, but he had lost it—one, two, or three weeks ago—and it would never return. There was no reason to carry on with confidence lost, the spirit dried and impotent, and courage a false conditioning that he once had hypnotized himself into believing he possessed.

But there were medals and no one would believe, when he told them, that he had cracked and was not a hero; and that the Silver Star, and the Purple Heart received on the beach for a scratch, were only pieces of engraved metal without meaning. They would laud him, and shake his hand, and clap him on the back, and say they always knew he had it in him. But he wouldn't show them.

Yet Ellen would make him drag them out into the clear light of day, and she'd be proud of him, and no words ever created would make her believe that he was anything else but a hero. She had a way about those things, and she'd protest that everybody felt fear, and that the hero was the man who could continue onward even though his knees were trembling.

Still that wasn't the way of things. What he felt and knew couldn't be put into words. They were too deeply entrapped in recesses of his mind where they could not be clarified. He felt fear, but his courage was false and his confidence and strength a weak mask, attributes that he never had, but forced himself to acquire. The whole chapter was a lie.

He was no hero. He had receded back to that small trembling boy who jumped at shadows, screamed in fright at his over-magnified dreams, and grew red-faced, tongue-tied, and impotent at any suggestion of violence. His entire life had been a masquerade of compensatory actions. Football, when he was too clumsy to get out of his own way and vomited behind the stairs every afternoon after a game in the park; acting a part all the time, always trying to be what he wasn't....

And there was no way back. He had had it, and it was gone; but the husk remained to cry alone at break of dawn and quiver emptily during shadowed nights. He couldn't go forward, and he couldn't go back.

He sat up and lit a cigarette; no sense in trying to sleep. Everything was quiet, too quiet for the middle of the day. It was a screaming silence more promising than a battalion of artillery coming directly down on a target.

Potter lay curled up in the hole next to Roth's. He had a slight smile turning up the corners of his mouth and he looked unusually happy, not like the frightened little gamin who had huddled in fear that morning. He could be dreaming of home, and of his mother's pies. That's what the papers said soldiers dreamed about and fought for: their mother's apple pies, icecream sodas, the home-town team winning the World Series, hot dogs, and a five-buck raise when they got back to the office. They fought for their Momma's apron strings, and for wonderful Sunday picnics with the girls of their dreams down at Anderson's Creek in a thousand counties of America.

Roth felt hungry. He went to his pack and removed a K-ration package. He opened the waxed cardboard and lifted out the assorted containers within. He found cheese, dog biscuits, a lump of sugar, a small paper filled with bouillon powder, and a piece of hard candy. He threw the bouillon over the hedgerow, put the candy and the sugar in his pocket for later, and began to open the can of cheese.

Hungrily he munched on the dehydrated biscuits and the dry cheese, taking swallows of warm water from his canteen after each few mouthfuls. When he finished, still as hungry as when he started, he threw the cardboard and other debris into a pile of garbage near his foxhole.

He watched Saunders greedily counting and arranging in neat piles a small fortune in French paper francs. He thumbed each bill carefully, setting them in the proper denominations, and when he had a pile ready he wrapped it with a length of dirty string and replaced it in his pocket. From the enemy, and sometimes Allied, bodies that he rifled, the man would be rich if the war or he lasted long enough.

McCrea had awakened and was concentrating over a V-letter sheet. He used a small issue Bible as his desk and seemed tranquil while he wrote. A few times he gazed up at the sky in thought and then went back to his paper and scribbled hurriedly. It seemed as if he had so much to get down that he felt the day would quickly end before he could say what he wanted.

As he watched the scenes around him, a spark of awareness flashed in Roth's mind. He still had a job to do, and responsibility began to tickle his conscience. He knew he'd have to play it out until the final card was dealt.

"Rodriguez! Rodriguez!" called Roth.

The Platoon Sergeant was seated upright in his foxhole reading a ragged copy of the Stars and Stripes. He lowered the paper and looked toward the Lieutenant.

"Will you come over here a minute?" said Roth.

The Sergeant placed the paper under his pack and in slow dignity walked over to his platoon leader.

"Do you have any suggestions for a man to take Jamborsky's place?" asked Roth.

"I can think of a couple of guys, but we still don't have too much choice," said the sergeant.

"What do you think of Motoya?" said Roth.

"I don't know," mused the sergeant. "Can we trust him?"

"I think so. There's no better combat soldier in the outfit," said Roth.

"Yeah, but how many times has he gone over-the-hill?" Roth laughed scoffingly. "That doesn't count out here! You're long enough a soldier to know that!"

"Yeah, but he's too wild. Even out here he's liable as not to disappear on us one of these fine days."

"I don't think so," said Roth. "I think he's just the man to run the second squad."

"How about Reilly?" offered Rodriguez.

"He's a good man, but I don't think he has enough common sense," said Roth.

Rodriguez puffed thoughtfully on his pipe. "Greenberg?"

"Not bad. But I still think Motoya is the best bet for the job."

"I don't know," Rodriguez said. "I wonder...."

"What do you say we try him?" said Roth. "Nothing has to be permanent...."

"Well, if you want him...."

"Good! I'm sure he'll make out!"

"How about assistant squad leaders?" asked Rodriguez.

"I don't know how we can appoint any," said Roth. "We're so damn short now; if we try to get up to full strength on non-coms we'll have a platoon of sergeants with no privates."

"We should have a few ready to step in, just in case...

"I'll leave it up to you ... see what you can figure out," said Roth.

"Who would you want?" asked the Sergeant.

"You know the men as well as I do," said Roth. "If you come to a decision, pick who you think is the best."

Rodriguez nodded his head, and turned to leave.

"One more thing, send Motoya over," said Roth.

Roth wondered how he would word the proposition to Motoya. The man was cynical and bitter and desired only to remain in the anonymity of the ranks. He once had been a staff sergeant but, due to a controversy with the former commander of B Company, he had turned in his stripes and had since been a bad actor: twice charged with desertion, and four courts-martial for AWOL.

Motoya stood in front of the Lieutenant. His hands were thrust in his pockets and his strong chin inclined at an arrogant angle. His head was bare, and his long straight black hair hung over his eyes.

"You sent for me, sir?" said the Mexican. There was an unreadable twinkle in his eyes.

"Where's your helmet?" said Roth sternly.

Motoya raised his hand to his head. "Oh, I must've left it in my hole," he said smiling.

"What's the order about steel-helmets?" said Roth.

"That helmets are to be worn at all times," said Motoya dryly.

"Don't let me catch you without it in the future!" barked Roth.

"Yes, sir."

"You're taking over the second squad," said Roth matter-of-factly.

"What do you mean?"

"I'm making you a squad leader."

"Me a squad leader?" said Motoya in exaggerated disbelief. "That's right. You're taking Jamborsky's place."

Motoya shook his head stupidly. "But I don't want to be a noncom."

"Why?"

The handsome Mexican shrugged his shoulders and held out his open palms.

"I know you've been carrying a grudge about what's happened in the past, and maybe I can't blame you for feeling the way you do. But this is more serious than personal feelings, and I'm asking you to do a job!"

Motoya's lips drew back in an ugly smile. "I don't want any goddam stripes.... I don't want nothin'."

"You're one of the best men we've got," continued Roth. "We're going to attack in a little while, and you're needed badly in charge of the second squad!"

Motoya remained silent.

"You know, I can order you to do it, but that isn't what I want. Forget the past... it doesn't exist here. How about it?"

Motoya pursed his lips solemnly. "I'll take the squad, but I don't want the stripes," he said impassively.

"Why not?"

"I don't want nothin' from the army!"

"It'll mean more money," said Roth.

"They can take their money and shove it!" spat Motoya.

"Give me the squad, and you can give someone else the goddamned stripes!"

"Just as you say," said Roth. "Thanks a lot, Motoya."

"When do you want me to take over?"

"Right away. I don't have to worry about your doing a good job."

Roth stifled an impulse to slap the man's back. With him at the head of the second squad, the toughest missions would be a lot easier.

With no more words, Motoya walked back to where his equipment lay. It was what he wanted, but he couldn't show the Lieutenant that he was too eager. He didn't want their goddam stripes, but he did want a squad. Then he'd get some action. The other squad leaders were too careful, too slow when opportunity came their way. Now he could really operate.

Roth watched the broad-shouldered Mexican until he disappeared around a slight bend in the hedgerow. He smiled sympathetically at the man's sense of justice. He wanted nothing but to be left alone and to do his job which, in his case, was to kill as many of the enemy as possible. The more he killed, the sooner he would get home. It was simple.

Chapter Eight

A GROUP OF YOUNG MEN, led by Sergeant Hannegan, marched across the field from the direction of the company command post. Roth stared with amusement at the collection of soldiers. They were encumbered by full field packs topped by two blanket rolls; an extra pair of shoes hung down from each pack; and some of them carried in their free hands assorted bundles and packages.

"Hup, two, hee, haw . . . hup, two, hee, haw!" shouted the First Sergeant. "Pick up the step . . . you're in a war now! Hup, two, hee, haw! De . . ta . . il . . . HALT!" He stopped the men near Roth, who watched with an uncontrollable smile on his face.

"First Sergeant Hannegan reporting with replacements!" he said in a loud, clear voice, and saluted briskly.

"Watch the saluting, Hannegan," whispered Roth gayly. "You'll have a hundred snipers on me in a minute." Then in a normal voice. "Replacements? Good! How many are there?"

"Fifteen. All plucked and fresh!" The sergeant turned to the men who were staring at Roth. "Nobody gave at ease! Stand at attention!"

The new men snapped back their shoulders as best they could under the weight of all their equipment. They grew red-faced and hot.

"Why don't you take it easy on them?" whispered Roth.

"Ah, it'll do them good," the sergeant whispered back. "Let them know they're still in the army."

"Do you have a roll?" asked Roth.

Hannegan reached into his back pocket, pulled out a crumpled sheet of typewritten paper, and handed it to the platoon leader.

Roth walked over to the men. They all looked fresh and young and recently shaven, and their equipment and uniforms were of recent issue. They stared expectantly at the Lieutenant. A few had worried wrinkles at the corners of their eyes.

"At ease, men," Roth ordered kindly. "And take off all that junk, and spread out. The first thing you learn . . . dispersion and more dispersion!"

The men still looked at Roth questioningly without moving.

"The Lieutenant said at ease, and remove your equipment!" Hannegan shouted.

Roth laughed in realization. "That's right, fellows. I'm your platoon leader. We don't wear insignia in combat. Snipers have a well-developed appetite for American lieutenants."

The men laughed self-consciously, trying to place this bearded, dirty, ragged-kneed person who was responsible for their welfare from then on. He didn't much look like the gravel-voiced martinets who had been on their tails from the New York Port of Embarkation through to the beachhead at Normandy. They removed their heavy packs and blanket rolls, and sighed with relief as new life flowed through their tired shoulder muscles and beaten backs.

When all the equipment was on the ground, Roth ordered the new men to be seated and started to call the roll.

"Appleby!"

"Here, sir!"

"How long have you been in the army?" Roth questioned.

"Five months," answered a youth with straw-colored hair.

"Where did you get your training?" asked Roth. Five months against the best trained army in the world.

"Fort McPherson, sir," answered Appleby, wondering why the Lieutenant asked such questions.

"McCarthy!"

"Here, sir!" A short, heavily bearded man.

Roth looked at him for a second. "How old are you?"

"Thirty-nine, sir," answered McCarthy.

"I thought they weren't sending down men over thirty," said Roth.

"So did I," laughed McCarthy. He looked like a man who had done heavy labor all his life. The others laughed with him. Roth smiled.

"Schonbrun!"

"Here, sir!" The man had a quavering, plaintive voice. He was thin, and his back bent as though he had a bad curvature.

Roth stared at Schonbrun. The man looked very familiar.

"Where are you from?" asked Roth.

"New York, sir," answered Schonbrun.

Roth felt sure he knew him from some place. He continued down the list.

"Abbruzio!"

"Here, sir!" A well-built, olive-skinned fellow who didn't appear to be more than eighteen years of age. He smiled openly and cockily at the Lieutenant, a warm friendly light in his eyes.

"How long have you been in the army?" asked Roth. The kid had a nice smile.

"Four months, sir," said Abbruzio.

"Where were you trained?"

"Camp Howze."

"Are you good with a rifle?" asked Roth.

"Yes, sir! I fired expert!" boasted Abbruzio.

Roth continued on with the list.

"Kimmel!"

"Here, sir!"

Roth gazed at the list again. "Sergeant?" he asked.

"Yes, sir," said Kimmel, a tall rotund man who would have looked at home behind the metal grille of a bank teller's window.

This was the first replacement noncom to be assigned to Roth's platoon. "How long have you been in the Army, Sergeant?"

"Three years."

"Infantry?"

The Sergeant appeared slightly uncomfortable. "No, sir. Air Force."

"Had any infantry training?" asked Roth.

"Six weeks." Kimmel's face grew red.

Roth pondered. It would be murder to place the man in charge of a squad.

"Sergeant Hannegan," Roth called, and the First Sergeant stepped up to him. "Put Kimmel in one of the squads as a . . . well, a trainee for squad leader," he whispered. "Maybe he'll learn quickly, and we can give him an assistant's job later on."

"I'll make him Olivet's shadow," Hannegan whispered back. "Christ, I don't know what the army's coming to when they have to send the country-club set down to the front!"

The First Sergeant stepped back, and the platoon leader continued on with the roll.

"Wong!"

"Here, sir!" A slender, scholarly looking Chinese.

"Been in the army long, soldier?" asked Roth.

Wong smiled and showed a neat array of large white teeth. "Four years, sir."

"That's a long time," said Roth. "Infantry all along?"

"Yes, sir." Wong spoke eagerly. "Sir, but I'm supposed to go to the Pacific. Interpreter."

Roth felt embarrassed. "This is quite the opposite, I guess. But there isn't much we can do now."

"But I've been trained as an interpreter. . . ." The man seemed to plead.

"We'll see what we can do," mumbled Roth, avoiding any further glances at Wong.

"Wolcott!"

"Here, sir!" snapped a morose looking man in his early thirties. He seemed worried and disconsolate.

"Williams!"

"Here, suh," came the reply in a musical, southern voice. The man had pale blond hair and a tremendous physique, with huge shoulders that tapered down to a needle-thin waist. When he spoke, he held his head down and peered at Roth from between his eyebrows.

"Where are you from?" asked Roth.

"San Antone', sir," answered Williams.

"Been in the army long?"

"Yes suh! Seven years!" smiled the powerful fellow.

"Hmm. Where're your stripes?" asked Roth.

"A woman got 'em," said Williams cheerfully.

"What do you mean?"

"Gol-danged woman upped and give birth just when we were ready to leave Fort Sam. . . ."

Roth laughed. "You mean you went over-the-hill?"

"That's part of it, suh," stated Williams.

Roth's eyes went down the list. An ex noncom... would pay to keep a lookout for him.

"Meyers!"

"Here, sir!" A man with thick, steel-rimmed glasses and a heavy European accent.

"Where did you take basic?" asked Roth.

"Camp Wheeler," the words were guttural. "Cooks and Baker's school."

"You had infantry training, though, didn't you?"

"Yes, sir. Thirteen weeks."

"Are you a cook?" questioned Roth.

"Yes, sir. One year."

He was the third cook received in as many weeks. No wonder the hot food, sent down occasionally, was so lousy.

"Abadjian!"

"Here, sir!" answered a sleek soldier, as neat in his uniform as if he were shined up for a Saturday night date.

"Stepkowicz!"

"Present!" called out a red-cheeked soldier.

"Repeat that!" said Roth.

"Here, sir," said Stepkowicz, his face a bit brighter.

"That's better," said Roth, stifling a smile. A comedian in every lot, always a guy who strives to preserve his individuality.

"Northrup!"

"Here, sir!" in well-enunciated tones. A college man, probably yanked out in the middle of his junior year.

"Higgins!"

"Here, sir," in a dull spiritless voice. The man was pale and colorless, and his cheeks were indented with acne pocks.

"How long have you been in the army?"

"Six months," said Higgins in a monotonous drone.

"Any bazooka training?"

"A little."

"We might be able to use you on one," said Roth. It didn't take much initiative, only the ability to hold the weapon while the gunner aimed it and to assist in carrying the thing on long marches.

"Wysocki!"

"Here, sir!" A tall farmer with faded hair, gangling arms and legs, and an exaggerated Adam's apple that fluttered when he spoke.

"Can you handle a BAR?" asked Roth.

"I fired expert," said the tall man in a mid-western drawl.

Roth made a checkmark beside the name. Big men handled the BAR much easier than smaller fellows. And Wysocki looked like a cool individual.

"Murphy!"

"Here, sir!" Murphy bellowed as if he knew it was the conclusion of the list. It was a New York voice.

"Been in the army long, Murphy?"

"A year last week, Lieutenant," said Murphy crisply.

"Infantry?"

"T'ree months in Ordnance, and the rest of the time Infantry."

Roth made a check next to Murphy's name. He looked like good noncom material.

The Lieutenant folded the list and placed it in his pocket. He walked past the large assortment of equipment piled on
the ground and prodded a few of the packages with his foot. "What's in this package?" he asked.

"Candy, sir," answered Abadjian.

"Do you expect to carry it with you into the attack?" said Roth.

"I don't know," said the sleek soldier.

Roth stood back and again addressed the group. "Fellows, you're carrying a lot of junk that'll do you more harm than good. Get rid of those blanket rolls, extra shoes, candy, knitted socks from home, extra cartons of cigarettes, and anything else that might add one extra ounce of weight on your backs. Pile all the crap right here, and when you've been assigned to your squads a detail will be picked to carry it all to the rear. You're to carry nothing but combat packs . . . and those to be light as possible . . . and your weapons and ammunition. In case blankets are ever needed, they'll be issued to you. And you'll get all the candy you need with your rations."

Abbruzio raised his hand. "How about stationery, sir?"

"You can take a few sheets . . . you won't need more," said Roth. "You won't have much time for letter writing."

"Thank you," said Abbruzio.

"I don't like to make pretty speeches," continued Roth. "But there're one or two final things I have to say. Combat is no bed of roses, but if a man pays attention and doesn't forget the things he learned in training, he'll come out all right. Keep your eyes on your squad leaders at all times, and follow to the letter their orders. When you're moving, keep dispersed; and when you're stopped, dig your holes deep... the way you dug them in basic training. Keep alert and stay on the ball, and I'm sure you'll be okay. Good luck."

Roth turned to the First Sergeant. "Hannegan, march these men to Sergeant Rodriguez, and tell him to assign them to squads."

"Yes, sir," said Hannegan, and turned to the men. "Pick up your equipment and follow me."

The new men secured their equipment, many of them casting last looks at the weight that had been with them for so many weeks. They swung off behind the First Sergeant.

Roth lit a cigarette and watched them as they walked off. The replacements lifted some of his cares, but still the outfit wasn't up to full strength. And it was hard to determine just how effective they'd be during the coming attack. New men were apt to get panicky... especially the younger ones... with many of them hitting the ground when they should run, and running when they should hit the ground. They looked like a nice group, though... young and fresh and still eager. In another week they'd be tired and old, covered with beards and dirt, their eyes showing the red of strain and fear and lack of sleep, and a thousand real and imagined worries.

The Lieutenant sat down and rested his back against the hedgerow, and was about to close his eyes when Wolcott, the morose replacement, came up to him and saluted.

Roth raised his head. "You can eliminate the saluting. We forget that at the front. What do you want?"

"The First Sergeant gave me permission to speak to you, sir," said Wolcott.

"Shoot," smiled Roth, attempting to put the man at ease.

"Well, sir... it's... it's this way," the man stuttered. "I... I think there's been a mistake in my assignment."

"Why?"

"Well, sir... it's... it's that I've been trained as... as a company clerk. It's my M.O.S.... it's even on my qualification card."

"That can't be helped, now," said Roth.

"But I'm not a rifleman," said Wolcott, the worried lines seeming deeper.

"Did you get infantry training?" said Roth.

"Yes, but... but I've been working in the personnel office for more than six months before I came over."

"Did you fire for record before you left for the port?"

"Yes, sir."

"Did you run the infiltration course?"

"Yes... but..."

"Then you're in the same boat as all of us. We've got cooks, drivers, clerks, typists, and a lot of other things fighting here at the front," offered Roth in a kindly voice.

Wolcott swallowed nervously. "But I'm not really a rifleman. I'm a ..." His voice trailed off.

"Anyone who's had three months of basic training is considered a rifleman," said Roth.

"Look sir, I'm a lawyer in civilian life!" the man began to plead. "I'm not like these other fellows! My whole background is against me!"

"Do you mean that a farmer, or a laborer, or a mechanic makes a better soldier than ... than an *educated* man?" said Roth.

"Well ... something like that," agreed Wolcott.

"I hate to tell you that you're wrong," said Roth, his temper growing. "We have lawyers, engineers, even college professors, fighting in the infantry. I ... I'm in advertising myself. The Company Commander's a singer. Look around for yourself, soldier, and count the number of farmhands and the college degrees!"

"But...!"

"That's all. Return to your squad!" ordered Roth.

"Yes, sir," muttered Wolcott, his lips tightening. He quickly walked away.

Roth shook his head angrily. There were twelve lawyers distributed within the four companies comprising the First Battalion, and all of them mis-assigned. Three had Silver Stars, one had won the Distinguished Service Cross, and two already had received battlefield commissions.

A company runner trotted across the field, and when he neared the hedgerow he slowed down to a walk and finally stopped in front of Roth. "The Company Commander wants all platoon leaders right away," he said, his voice heavy from exertion.

"I guess this is it," muttered Roth as the runner trotted off to the right.

Roth walked quickly toward the rear. When he was half way across the field, he looked back over his shoulder and surveyed the platoon sector. It had the peaceful aspect of a day astonishingly remote from violence. A few men talked lazily; those on post nodded as their eyes sought the distance; and the others peacefully slept in their foxholes. A soft, damp breeze trickled over the pointed-tips of the meadow grass, parting it and baring the deep green of the stems, like a shadow moving on the field.

From the rear areas, behind the company, battalion, and regimental command posts, Roth could hear the low clanging of truck gates and the rumble of motors being warmed up. Shouts, still like whispers from the distance, floated down to him vaguely.

Roth reached the company command post and joined the officers gathered outside the dugout. Lieutenant Dougall was at the center of the group; he held five long white tubes under his arm.

Dougall nodded to Roth and cleared his throat. "Here're the new maps," he said, and handed a cardboard tube to each of his officers.

The officers removed the large-scale maps from the coverings and dropped the tubes on the ground. They opened the vari-colored, symbol-marked sheets and began to examine them.

"Spread your maps on the ground," said Dougall. "We have a lot to cover."

The platoon leaders opened the maps, placed stones and rocks in each corner to keep them from blowing, and squatted or kneeled over them.

Lieutenant Dougall glanced at his wrist watch. "We're going to attack, and all we have is half an hour. We move out at 1300. Get your pencils, and I'll give you the order."

He waited until they all had taken pencils and pads from their pockets and then continued. "Our information is that the enemy is situated in well-dug-in positions starting at St. Mère du Prée, with small holding forces distributed back about three miles. They're entrenched in the ground, in farmhouses, and there may be a few pillboxes. Strength, about a battalion. They've got a lot of artillery, and plenty of machine guns and mortars.

"A Company'll be on our right, and C Company in Battalion Reserve. Two heavy machine guns will be attached to us from D Company. Our left flank is open, and the main flank guard will be supplied by C Company, but we're also going to have to watch it ourselves.

"Our mission is to take this high ground to the right of this crossroads." He held up his map and pointed to an elevated portion three miles south and one thousand yards to the right of a blurred net of roads. Wide-spaced contour lines on the map showed a valley to be directly in front of the high ground.

Dougall continued. "Intermediate objectives will be, One: St. Mère du Prée; Two: this group of farm buildings." He again held up his map.

"We move off in a skirmish line across the fields, until we're past the village. Second Platoon on the right, First Platoon on the left, and the Third in support. Third Platoon put out about five men to watch the left flank. Third Platoon will be informed when they're to be committed. When we pass St. Mère du Prée... if the Jerries pull back ... we'll take up approach-march formation on the road. First Platoon will take the point, followed by the Second, and then the Third.

"Weapons Platoon will stay behind the Third, directly in front of the Command group. The two heavies we're getting from D Company will stay with the Weapons until we need them.

"The battalion aid station will move up to where the First Platoon now is. They'll keep following behind as the battalion advances, and further word will be sent up as they displace forward.

"Ammunition dump is mobile and will move to the left of Battalion Headquarters.

"At 1245, Division artillery opens up with a concentration that'll continue until we near the village. Green parachute flares to be used when you want the artillery lifted. We're also getting a battery of one-fifty-fives from Corps which will lift at 1300."

Dougall looked at his watch. "It's now 1237. Set your watches."

The officers adjusted their timepieces.

Dougall continued. "We attack at 1300. Move out when ready, and don't forget to keep contact. Any questions?"

"Do you want me to stay with the mortars, or with the thirties?" asked Lieutenant Carter, the Weapons Platoon leader.

"Stay with the mortars," said Dougall. "Put one of your noncoms on the thirties."

"How will I know when I'm to be committed?" asked Garvey, one of the newer officers who had the Third Platoon.

'Til send a message, or it may be that Roth or Hartley will have direct need for you and call you themselves. It all depends on the situation."

Two other officers, McNamara and Kalman, remained silent in the background. They were extra officers, recent replacements who stayed behind to be used in case of casualties among the regular platoon officers.

"Any other questions?" asked Dougall. No answer. "Okay. Move out."

Chapter Nine

PAUL ROTH RAN BACK across the field. Hurry up and wait. Two days in a static position and then one half hour or less to prepare for an attack.

"Potter! Potter!" Roth shouted at his runner.

Potter awoke with a start and sprang out of his hole as if a shot had been fired at his head. He rubbed his eyes and scratched himself under his armpits. "Yes, sir," he mumbled.

"Get me all the noncoms! Quickly!" Roth ordered.

Potter hurriedly placed his helmet on his head, secured his rifle, and scurried away.

Roth put his arms through the straps of his pack, adjusted the weight high on his back; pulled the bolt back on his carbine, let it shoot forward, and locked the piece. He removed the new map from his pocket, the notes he had taken at the CP, and placed both on the ground.

The squad leaders, the platoon guide, and the platoon sergeant came running towards Roth. They were buckling on their helmets, and a few already had their packs adjusted. The news had spread quickly, and most of the men knew, after Roth had been called to the rear, that an attack was imminent. It was an element present in the air.

"All here?" said Roth. He glanced over the group. "Where's Motoya? ... Oh, here he comes...." The new squad leader was last, and came running with his helmet in his hand and his trousers half-buttoned.

The men laughed.

"You'd better watch out," said Warner. "That nice round ass of yours makes a good target."

"You're just jealous of this butt," said Motoya.

Roth held up his hand. "All right! We don't have much time. We're moving out in a few minutes. Here's your order."

The squad leaders began to write on bits of scrap paper or message pads.

"The enemy is to our front . . . well-dug-in positions starting back from St. Mère du Prée. Strength, about a battalion. They've got plenty of artillery and mortars and machine guns.

"The Second Platoon is on our right, and the Third supports."

"Come in closer," Roth ordered. The men crowded close to his map. "Here's our objective," he pointed. "This high ground. Intermediate objectives, just beyond the village and these farm buildings.

"We skirmish across the fields until we're past St. Mère du Prée. First squad on the right, second on the left, and the third in support. Warner, put two men as a connecting patrol with the Second Platoon. We want contact at all times. When we pass St. Mere, we may move off the fields to the road. I'll let you know about that.

"Battalion aid station will move up to this line, and then displace forward as the battalion advances. You'll get more information later."

The air above suddenly started to burn; by instinct they all hit the ground. Shells in a constant stream fluttered and whispered, and crashed with blasting roars in and around the little village of St. Mère du Prée.

The group lifted themselves up off the ground. "That's us," said Roth. "We've got Division and Corps artillery support. I'll fire green parachute flares to lift the fire when we approach the village.

"Watch me closely. I'll use arm and hand signals, or the whistle." He looked at his watch. "We move out in fifteen minutes. I'll blow my whistle, and it's over the hedge. Are there any questions?"

The sergeants shook their heads negatively.

"All right, get your men set. And for Christ's sake, keep them spread out!"

All except for Rodriguez, they trotted back to their squad areas.

The Platoon Sergeant lit his pipe. "Where do you want me?"

"Stay near the rear," Roth said. "Oh yeah, one more thing. Tell Saunders I want him up close to me."

"Yes, sir," said Rodriguez, and walked away with blue ribbons of smoke rising from his pipe.

"Potter, keep close to me with the 536 radio," said Roth.

The platoon runner, who was adjusting his equipment, glanced up and nodded.

The artillery concentration flew over in a steadier, constantly increasing hose of destructive violence. There was a newer and faster sound, that of the long-range rifles from Corps, whining hotly within the slower moving high trajectory flutters of the Division projectiles. The fields to the front were blanketed with smoke, and when the clouds momentarily dispelled new excavations magically appeared. The small village rocked and burst under the explosive fury of the preparation, and dense gray fogs rose up as the shellfire landed on the dwellings, smashing and pulverizing the ancient stone structures. A few fires broke out, and the air shimmered murkily.

The sound of a rusty washing machine was overhead, and Roth looked up to see two Piper Cub observation planes circling about. They were directing the fire by radio on to the pin-point targets. Round circles of smoke, with blank holes in the center like the rings a cigar smoker makes, began to pepper the sky, gradually searching in on the two tiny planes.

The Cubs flew in slow-moving swoops. After each series of bursts in the growing circle of ringleted puffs came the dull belching of the German antiaircraft guns and then the moaning wails of shrapnel eddying towards the ground. In ever-narrowing fingerings the puffs came closer to the planes, until the two toylike machines, in final dips, turned around and headed back to their base with the Division artillery.

The men of the First Platoon rushed up and down the hedgerow, buckling on their helmets, adjusting their packs, loading their weapons, and shouting incoherent phrases. They joked crudely, swore, and shouted in loneliness and fear.

Shells came closer to the hedgerow, and a few large clots of blasted earth fell behind to land directly in the platoon sector. After one tremendous explosion the ground heaved and rolled, and Roth was lifted from his feet by the concussion and thrown on his back. He raised himself up and shook his fist in the direction of the rear.

He looked at his watch. Twelve fifty-eight. He rolled his tongue over his caked lips and looked around at his men. They were lined up at the hedgerow, with their rifles held in readiness and the bright bayonets fixed to the studs. The air was hot and thick with smoke and dust, and heads hurt from the force of soundwaves breaking against tender eardrums. A hundred yards ... fifty yards in front of them ... closer than fifty yards ... the blasting of huge shells tore a choppy pattern through the field. Much too close, but maybe it would lift at 1300.

Twelve fifty-nine. Roth felt for his whistle and clenched it tightly in his free hand. His fist sweated around the stock of his carbine. The shells from the rear came closer. He began to duck as did the other men, and a few hurled themselves to the ground and clutched the earth with trembling hands.

Thirteen hundred; but the concentration still completely covered their route. Left and right, and to the front, the earth was one exploding corruption.

Lieutenant Dougall came lumbering over. "Get going!" he shouted above the bedlam.

"What the hell's the matter with that artillery!" Roth shouted back.

"You've got orders to move out at 1300!" shouted Dougall, his eyes reddened from smoke and dust. He peered over the hedgerow and ran his fingers angrily over his face. "Goddamit! Let's wait a minute and see if they lift it!"

Roth felt the breath torn from his lungs, and his throat contracted in a choking gasp, as the blow of another concussion hit him in the pit of his stomach. Another series of shells had landed directly on their position.

A roar of pain pierced the tones of the explosions, as some man over on the right was torn apart. The air grew momentarily black, before the smoke cleared away and daylight again appeared.

"Come with me!" shouted Dougall, and started running towards the rear.

Roth trotted after the Company Commander and, as he passed, shouted to Rodriguez. "Keep the men down, and don't move until I get back!"

They reached a small bush behind which lay a few members of the company command section.

"Get me Battalion!" ordered Dougall.

Kaplan, the communications sergeant, spoke into the field radio. "Charley One to Red One, over.... Charley One to Red One, over...."

Roth lay on his stomach and trembled as he watched the field in front; the ground was studded with newly torn craters, each one appearing a second after the other. It was much too concentrated for Division artillery: Corps must have had their signals screwed up.

"Wormsley!" Dougall screamed into the radio. "Get that goddamned artillery off my position!... Get it off, I tell you! We can't move out under this fire!... No! No! No!... Then it must be Corps! Those bastards never know what they're doing!... What can you do? What can you do! You dirty son of a bitch, you have communications with them, haven't you? Get hold of Corps and give them the right grid zone! And do it quick, or the next time I see you I'll tear your rotten heart out of your chest!"

Dougall crawled over to where Roth lay huddled. His face was livid with passion. "Dirty sons of bitches! Lousy Corps sons of bitches won't even send down an observer! No, they have to work by map!"

"Watch it!" screamed Roth.

They buried their heads between their arms and held their breaths, and felt themselves lifted and held motionless in the air for a paused second, and then slammed cruelly to the ground.

Dougall spat some earth from his mouth. "Jesus, would I like to get my hands on some of those rear-area bastards!" Roth lifted his head fearfully. "What the hell are they trying to do?" he cried. "Every time there's an attack they kill half our men before we even jump off! Jesus Christ Almighty!" His voice shook.

"Get back to your men," Dougall ordered. "It should lift in a minute."

Roth sprang up and zig-zagged back across the field. Three yards from the hedge he hurled himself to the ground, and slid in on his stomach. Another shell had gone off behind him.

The men crouched or lay prone behind the hedgerow. One man at the far left corner of the line moaned pitifully for help, and rolled and writhed on the ground, clutching with both hands at his leg. It was doubled up under him, with the toes touching his buttocks.

The blasts on their side of the line became fewer, and finally stopped.

Dougall came running up. "Move out! Move out!" he shouted.

Roth jumped to his feet and applied all the power in his lungs to the whistle. The men rose dazedly. Roth continued to blow his whistle, and the squad leaders began to shout: "Move out!" "Stir your asses!"

"Move, goddamit, move!"

Reilly and Greenberg, the two scouts, climbed over the hedgerow and started moving forward. They held their rifles at high port. The others followed, and soon there was an extended line of men spread across the field.

Roth maintained a close check on his men. He saw four bunched up, almost touching one another. "Spread out!" he shouted. "Goddamit! Spread out! How many times do you have to be told!"

The men looked his way and dispersed slightly but not enough. "You dumb bastards, take ten yards!" Roth screamed.

They were from Motoya's squad, and when he heard Roth's shouts he jumped between them and shoved and kicked at the four until they were sufficiently dispersed. "The next man I see bunchin' up, I'll break his neck!" he threatened.

The scouts slammed to the ground, and the rest followed. The Germans were blasting with eighty-eights.

Roth blew his whistle and shouted, and blew his whistle and shouted: "Double-time! Get up and through it!"

They started to run madly through the narrow strip of shelled earth. Another man went down. He stopped suddenly as though he had brakes, floundered with his arms in a pawing motion, and slipped to the ground and lay still. A large stain spread over his clothing.

The shellfire stopped as quickly as it had started.

"Slow down!" Roth shouted, and the sergeants took up the call. The men walked as though they were dazed, and stumbled in the ruts and holes made by the shells, and tripped over knotted strands of grass.

Three hundred yards from the village . . . two hundred and fifty yards . . . and the concentration from Division still pulverized the ancient place. Roth felt for the flare gun in his belt.

Two hundred yards and sporadic machine gun fire began to spray the earth, and the men dodged like dancers.

Roth clapped his hand to his arm and almost stopped. He drew his hand away. No sign, but a round had passed through his green denim sleeve.

One hundred and fifty yards. Roth raised the flare gun and squeezed the trigger. There was a quick whishing noise and, hundreds of feet above, a green light flamed into being, held almost stationary by a tiny silken parachute.

One hundred and twenty-five yards and the concentration still excavated the village. Roth loaded another flare and fired it into the air.

Gradually, the concentration lifted. For another few seconds some scattered shells fell, and then there was a large silence broken only by the spattering cracks of machine guns in the distance, firing ineffective, harassing bursts at the advancing American troops.

"Keep your eyes open!" called Roth. "We're going in! Search every house carefully!"

The squad leaders took up the cry, and shouted orders to their men about respective areas that were to be covered within the village.

They increased their pace until they arrived at the outer edges of St. Mère du Prée. On the right they could see the extended skirmish line of the Second Platoon, led by Lieutenant Hartley, parallel with them in the line of advance.

Roth held up his arm. "Hold up!" he ordered. "Move in two at a time, scouts first! BARs cover!"

Reilly and Greenberg slowly advanced into the torn village, treading nervously over the rubble and cautiously avoiding the cratered holes caused by the artillery's blasting.

Sanchez, Hohmeyer, and Coombs . . . the BAR men of each squad . . . opened the bipods of their automatic rifles, dug them into the earth, and covered the approach routes leading into the village.

The streets were crumpled piles of stone and masonry. Gaping holes displayed the skeletal structure of the houses that remained erect.

Furniture littered the street. A child's rubber ball, colored with orange, brown, and blue stripes, sat on a pile of rags. A dead German soldier lay next to the rag-pile, his ripped face exposed to the sky, the tip of his finger touching the striped ball.

Reilly took the right side of the single street in the village, and Greenberg took the left. Their eyes quickly searched the debris, the shattered buildings, and the two houses that had remained standing. Reilly turned his head and beckoned for the platoon to follow.

The First Platoon men began to tiptoe into town, and the automatic rifles covered their advance.

A single shot rang out from the intact house on the left side of the street. Greenberg and Reilly dropped prone to the cobbled street and quickly dragged themselves to wall cover.

Greenberg felt in his pocket, removed a grenade, pulled the pin, and rose to his knees. With a long sweeping motion, he hurled the grenade up and over his head into the top floor window of the little building. There was a tinkling of glass and a dull explosion.

Greenberg rose to his full height, and hurled another grenade into the bottom floor. He waited for the explosion and hurled a third, the last again into the top floor. After the explosion he rushed into the building, holding his rifle at hip level with the bayonet pointed to the front.

A few seconds later his smiling face appeared from the shattered top story window. "I got the bastard!" he shouted triumphantly. "Right in the puss!" he added as a joyful afterthought.

"Anything in there?" asked Roth from the street level.

"Yeah, look what I got!" Greenberg held out a black leather binocular case.

"Hold on to it!" Roth called.

"You bet I will!" Greenberg shouted.

The three squads dispersed through the streets of the village. They kept close to the walls and kicked and prodded all piles of rubble and debris. Every few yards dead enemy soldiers lay sprawled. Two badly wounded Germans were huddled close together behind an overtipped rain barrel, weakly whispering for help.

Reilly stood anxiously before the second upright building. He skirted the house and nervously peered into each groundfloor window.

Lieutenant Roth came over to him. "Go ahead... I'll cover you from the front," he said.

The scout looked at Roth with frightened eyes. He made a vague movement as if to enter, but held back. The Texan was excellent in open country, but he froze when he had to enter buildings.

Roth felt as nervous as Reilly, but with an impatient gesture he brushed past him and entered the house. He held one hand on a grenade and lightly trod over the bottom floor.

The home appeared to have been evacuated in a hurry. Except for a broken chair that leaned precariously in the kitchen, the furniture had all been removed. Old newspapers, a few rags, a piece of broken crockery, and a broom with worn bristles lay on the dusty floor. In the front room a pile of logs, still smoking from a recent fire, was pyramided high in the soot-blackened fireplace. The Germans probably had used the house for one of their billets.

Roth nervously searched the bottom floor and then began to walk up a flight of rickety stairs to the top floor. The warped wood of the winding stairway creaked as he climbed, and each creak chilled his spine. When he reached the top, a half-opened door was before him. He pumped two shots through the thin wood panel and then stood back and delicately began to open the door with the barrel end of his carbine. He opened it slowly, stopping each few inches to see if there was any sign of tension caused by booby-trap wire. The door finally swung fully open, and he entered a small bedroom.

The room was bare. A dirty towel lay on the floor, and a broken wine bottle stood on the window sill. A black shade fluttered in the breeze. Roth backed out of the room and examined the rest of the floor.

There was another room with the door wide open. He walked in and almost squeezed the trigger of his carbine. A figure leaned over the window, elbows spread wide on the narrow sill, seeming to peer into the distance in an attitude of cautious reconnaissance. But it was as still as the air. A fresh pool of blood shone between its legs.

Roth backed out of the room and took the stairs down two at a time. When he reached the street, his men were already clustering in small friendly groups, all chattering rapidly in nervous, happy voices. They laughed and made crude jokes, the strain of the first advance removed for the time being. They poked about the rubbish and debris in search of souvenirs. A few men rested their backs against the walls and peacefully smoked.

The Second and Third Platoons had taken up positions on the outskirts, dispersed in a semicircular defense covering all approach routes. The light machine guns and the two heavies were set up on tripods, ready to lay down a hail of crossfire in the event of any possible counterattack from the enemy.

Lieutenant Dougall strode into the village, his large face steaming with sweat. He reached Roth just as the platoon leader stepped from the house.

"All clear?" asked the Company Commander.

"It looks okay to me/' said Roth.

"Start your men down the road," said Dougall. "Move out in platoon column, and you take up the point."

"How about a short break?" asked Roth.

"When we get a distance away from here," said Dougall. "They'll have this place zeroed in. . . ."

A distant series of plops were heard, and a few seconds later six shells exploded near the village.

Roth blew his whistle. The men scattered for cover. "On the double!" he shouted. "Platoon column!"

The First Platoon formed quickly and began the exodus from St. Mère du Prée. Mortar explosions became more violent, and the newer, sharper sound of artillery added speed to the exit from the village.

The other platoons followed close behind, and each succeeding company of the battalion came after.

As Roth ran behind the two scouts, he noticed two very old people, a bent wizened man and his tiny gray-haired wife, standing amidst a pile of shattered stone, waving their hands in greeting as the troops went by. The man cried and laughed in turn, and the woman merely cried as she waved a wrinkled, blue-veined hand weakly in the air. They shouted words which were not discernible under the sounds of shellfire. Shrapnel screamed all about the two old people, but they seemed impervious to everything except the joy of seeing the advancing troops running through their lost village.

The terrain past the village was more expansive and far less verdant than that which they had left behind. The fields were wider, and the hedgerows were lower and spaced from six hundred to eight hundred yards apart. The meadow grass was close-cropped and seemed lawnlike by comparison with the tall, saw-toothed growths of the fields behind St. Mère du Prée. Roth ordered the scouts to slow down to a walk and called back for the troops following to take ten yards between men. They pushed on up the road at a steady pace.

Suddenly a gray clad figure rose from a prone position in the narrow drainage ditch. He sprang up quickly, his hands partly raised, and advanced smilingly toward Lieutenant Roth.

Roth stared with surprise at the moving soldier. Then, without hesitation, he brought his carbine to his hip and fired three shots. The German appeared amazed after the first shot, bubbled "Kamerad," and fell to the ground. He lay still after the last bullet had passed through his body.

Roth shook his head in an effort to clear his brain, shrugged his shoulders, and continued on without pausing. It was an error, one of many that a man was bound to make. The German should have made his desires clearer.

He glanced at his watch and then hastily surveyed the surrounding terrain. It was open enough for a break. He raised his arm and blew a short blast on his whistle. "Side of the road!" he called. "Flank guards out... all noncoms this way!"

Like a wrinkled ribbon spreading out under the pressure of a hot iron, the troops left the road and took to the protection of the bordering drainage ditch. They voiced a group sigh and sank to the earth and lit cigarettes. They loosened their packs, sucked their canteens, and scratched at the sweated parts of their bodies. A few ate the bowel-gluing, dry chocolate ration.

The noncommissioned officers gathered in a group at the side of the dusty road. Their faces were streaked with sweaty mud; their eyes looked tired.

Roth puffed anxiously on a wet cigarette. "How did you make out?" he asked.

"I lost one man," said Warner.

"Who was he?"

"Appleby," offered the short sergeant.

"Appleby? Which one was he?"

"The young kid. The new replacement who came in a while ago," said Warner.

Roth shook his head. "Anyone else?" he asked.

"Higgins . . . new man," said Olivet. "Leg broken in a couple of places."

"Did they pick him up?" asked Roth.

"The aid-men got him before we went over the hedgerow," said Olivet.

"He'll be okay. At least he's out of it," said Roth a bit enviously. "Anybody else?" he continued.

The others remained silent.

"I guess there's no replacements to make, then," said Roth. "Keep on their tails and make sure they're spread out. Watch the new men especially, and when they're to hit the ground they're to do it immediately . . . even if you have to jump on them with both feet. And when they're to move, well . .

He suddenly seemed embarrassed. There wasn't much more for him to say; it was the same old story repeated time and again. The squad leaders knew their jobs.

Lieutenant Dougall walked up to the group. "How're you doing?" he asked Roth.

"All right," said Roth.

Dougall addressed the entire group. "We're going through regardless of the cost. Spread the word to your men. There'll be no stopping, today... no matter what happens."

"I don't get you," said Roth. "Isn't that what we always do?"

Dougall smiled faintly. "I guess it is. But somehow this is different. Orders have come down from Regiment that we're to get through to the objective no matter what it costs. It means the eventual breakthrough to St. Lô."

"What if we're stopped, sir?" asked Rodriguez.

"We won't be stopped," said Dougall.

Rodriguez shrugged his shoulders and applied a fresh light to his pipe.

Roth laughed. "I've heard *that* before!"

"Those are the orders," concluded the Company Commander, and turned back towards the rear.

"That's all, fellows," said Roth. "Tell your men what you've just heard."

The squad leaders returned to their squads. Rodriguez and Saunders remained near their platoon leader and smoked in silence.

Roth angrily puffed on his cigarette. St. Lô again. For weeks they had been hearing about that place, and every time they made an attack it was for some future mission of eventually getting through to the three hills. And every attack was made at all costs; and all costs was a dark phrase of mysterious connotation. In a static position they would hold at all costs; on a patrol it was all costs; and during an attack it was all costs. He wondered whether there ever had been a war not fought at all costs. Each time they moved the costs went from fifty per cent on up the scale. Normandy paid off at a high rate of interest.

Wolcott, the worried replacement, sat in the ditch and trembled. He smoked with difficulty. It was an effort to direct the cigarette into the small quivering target. His hands sweated and his eyes stared at the ground in front of him. He wanted to run back and get miles away from all the hell that was sure to come, and from the hell that he had gone through just a few minutes before. The shellfire and the spattering spitting of the blazing tracers still pounded painfully against his eardrums.

He dreaded what was to come and knew that he couldn't go much further. What he had feared for months . . . the nightmares that filled every dream . . . had become a vivid reality. He felt them rising over him like a smothering cloud. The jokes of the men . . . their whistling in the dark as they were coming over . . . had never been funny to him. His intelligence and his imagination and what he knew from all he had read told him that war was this way. Now he was in it, and he saw no way back.

Motoya stood over the trembling soldier. "What's the matter, soldier?" he asked kindly.

Wolcott looked up at the strong Mexican. "Nothing," he said unconvincingly.

"Don't worry. The first attack's the hardest," Motoya said.

"I'll be all right," said Wolcott, shivering more spasmodically.

"You just got a chill," said Motoya. "You'll warm up when we move out."

"Yes, that's it," said Wolcott. "I guess I got overheated."

Motoya laughed self-consciously. "Think of some broad you used to lay . . . or something . . . get your mind . . . you know. . . ."

Wolcott gravely nodded his head. That was it. To get one's mind on other things. To hypnotize one's self into believing that reality did not exist, and that the world was only a dream.

Motoya walked away and knew that Wolcott didn't have far to go. He'd seen them like that before. One attack and they were through. They had themselves primed for it, with months and sometimes years of worry behind them, all adding up to their final explosion. Like a clock spring that's been overwound. One noise . . . one close shot past their ears . . . and the spring snaps.

The tall Mexican came up behind Warner, who, in a serious voice, was haranguing his squad. Motoya slapped the short man on the back and in a loud voice shouted: "Are you still beating your gums, you little bastard?"

Warner spun around, his lips narrowed in an angry snarl. "Why don't you get off my ass, you lousy spic bastard! Can't I ever get away from you?"

Motoya laughed and poked his fist into the little man's stomach. "Don't get your balls in an uproar, Shorty! You know I love you!"

Warner clenched his fists. "If I didn't have work to do, I'd break your goddamned black neck!"

Motoya laughed louder. "If you lay a hand on me, I'll report you to the Company Commander!" he said in mock fear.

"When I put my hands on you, you won't be able to report to the Company Commander!" said Warner, the anger beginning to leave his face. He turned abruptly back to his men before his friend could see him smile.

Motoya continued to laugh and walked down the road towards his squad. A guy like Warner was a relief after Wolcott.

Roth removed his map from his pocket and spread it out on the ground. He traced the various contour lines with his finger and tried to find his exact position on the terrain. He surveyed the fields on both sides of the road and returned to his map. The map showed heavily foliaged ground, and where they were then the land was comparatively open and clear. He looked into the distance and wondered how far it was to the next intermediate objective.

"Rodriguez," Roth beckoned to the Sergeant.

"Yes, sir," replied the Sergeant.

"Take a look at this map. It seems to be a little off. I can't find our exact position."

Rodriguez squatted and examined the map. He looked up at the Lieutenant. "Right here, sir," he said, and pointed with his finger at a green section of the map.

Roth again examined the map. The Sergeant had the position. It was a small spot of pale green, symbolizing lightly foliaged terrain, which he had overlooked during his own examination. He had missed it at least three times.

Rodriguez stuffed some fresh tobacco into the bowl of his pipe and puffed thoughtfully. The Lieutenant certainly was forgetting himself. It must have been the tenth time during the past week he had consulted him about his map. During maneuvers . . . down in Louisiana he remembered . . . Roth was an excellent man on terrain. He could get through the most thickly wooded areas, scarcely referring to his map or compass, and he seldom made an error. The strain was showing. The man needed a rest.

Chapter Ten

LIEUTENANT DOUGALL blew his whistle, and the signal was relayed along the line by the platoon leaders. The men reluctantly rose to their feet, tightened their equipment straps, and grasped their rifles.

Roth signaled his scouts, and the brown column moved off down the road. The men were quiet as they searched the fields with their eyes. They shuffled their feet in the dust and tried to visualize what lay beyond the immediate horizon.

Roth's feet felt like weighted diver's shoes. A dull numbness began to possess him, and each step that he took was a new struggle, a distinctly separate operation. He no longer felt nervousness or concern, or interest in what the next few miles might bring. His system was drained. A foreign force propelled him onwards. If the force had not been present he would have thrown himself into the ditch at the side of the road, to lie there until the blank dark crept over him and covered him forever. His body was not his own, and the legs under him were two stumps of dead flesh that moved as a snake's body twitches after life has gone out of it.

He turned his head, and automatically... the voice coming from some strange being... croaked dryly: "Spread out!"

He turned his head back to the front and wanted to laugh at the weird voice... the voice of habit, of loss of will, of death of soul while the body still lives on, vague, impotent, and alone.

"More distance between scouts!" the voice again called and cackled a hollow laugh heard only by himself. More room between scouts, the eyes and ears of the platoon, the tentacles of the octopus reaching out toward the enemy. All scouts should get the Congressional Medal. They stuck out in front as bait and, when the hidden enemy opened up, went down like wob. bly-legged calves. Two to four scouts per day was the usual quota; they were more expendable than thirty caliber ammunition. Funny how Reilly and Greenberg had lasted nearly a week. But of course they hadn't been attacking as often as in the weeks past.

During basic training he too had been a scout. But that was basic training and there was no enemy, and no bullets or shrapnel or strafing. Still, during many nights, spearheading a column of men through a dark wooded wilderness, it had been as fearful and lonely as sleeping in a haunted graveyard. He couldn't understand how Greenberg and Reilly could take it for so long. Young, maybe. They were younger than he. Two or three years younger... but was that a long time in the life of a man? In combat, yes. He had lived longer than the two of them, and therefore had better reason to die before they did.

Rodriguez strode along the column from the rear. He spoke to the men and asked some to spread out and told others to close up. He drew up beside Sergeant Saunders. "Look at Roth," he half whispered.

"Goin' from side to side, ain't he?" said Saunders.

Rodriguez shook his head commiseratingly. "I hope he makes it!"

"Shore he will," said Saunders. "He's been a goin' like that for a week. He just don't get 'nough sleep, that's all."

"He's got me worried," said Rodriguez. "He's losing his memory, and half the time he don't know where he's going."

"He's still the best damned platoon leader in the outfit!" avowed Saunders. "He stays with his men."

"He stays with his men," said Rodriguez. "But I'm afraid someday he's going to lead us where we just don't belong!" Saunders grinned and showed his large buck teeth. "A coupla nights sleep, and he'll be in fitten shape. Christ, the man never sleeps. Ever' time I look up he's runnin' 'round the platoon, checkin' on this or that squad, or back at a meetin' in the CP, or out on patrol.... Man, he's jest tired!"

"That's what I'm afraid of," said Rodriguez. "Look... up there!"

Roth had stumbled and almost fallen into the ditch at the side of the road. He caught himself drunkenly and returned to the center of the road and, with what looked like an effort, straightened his shoulders and took deep draughts of air into his lungs.

"He's jest tired," insisted Saunders.

Rodriguez returned to the rear of the platoon, shouting orders and encouragement at the men as he walked back. All platoon leaders stayed with their men; that was no indication of a man's fitness for leadership. He never heard of a platoon leader in the outfit who wasn't up in the thick of it with his men. But Roth was going the way Bartel, the man who once had the Third Platoon, went. One day he led his platoon into an ambush, and three out of thirty came back. They couldn't afford to have a lieutenant as tired as Roth leading a platoon of men.

The long column moved on. Clouds of smoke swirled on the distant horizon, and the dull thuds of bursting shells could be heard from other battles. The sun was hot in the sky, and the breeze which had blown that morning was gone. Reilly and Greenberg almost imperceptibly slowed their pace as they sighted a crossroads thousands of yards away. The entire column tightened up, and each man strained his eyes towards the junction. They slapped the flats of their bayonets, unlocked the safeties on their weapons, and held each breath to the ultimate.

Suddenly a section of machine guns from the crossroads blazed open, and, as if the instant of the firing was expected, the column immediately took to cover off the road. The tracer fire spit a cadenced stream of blazing steel and then stopped as quickly as it had started.

The First Platoon lay in the ditch on the left side of the road, and behind them on the right, deployed in depth, lay the Second Platoon.

Roth tried to pick up telltale smoke from the distant machine guns, but the only tangible presence was the hovering stillness.

The call came down from the Company Commander at the rear, and was relayed by voices within each platoon: "Off the road... off the road, and keep moving ahead!"

"Reilly... Greenberg! Hit the field!" Roth shouted to the scouts.

The scouts rolled out of the ditch and into the field on their left. They sprawled awkwardly, first on their backs and then on their stomachs, until they lay flat in the short scrub grass of the meadow.

"Everybody... into the field!" Roth shouted to the others.

The men behind rolled, crawled, crept, and stumbled into the meadow.

"On your feet! Spread out!" ordered Roth. He stood erect and his men followed.

Reilly and Greenberg had begun to move ahead when more machine guns opened up and sprayed the open field. The men went down again and buried their faces in the rough texture of the earth.

Roth cursed and prayed. They were pinned down; the Jerries had the ground completely organized. He turned his head and called to Potter. "Give me the 536."

Cradling his rifle in the crook of his arms and holding the small carton-sized radio in his extended right hand, the runner crawled up to the platoon leader.

Roth pressed the open lever down and growled the repetitive call letters. He heard a series of grating sounds, followed by the indistinct voice of the Company Commander.

"Roth... Roth?... come in Roth . .. !"

"This is Roth... Rothspeaking... we can't go ahead... too much fire...!"

"I'm coming down... hold where you are... hold where you are. ..." Dougall's voice died off, and there was a final click.

Roth handed the radio back to his runner and anxiously searched toward the rear for the arrival of Dougall.

Warning plops sounded, and a few seconds later mortar craters began to decorate the field five hundred yards to their front. The flat explosions came in series of three, until there were twelve thick circles of smoke where the shells had landed. Another few seconds went by and twelve more landed, the twelve bursting many yards closer but still enough distance away not to be of immediate danger.

Dougall came running along the edge of the field. He ran low with his shoulders thrust forward, his back bent, and his knees pumping high. A short burst of machine gun fire rattled when he neared Roth, and he plunged to the ground with a solid thud. He panted hoarsely. "Can you see where they are?" he asked.

"I'm not sure," said Roth. "They're some place near or behind the crossroads."

Dougall raised his head and surveyed the crossroads in the distance. "It's the only place they can be. Goddam, they should have expected this!"

"What's going to happen?" asked Roth.

"I just had a message from the Colonel," said Dougall. "They're sending a gun down from Cannon Company to try and knock out a few of them."

"What's the matter with the artillery?"

"We can't get them now."

Roth laughed cynically. "Whose crazy idea is it to use Cannon Company?"

"Captain Sanborn's, probably. I guess he wants another medal."

"Direct fire?"

"What do you think? Listen, get your men back in the ditch on the road. When Cannon Company's done, we're moving off to the right."

"What's the idea?"

"The bastards are wised up that we're coming this way. We hit off on a ninety-degree azimuth until we come to another road that's supposed to be clear, and then move south again.

We come to a hedgerow, and right beyond that are the farm buildings we're aiming for."

"What happens then?"

"We take the ground and move on to the final objective."

"They still expect to do that all in one day?"

"In one day," concluded Dougall.

Roth pulled his map from his pocket. "I'm not so clear on the route."

Dougall traced the new route with his finger. He pointed out the direction across the field to their right; a narrow country trail one thousand yards away; and the wooded area that would have to be passed through before they arrived at the hedgerow which was the line-of-departure leading up to the second intermediate objective.

"Get your men in the ditch, and when Cannon Company's finished move out as fast as you can," said Dougall. He jumped to his feet and ran to the rear.

Roth shouted the new orders, and there was a hasty scramble as the men rolled and crawled back into the ditches bordering the road.

They heard the roar of a motor on the road, and a ton-and-a-half truck, pulling a one hundred and five millimeter field piece, rolled into sight. Five men were in the vehicle including the driver, the gunner, the assistant gunner, an ammunition bearer, and Captain Sanborn, the heavy-set commander of Cannon Company.

The truck jammed to a stop a few yards behind Roth and, in one organized movement, the team jumped to the pebbled road. Captain Sanborn waved his arms grandiloquently as he shouted orders, and his men unhitched the weapon from the vehicle, swung the blunt nose towards the front, and spread the sharp trail-legs.

The enemy machine guns opened fire, and dust and pebbles kicked up a dangerous cloud around the men of the gun team. Captain Sanborn bellowed fire orders, and the weapon was loaded and locked and aimed in a series of miraculously speedy actions.

Roth watched Sanborn. The heavy-set man's face was red and tense, but he seemed to be thoroughly enjoying the action. He dropped his arm stiffly, and the seventy-five roared.

Roth felt a stab of pain behind his neck, and his eardrums seemed crushed. The force of the blast caught him and raised him inches into the air and slammed him back to the ditch.

Sanborn again bellowed fire orders. "Let's show these line bastards what Cannon Company can do!" The machine-gun bullets tore up large chunks of the road, and the heavy man twirled and danced around his men. He raised his arm and quickly lowered it.

This time Roth pressed his fingers tightly against his ears, but he was again lifted up and smashed back by the appalling closeness of the concussion.

The storm of tracers was thicker. A dark angular man, the assistant gunner on the weapon, clutched at his right side with his hand and started to slump to the ground. Captain Sanborn sprang to the wounded soldier and supported him under his armpits.

"We're going back!" the Captain howled. "Let these bastards fight their own battles!"

They lifted the wounded soldier into the back of the truck, swung the field piece around and hooked it to the rear of the vehicle, and rapidly took their former positions. The truck roared as the throttle was jammed down, veered and careened around, and sped away under a solid stream of tracers.

Roth sadly shook his head. Two rounds from a one hundred and five with nothing proven; a man wounded and another medal for Captain Sanborn. One battery of artillery from the rear could have done the trick.

"We're going directly right...across the field!" Roth shouted. "Pass the word back! Across the field as I told you! Greenberg! Reilly! Move out! Across the field!"

The two scouts sprinted wildly across the road and into the field on the right. As the first two men rose into sight along the skyline the machine guns spat hot defiance and continued to rattle their message as the others chaotically left the road for the adjoining field.

The exploding mortar shells came closer and began to blanket the road. Eighty-eights started to whish overhead and drop among the companies and battalions behind B Company. Shouts and screams, filtering down from the rear units, added speed to the scrambling of the men in front.

Artillery and mortar fire blanketed the entire field. The smoke was thick, intermittently illuminated by the flaming tracer tails of the machine-gun projectiles. The ground rolled and rumbled and rocked with shock, and men stumbled and tripped and clawed in their panic to clear the area. The enemy must have been waiting for just such an opportunity.

Shell and mortar fire intensified until there was not an inch of ground that did not seem an exploding atrocity. Geysers of earth and rock vomited into the air, fell back down upon the shoulders and heads of the running men, choking their nostrils and throats with the graveled dust.

Roth ran with his men. He had given up trying to shout orders. They knew where they were going—to safety beyond the blazing field.

Wolcott, the former lawyer, stumbled and fell to the ground.

A mortar shell burst yards from him, and he screamed and felt his brain split open. He started to crawl toward the rear, fearing to rise to his feet and expose himself more than was necessary. He blubbered and phlegm rose to his lips. He crawled, hands and knees clawing into the tough grass, his extremities revolving like those of a frightened crab. Another shell exploded nearer. The scream brought blood to his raw throat, and he jerked to his feet and ran toward the beach. He remembered the beach where they had landed that quiet day; it was miles away but he knew he'd get to it. He ran and there was no breath left in his body. He didn't have to breathe, nor see with his eyes, nor run with his legs. He was soaring in space and in a short time he'd be at the beach, miles away from the red blasting, and a boat would take him to safety. A blow caught him between his shoulders, and another heaviness landed on the back of his neck. He fell to his knees, but quickly struggled up and continued to run. Another weight caught him on the base of his spine, but this time he remained upright; he was on the beach and in safety. He was running in darkness, a wetness poured down his back and cooled his buttocks and his legs, and he laughed. He saw the cool green water at the edge of the beach and crying with relief he hurled himself into the all-enveloping, refreshing wonder of the Channel. The water rose over him, and he relaxed.

Roth ran and drank air in croupy suckings. He was running through quicksand; his legs scarcely moved. Yet all the men around him moved no faster than he. They floundered with their rifles held out in front of them, their mouths wide open, and their eyes filmed. He wanted to shout at them to move faster; but one release of his breath in the effort would mean the end. All about him the field was brilliantly patterned with crisscrossing tracers, grass fires, and bursting signal rockets of many hues. Shrapnel whined with siren noises. Roth could feel the wind of the jagged-edged steel fragments shrieking past his face. To the road, the new country road where there might be safety from the suckers' trap they had fallen into. To his left a man went down, his hands clutching at his groin. It was Meyers, the replacement with the accent.

Meyers jerked spastically. He bit through his lips until they were lacerated red meat flapping down over the cleft of his chin; he chewed into his tongue until the tip hung by a thin thread of torn flesh. His hands clutched the soft crimson mass of his groin. Shrieks came from his mouth. The pain moved up into his belly, and the white hot fire blazed into his intestines and emptied his bowels in a loose gushing hemorrhage. He groveled and bit into his arm and screamed until no voice was left in his torn larynx, and then he whimpered.

Sergeant Warner scampered along on his short legs, shouting angrily at his men as he tried to organize them into a squad. "Close up! Close up, you dumb bastards!" he screamed in the uproar of the bursting shells and the spatter of machine-gun bullets.

He moved up alongside Groggins, and yelled in his ear. "Close up! Ten yards's enough!"

Groggins stared stupidly at the squad leader and continued to run at his wide-legged fear-impelled pace. His jaw was slack, and his straight hair hung out of his helmet and trickled down over his glassy eyes.

Warner sped up and down the disordered line of men. "Sanchez, get your BAR up in front!"

Sanchez tried to grin to show that he understood, but he didn't have the strength to add speed. The fourteen-pound weapon slung over his shoulder cut into his back, and he knew there was ho hope of him getting up ahead unless the whole platoon slowed down. He wanted to explain to Warner, but he lacked the breath.

Schonbrun struggled ahead, his neck screwed down into his hunched shoulders like that of a frightened tortoise. He couldn't see where he was going, and it was far worse than the times he had been chased when he was a kid by the gangs from around the corner on Eighth Avenue. He was afraid to even breathe, afraid that the freshening air might awaken him to the full realization of all the noise and smoke and men falling to the earth. His eyes were half-closed and he was like one gone blind; he could hear his heart beating and strange voices whispering.

Abbruzio ran as fast as his legs could revolve, his lips moving in reverent prayer. The Latin words came back to him as if parochial school were only a few hours away and he were rehearsing for the exam given by Father Sheehy. But the prayers were uttered in passionate hope that he would be saved, because he knew that once he got through this he would never again fear. The rest of the combat to come would be a lead-pipe cinch. After this was over he'd be a good soldier and do his job. His lips moved faster as the prayers became more fluent, but still he couldn't rid himself of the icy feeling in his spine.

Sergeant Kimmel panted and wheezed, knowing that one more step would be his last and he'd fall to the green earth with the breath gone from his short-winded body. He had always been a poor runner . . . even as a kid he was last in everything . . . and now this mad sprinting away from certain death brought fire to his lungs. The rolls of fat on his stomach knotted and contracted, and pain surged up to his heaving chest. He could think of nothing but air, fresh reviving draughts of air to bless his lungs and give him new strength to move. His eyes were inflamed, and his tongue hung out over his teeth, dried and sucking the dust and smoke of the blasting destruction. With all the young, well-muscled men in the Air Force, they had to choose him for the infantry.

Profanity rolled off Motoya's tongue as he ran with the men of his squad. He roared the words, trying to obliterate with his voice the vivid thunder of the enemy fire. "German sons of bitches too goddam stinking yellow to fight!" He peered through the smoke and tried to distinguish the figures of the men in his squad. "Get together and watch where you're going!" he shouted. "Keep your eyes open, you bastards! You ain't on maneuvers! They play for keeps here!" He laughed huskily and continued to shout and scream, his dark face inflamed with hatred, concern, and fear.

The long field was a nightmarish kaleidoscope of running stumbling troops, exploding eighty-eights, one-fifty-five's, mortars, and an unbroken network of flaming tracers. To escape the prepared area the entire battalion together was making the right flanking movement, and hundreds of men went down under the storm of steel. Jeeps and trucks rocked precariously over the blasted earth, and many overturned as they rolled into unseen shell-holes. One vehicle which carried mortar ammunition blew up. As though carried by some monstrous Kansas twister, bodies, machinery, wheels, and shells were flung high in the air and scattered like chaff.

Surrounded by the overpowering force and noise, McCrea ran and forced his mind to his home and family, but the blasts kept intruding. His mind was a cracked mosaic of smoke, exploding sounds, and the blank featureless faces of blond children devoid of expression and name. They held out their arms and embraced the smoking earth, their voices shrill within mushrooming mortar bursts. He closed his eyes to rid himself of all imagery, but the picture was of blood smearing the young blond bodies, and he quickly opened them again to the sight of the field madly rushing by. The pleading hands, the featureless faces, the swollen belly of a pregnant woman, and the birth of open shells became an insane spectrum of whirling color that made him want to shriek out in horror.

Reubens struggled with the heavy bazooka. He shifted it from side to side and tried carrying it on his shoulder, but it continued to add more weight with each clumsy step he took. He recognized Schmidt's slender figure about ten yards in front of him. "Schmidt! Schmidt!" he screamed.

Schmidt moved on without looking back. His arms moved in a steady piston motion, and he ran on the balls of his feet.

Reubens shouted again. Tears of frustration and exhaustion rose to his eyes. "Schmidt! Schmidt! You're to help carry this bastard ...!"

Schmidt heard nothing but the shirring of the shells and the roars when their sensitive noses crashed into the earth.

Reubens' lower lip trembled and he sobbed in desperation. He forced his heavy legs to the ultimate and finally drew up alongside the redheaded soldier. He held out the long weapon. "Take this son of a bitch.... I had it long enough!" he panted.

The freckles stood out in dark clusters on Schmidt's pale frightened face. He stared blankly at Reubens, and kept on working his arms in steady rhythm.

"Are you gonna take this thing, you lousy bastard!" screamed Reubens. "You're assistant gunner ...!"

Schmidt slung his rifle on his back and grabbed the bazooka. His lips, as white as his face, were drawn back in a thin wrinkled line over his teeth. He was a truckdriver. He had to carry a bazooka when he should be bent over the wheel of a two-and-a half-tonner.

Reubens ran easily. Shells, machine-gun fire, mortars ... all meant nothing now that he was rid of the heavy beast he had carried for so long. He ran faster and began to approach the head of the platoon. Every worry that ever existed was gone.

Private Hohmeyer muttered as he ran. "Holy good Jesus Christ! Holy good Jesus Christ!" For hours it went through his head and no longer had any meaning, but the sounds were comforting. "Holy good Jesus Christ!" he said over and over again; and he tried to run faster than he had ever run in his life.

Wong tried not to hurry, not to become too excited, and to obey all he had been taught in training; but he couldn't control forces stronger than himself. The tip of his tongue stuck out from between his tightly closed lips, and sweat rolled down his face. He wanted control, discipline so that he could be ready for any eventuality. Eyes and ears open, and watch for the enemy: the primary rules of infantry fighting. His eyes and ears were open... to the madness of the bursting, smoking, rocking field. Control. A day or two and they would discover that he had been assigned to the wrong outfit, and then he would be sent to the Pacific to interpret.

Verne Potter kept as close behind the Lieutenant as possible. The SCR 536 radio slammed against his sore side and periodically swung around to hit his tired back. He cried freely now, great choking sobs issuing forth after each explosion. He no longer feared but felt that a vast sadness had overcome him and that death, before he had even known his youth, would soon take him away. He tried to stop the formation of the word but restraint was gone, and the name of his mother came out as clear and distinct as though he were home and had just awakened from a fevered nightmare and called for her comfort.

Williams, the ex-sergeant from San Antonio, sped along rapidly, his tapered legs moving almost effortlessly over the earth. He kept his broad shoulders straight, and his chest high. His M-1 was held in a trailing position with one hand while the other arm pawed the air easily. As a result of all the years of training and maneuvers in the Southwest, the strain of the run hardly bothered him. He had often maneuvered under live shellfire . . . not as closely as this . . . but the indoctrination had been fairly complete. He tried to think of it as only training, and the smoke and blasting all around him as harmless blanks, but little warning notes kept seeping in whenever the promising moan of a piece of shrapnel sang past his ear.

Abadjian's sleekness had disappeared. Large circles of sweat stained his back and chest; one trouser leg flopped loosely out of his legging; his helmet had fallen over his eyes. There were worried lines on his smooth olive skin, and his face no longer showed confidence. The sounds around him and in him were of death, of legs being torn off, of his heart stopping in full power. He ran as fast as he could because there had to be an other side, a hill or a crevice or a hole where his body would be safe, and his ears hear no other sounds but the pleasant hoarseness of his breath and the knowledgeable beat of the life in his chest.

Sergeant Olivet kept beckoning encouragement to the men of his squad. Running through a field saturated by shell and machine-gun fire was the worst. Complete disorder ensued, with the men losing the important energy and strength which could be used to greater advantage elsewhere. He ground his teeth until flakes of enamel chipped off and he prayed for the chance to meet the enemy in a small-arms fight, with his own skill and strength the deciding factor. This decided nothing but chaos and the loss of men's souls. One close-in-shooting, grenade-throwing fight would cleanse the ignominy of their mad, fearful, ratlike scurrying.

Private Coombs had lost his helmet at the beginning of the run through the shelled area. Seconds later a tiny shell fragment had grazed his skull and fresh blood trickled into his eyes. He kept raising the back of his hand to wipe away the wetness, and he cursed the heat and thought how it would feel to dip his head into a barrel of water which had a solid block of ice at the bottom. The red sweat from his brow seeped down under his shirt, causing the rough material to stick oppressively to his back. He wanted to tear his clothes from his body and run naked and in freedom away from the visual and audible hell surrounding him. He heard a moaning sirening sound coming closer ... the sound of skimming shrapnel that he knew so well ... and it suddenly made a whirring noise in his ears. It caught him between his eyes, above the bridge of his nose, and he went down and lay still.

Stepkowicz plodded, almost at a fast walk. He tried to increase his pace, but the effort was worthless; he had heavy muscular legs that were better on the football line or the wrestling mat, but not suited for sprinting. He was scared ... Christ, was he scared ... he never knew it would be like this with death in front of your face every single second. He always thought he was a pretty tough guy knocking around the South Side, but this ...

Northrup breathed regularly and deeply and felt his cheek muscles twist and knot under the strain of forcing every reserve of will power. Fear was the weak link of the mind over the spirit, and he did not choose to lose any spiritual grasp over himself. He was flesh and mind. . . a mind created for the sole purpose of checking the flesh and ordering it to act as the will ordained. He could not fear, now; not in his first battle when he needed every ounce of perception to discover the meaning behind the tumult. The confusion of bursting shells and the men dying were all essentials of knowledge, and he intended to utilize every part of his being to find some answer to even that phase of existence. His cheek muscles crawled and twisted, distorting his sensitive young face.

McCarthy barely could breathe for the pounding of his heart. His hands clawed out and his jaw hung low as he tried to suck the air which never contained enough substance. He felt sick and wanted to die, and would have dropped were it not for something that told him to go on. He was one who never shirked work and he would do his job like the others; but still he wished he could fall dead to the ground and rest without the tearing pains tormenting his narrow lungs. Each step was the last, and the one following the worst.

Wysocki flayed the earth with his long legs, his rifle held close to his chest in readiness. He was beginning to feel the run but he knew, if necessary, he could go on for many more minutes. It wasn't so bad as long as the shells didn't burst near him, and he tried not to think of any doing so. He had expected combat would be like this, and anything he knew about beforehand wasn't too bad. He was ready for whatever they had to throw at him. He knew he was stronger than those foreign bastards with their thick voices and pale blond faces. He never did like them since that family of sullen-faced clogs took the place down the road from theirs ten years ago. It couldn't all be like this. Soon they'd run out of ammunition and stop, and he'd get his bearings and find out what it was all about.

Murphy refused to think as his bowlegs chunked over the grass. He forced himself to forget he was scared and that the blasting sounds crowded against his brain worse than a thousand boiler factories. He even drove out sight, except for the few inches of green ground under his feet. Anyone who thought under this would go nuts; he would never be scared, for once a guy gets scared he's a goner... no good to himself or the world.

Rodriguez didn't like to lose his temper, but the crazy movement across the open field almost made him forget his principles. Like a bunch of rookies on a first maneuver they had been led straight into the trap. How many times had they been taught that open country was to be watched carefully and, when possible, avoided? From general on down to private they knew, and yet it never failed that during an attack they'd be caught with their pants down. The S-2 Section sure must have had their heads up their asses if they didn't know that the field would be zeroed in. Men were scattered from twenty to fifty yards apart, with complete disorder prevailing, and Christ only knew where they'd wind up. "Close up! Close up!" he shouted. His voice was lost in louder sounds.

Sergeant Saunders trotted behind the Lieutenant. He'd given up trying to help create order and only hoped they'd soon get into a safety zone where they could reorganize. He chewed his tobacco quickly, each few moments spurting a long brown stream along the path of the wind. He didn't like shellfire; much rather dish it out shot for shot with an M-1 or a Tommy gun. This way a guy never knew where it would come from, and if it caught him he'd go down like a goddamned fool with no chance to fight back. He'd as soon meet them on a dark patrol night and creep up on them and stick a long knife between their ribs.

Greenberg tried to motion with his arm, but he hadn't the strength to lift it. A new life was being born again and he saw it happening before his eyes and wanted to tell the world. The shelling had stopped in front of him and the ground grew fresh and green and pure. He wanted to laugh, to cry tears of happiness, and to embrace all his friends in the ecstasy of this rare delight. The shelling and the machine-gun fire had stopped as far as he could see, and everything was the most wonderful peace that God had ever given to a sore, tired earth.

Reilly saw the miracle. He began to giggle. The ground had ceased to heave, and the grass had a new softness as sweet and fresh as a field of grain ready for the harvest; it contained a coolness that was a blessing and a promise of new hope. He giggled and felt saliva surging up to dampen his dry tongue.

A few trees directly ahead formed a border around a sand-colored, narrow road. Shadows cast by the trees played a speckled pattern over the beige pathway, providing ragged circlets of shade rimmed by slender sun ribbons.

Reilly and Greenberg made clutching, swimming motions towards their goal, and their heads and shoulders shot forward in their last great effort to arrive at the oasis. They pounded onto the road, and allowed themselves the final realization of sinking to the ground. They lay there breathing noisily, the muscles of their diaphragms tightening under the pounding of their hearts.

Lieutenant Roth followed, but did not allow himself complete release. He squatted with the tips of his buttocks skimming the ground, his arms hanging loosely and trembling at his sides. A pool of sweat appeared between his legs. The sounds of shells and machine-gun bullets still danced in his head. He didn't know whether the cacophony came from the realistic distance, or was an impression forced into the soft filaments of his brain by the moments just passed. His head throbbed in an ebbing flowing tide of shimmering sound waves that made his body feel as though it were still being carried over the disintegrating earth.

His neck seemed to be on a pivot and revolved inches in each direction, quivering under the oscillations of an uncontrollable ague.

He tried to swallow, and his tonsils rasped against the granular matter clinging to his throat. He was alive again to reality... a feeling creature ... and aware of his responsibilities to the men who ran through the shelled field. A dim, reprehensible whisper began to warn him of his guilt as he remembered the mad dash; he should have done something to create order... to think clearly in the heat of such pandemonium... and acquit himself as a leader of a platoon. Lives could have been saved, wounds avoided, and discipline maintained if only there were something right that he could have done. But it was unexpected, and control was lost.

Roth changed to a sitting position and locked his hands around his raised knees. He wouldn't think of what had happened. He wasn't responsible for mistakes made higher in the chain of command; he couldn't undertake full responsibility for the life of every single man. They had been trained as he; and if they didn't know by then how to go through artillery fire, they'd never know. Where did responsibility begin and end for the lives of twenty, thirty, forty men? What guilt can lie upon the soul of a man when he too is human, and composed of flesh and blood and natural fears?

Leader or led, logic was a laughable word under the rain of a thousand hells. He would take care of himself and do the best he possibly could for the men, but he'd worry no more about each and every life as though he were the Maker who brought them into being. He was only a lieutenant... a ninety-day wonder because they needed fools like him to stand at the head of a group of men and shout meaningless orders. If it weren't he, it would be someone else; and if they couldn't get someone else they wouldn't be able to fight a war, because there always have to be symbols of authority for men to cling to, and look to, and be deceived by.

He looked at his watch: 1430. Eight more hours before dark.

Chapter Eleven

THE MEN OF THE FIRST PLATOON arrived at varying intervals. They straggled in, stumbled to the earth, and lay head to foot, squirming with exhaustion.

Roth raised his hand in an obscure signal for dispersion, made some weak, ill-defined motions, then dropped his arm defeatedly.

Sergeant Rodriguez was the last man to reach the road. His pace had slowed to a fast walk. He quickly strode among the panting men and irritably started to grasp shoulders and equipment straps. "Spread out!" he ordered. "Back along the road . . . five yards between men!"

The tired eyes of the men grew angry at their disturber; a few revolted audibly and were handled more roughly. Rodriguez had to drag Groggins and Sanchez bodily to their feet in order to add some distance between them. He sweated and puffed and cursed impatiently. "Spread out, you dumb bastards!" he grunted. "You'll be doing your fighting out the back of a meat wagon!"

Sergeant Saunders sat at the side of the road biting a chew from his tobacco plug. He smiled wryly as Rodriguez passed him. "Cain't you ever leave these boys alone?" he said. "You're the GI'st, Fort Sam, dress-parade sergeant I ever did see!"

"One shell and the platoon's wiped out!" Rodriguez stated seriously. "If you and the other noncoms would pay more attention to your jobs, we'd have less casualties!"

"Aw go on!" smiled Saunders. "These boys're plumb tuckered. Look at 'em . . . the life's done gone out of 'em."

"That's just the point," said Rodriguez. "It's always when they're done in that we're caught flat-footed. If we'd keep…" He went back to his work of separating the men. You couldn't argue with ridge runners who liked the army only for the three squares a day they got and the good shoes to keep them from cutting their feet on the rocks. . . .

Saunders laughed. Rodriguez was a good old boy and watched out for the men; but he made more noise about it than a cow pissin' on a flat rock. Take him, he'd like to see the fellows always keeping in formation and watching every detail, but when minds were sore and down from so much pounding, there wasn't much could be done. A couple of weeks back and the guys had it, just like they done in training; but now it was gone and they fought to save themselves. He couldn't much blame them. He didn't mind so much; trouble all his life was good training ground for war. He'd seen shooting and blood and thunder, and this was just repeating; a little noisier, but still the same.

Roth turned to Potter, who lay next to him wiping his eyes with a balled handkerchief. "Get me the CP," he requested hoarsely.

Potter switched on the tiny radio and began to repeat the call. When he heard the answering crackle, he handed the box to the platoon leader.

"Andy?" said Roth. "What're we supposed to do now?"

"Give your men a rest. They can eat if they want. I'll be down in a little while." Roth could clearly hear Dougall's heavy breathing.

"Do we move on from here?" asked Roth.

"I'll let you know when I see you," said Dougall. "Take it easy and get as much rest as you can."

Roth sighed and handed the radio to Potter. He'd have to get up and return to his duties. While the others reclined on their backs, he would have to offer them proof that he was still the leader; again he'd have to be both authoritative and friendly, demonstrate that he wasn't as tired as they. While they filled their lungs with the sweetness of the shade, he'd sweat again as he made his rounds. As he rose to his feet, he felt twinges of pain shoot through his stiffened knees. He removed his helmet and held it under his arm.

"Keep spread out and take a break!" Roth called to the men in a voice that raised and lowered from falsetto to hoarse bass. "Rations if you've got 'em, but watch out for the water. No water until I give the word!"

"How're you doing, Reilly?" asked Roth. The scout lay on his back, his eyes examining the thin blanket of leaves above him.

Reilly lowered his eyes. "I guess I'm all right, now. But I sure wish you could git someone else to be first scout!"

"We'll see," said Roth. "Maybe after we get relieved."

"Gee, I sure wish you could do it now," Reilly said. "I'm gettin' so's I don't know where I'm goin'."

"Finish out the day," said Roth. The young Texan had had it hard. It was no cinch being out there in front with nothing but the enemy and the first frightening sight of bursting shells. Scouts should get general's pay, generals . . . ?

"Holding up okay?" Roth next addressed Greenberg.

Greenberg stroked his nose with a grimy hand; he smiled shyly. He wanted to ask for relief as Reilly had done, but couldn't bring himself to do so. "Yes, sir," he said unconvincingly.

Roth looked toward Reilly for an instant and then back at Greenberg. "Maybe we can get you back in a squad soon. You're doing a good job . . . you and Reilly."

"Thanks. I wouldn't mind that," said Greenberg.

"I'll see what I can do," said Roth. "Maybe . . . everything'll turn out all right . . . I . . He wanted to say more, but couldn't piece it together. He half smiled at Greenberg and continued on up the road. He suddenly remembered a detail.

"Rodriguez! Rodriguez!" Roth called. "Set out some flank guards!"

"Already done, Lieutenant!" Rodriguez shouted from the rear. "I took care of it before!"

Another detail off his mind. "Who doesn't have rations?" Roth shouted, his question being lost to half the men. No answer. From experience they had learned to carry a chocolate ration or a small can of chopped egg or cheese somewhere about their persons.

Roth stopped near Abbruzio. The young, olive-skinned soldier had removed his helmet and his black hair showed even darker under the dampness of sweat.

"Making out okay?" asked the Lieutenant.

"Yes, sir," said Abbruzio, his mouth stuffed with food. He held a large chunk of cake in his hand.

"Where'd you get that?" asked Roth.

"I had it in my pack, sir," replied Abbruzio, trying to hide his embarrassment with a smile.

Roth laughed and went on. Always leave it to the new ones to stow away a piece of cake, or salami, or a handful of candy. He began to feel better; proud to be speaking to his men and looking out for their welfare, and of being an integral part of the unit. They were his friends ... men whom he had gone through hell with ... and he was one of them.

"How do you like leading a squad again?" he asked Motoya.

Motoya was lying on his side, eating with one hand and smoking with the other. "I'll have to see action first," he stated.

"What do you mean?" asked Roth.

Motoya gestured with the cigarette. "That was no leading. A position's what I want... a machine-gun nest, or a pillbox, or a houseful of snipers...." He waved the cigarette in a half circle.

"Is that all?" laughed Roth. The man was really cool; to run through one of the worst poundings and all he could think of was attacking a German position.

Roth sat down at the side of the road, removed a chocolate ration from his pocket, and slowly began to chew. He opened his canteen, and was about to swallow some water when his uplifted hand suddenly stopped. He gazed around at his men and noticed that a few were staring at him.

Roth uttered a discomfited laugh. "You can drink now," he called. "Pass the word along the line." He had almost broken his own order. He munched on the candy and listened to the contrast of the silence. Minutes, even seconds, were an entire universe of studies in contrast. In the compass of a moment a man gives himself up for dead and reverts to beasthood, a frightened animal of nerves and reflexes, without intellect. His soul leaves him and he becomes a creature of confused emotions, crying and screaming inarticulately for some god who never appears to save him from the awful fates which lie in wait at every turn. The past and the future are forgotten, with the present becoming the last and maddest dream before death.

Then suddenly the next moment is one of peace and silence; a peace so corporeal that one can hold it and fondle it; quiet that can be tasted and rolled about on the tongue, each taste bud exploring its structure in ecstasy approaching agony. Fine quiet ... rare jewel of silence ... the moment's relief from bamming, moaning, jagged-steeled death. Happiness of the instant so rare that it never can be recaptured.

The field on the left still exploded in occasional wide-spaced defiant orgasms. But the sounds were no longer of the present; they were of the past and merely the colored background of the vivid study in opposites. Roth listened and tasted the silence, knowing that it was only to last for a minute. He spaced the wondrous moment and divided it into ten equal parts, so that its beauty would last longer and time roll off the track. He counted the spaces slowly: One...two...three...four...five parts of the minute...on up to ten and then back to another, more miraculous minute.

A stray shell burst close by, and a single dry sob broke loose from Roth's throat. He again began to chew the bitter chocolate; the spell was ended and the present was once more his reality. He was back on earth fighting in a war, leading men through hell knows where. He was of the war world... dirty, bearded, and frightened of every strange shadow that appeared in his path. He was a soldier, a chewer, an eater, a runner, an excreter, a hero, and a coward. He was confused, wise, stupid, religious, and blasphemous. He loved and he hated. He loved himself and wanted to live, and hated himself for wanting to live when there was so much of more importance than his own meager little niggling self. He was a piece of flesh to be shoveled into the hungry maws of liberty, equality, democracy, fraternity, the brotherhood of man....

He wanted to die, and wanted more to live. He wanted to save his sanity, but was blowing his top. He was a leader who wanted to be led, a killer who had done his killing, and a dier who was afraid to shake the hand of death.

He was no better than the other men; he did not have the right to make decisions for them, to lead them into the face of the enemy. He was a feeler, a breather, an eater, an excreter, and a crier by night as much as any other dirty-faced, bearded, exhausted automaton. He could not raise his hands unto the heavens and by the utterance of magic words order the shells to change their path. He couldn't stand in the path of a stream of burning tracer bullets and deflect them with his chest. And he could not forecast errors which naturally happened as part of the chaos and confusion of a speed-paced war. He wore the insignia of authority, but he was not a savant. He was as foul and stinking as the others.

A few yards from Roth, Northrup, one of the new men, rolled up a piece of cellophane torn from a cigarette package and began to clean an annoying tooth cavity with the needle-point tip of the paper. He reclined on the road near Sergeant Olivet, who was eating a second can of chopped egg.

"Not very satisfying," said Northrup, his voice tired.

Olivet smiled. "You'll get used to it. It doesn't fill your belly, but it'll keep you going."

Northrup shook his head in exaggerated disbelief. "A quarter of a pound of concentrated sawdust... three times each day if we're lucky... to keep a man alive! Frankly, I can't believe it!"

"You'll soon learn how little a man needs to keep moving," said Olivet. "There was one time, the first week off the beach, when we only had one ration a day; one ration and a canteen of water."

"At least a man won't get fat," stated Northrup.

"No, he won't," said Olivet. "It still surprises me to think how much the human body can take. I've gone for three days without sleep and then marched ten miles into an attack."

"How did you feel?"

"Like in a dream. My eyes were numb and half-blind, my legs didn't seem to exist. When the attack was over, late that night, I didn't even have the strength to dig a hole. I fell on my back and slept through the damnedest concentration and strafing you ever saw... so they tell me ... and I never stirred once till dawn."

"Is it always that rough?" asked Northrup.

"Well, if it isn't one thing, it's the other."

"What do you mean?"

"If you're not attacking, it's a patrol. And if it's neither of the two, the enemy is attacking or strafing or shelling. Oh, we have moments of quiet, but sometimes that's even worse than the action."

"I see what you mean."

"Don't worry, though," said Olivet. "We're all in the same boat... you know, misery loves company...."

"Tell me, do we ever get relieved?"

Olivet laughed bitterly. "We're supposed to; but I guess the brass hats must have forgotten this outfit. We've been in the lines fifty-eight days, and ever since the first week we've gotten a rumor a day about our moving to a rest area." Olivet laughed again. "The only rest we ever get is when we knock off for five minutes on a road like this!"

"How do they expect men to keep going?"

"We're going... and here we are!"

Sergeant Warner was standing near the ditch, haranguing his squad. He shook his finger angrily at Groggins. "For the last time, when in the hell are you going to wise up?" Groggins sprawled comfortably in the dust at the side of the road. Sanchez sat beside him, listening with amusement to what the sergeant had to say.

"Geez, Warner, I didn't even know where he was!" said Groggins.

"You didn't even know where he was! You didn't even know where he was!" shouted Warner. "How long you been in the outfit?"

"I don't know... three years maybe," said Groggins. "Three years," continued Warner. "And what's your job been all that time?"

"Assistant gunner on the BAR," said Groggins, smiling benignly.

Warner turned to Sanchez. "What are you going to do with a guy like him? Tell me... what are you going to do?"

"Aw, lay off him, Warner!" Sanchez said. "The kid's got enough troubles."

"He's too dumb to have troubles!" said Warner. He returned to Groggins. "From now on I want you to stick to Sanchez like he's your twin brother. And when the going gets tough you're to help him carry that goddam BAR... or so help me Christ I'll stick a bayonet six inches up your ass!"

"Geez, I couldn't even see him with all that smoke!" argued Groggins. "How do you expect a guy...?"

Warner dropped his arms limply to his sides. "Balls!" he murmured, and fumbled in his pocket for a cigarette. "Tell you what, I'll tie you two together and then I'll be sure you're there...."

"How about him carrying the BAR and me helping him when he's tired?" Sanchez offered slyly.

"Yeah, then what do we do when we need the weapon in a hurry?" said Warner. "Leave him alone with the thing and he'd turn it loose on us!"

"I'd like that!" said Groggins. "Geez, I could do okay if you'd gimme the chance! Geez, I could really knock 'em out!"

"Listen!" Warner concluded. "You're assistant gunner and that's what you'll stay! All I want is for you to stick with Sanchez like glue and give him a hand when he needs it! Remember, stick with him! That's all I want!"

"Yeah, I know! But there was so much smoke...!" Warner threw his cigarette to the earth and walked away. You couldn't squeeze blood out of a stone, and you couldn't put brains into Groggins.

Motoya's squad was at the side of the road, some talking, some listening.

"What good's it going to do us if we do get to Paris?" said Reubens.

"There's lots of tail... these French mam'selles just waiting for us," said Hohmeyer.

Reubens waved his arm contemptuously. "Nah, the first thing they'll do is put it off limits... only for the S.O.S. and the brass hats! We won't stand a chance!"

"I'll get there!" said Motoya confidently. "There ain't a place yet they could keep me out of!"

"Sure, walk in and the first thing you know you'll be nabbed by the M.P.'s!" said Reubens. "I tell you, Paris ain't for us! I know... my old man told me how it was after the last war." Motoya thumped his chest boastingly. "When there's tail around, this guy's going to get it! Christ, how're they going to keep a million of us from getting laid after it's been so long we haven't had a piece?"

Reubens laughed raucously. "You ever hear what they did to the guys in Italy and North Africa? When the shooting was over, they gave them close-order drill and squad tactics to take the starch out of them!"

"Not line troops! I don't believe it!" said Motoya.

"I swear it!" avowed Reubens. "My cousin was in Tunisia and Italy with the Thirty-Sixth... he wrote me. Every time the fighting was over, the towns were put off limits... and the guys who done the fighting for them were started all over again with basic training! Sure, the S.O.S. and the M.P.'s and the brass hats get into town, but not the guys that done the fighting!"

"They won't keep this old boy out!" stated Hohmeyer. "I'm sharp now, and I'll be a lot sharper when we get to old Paris. They won't keep me out!"

"I'll get me a suit of civilian clothes," said Motoya reflectively. "I've done it before."

"Yeah, but that was Ireland," said Reubens. "Here they ain't even got what to wear."

"There's always a way," said Motoya.

"You'll see," said Reubens. "You'll be doing close-order drill with the rest of us."

"They're going to have to catch me!" exclaimed Motoya. "I'm willing to fight their goddamned war... and the more I fight the sooner I get home . . . but I'll be frigged if they're going to take away my fun! They never did it, and they never will!"

"Yeah, that's what the guys who fill up the guardhouses say too!" said Reubens. "They're never caught until they find themselves breaking rocks."

"They ain't built the guardhouse to hold me!" Motoya said. "What about the last time?" said Reubens.

"I didn't stay, did I?" said Motoya triumphantly. "I'm here, ain't I?"

"Yeah, but they let you out to make the invasion," stated Reubens.

"That's what you think!" argued Motoya. "They didn't have a goddam thing on me! That's why they let me out!"

"I heard different," said Reubens.

"Are you calling me a liar?" said Motoya.

"Sounds like it," offered Hohmeyer.

"No, I ain't calling you a liar . . . but you know how it is," said Reubens. "A guy just doesn't walk out of the guardhouse. . . ."

"Listen, I said they didn't have a thing on me!" Motoya began to display growing anger.

"Aw, I can't believe that," said Reubens lazily.

"You son of a bitch! You're looking for a fractured skull!" said Motoya. He rose to his feet and glared down at Reubens.

Reubens suddenly became aware of Motoya's temper. "That ain't what I meant! I mean . . . hell, sure they didn't have anything on you!"

Motoya dropped his raised fists. "Well, okay. But don't give me any of your frigging arguments! I ain't in the mood today. You always got too goddamned much to say anyway!"

Reubens lowered his eyes. "Okay. That ain't what I really meant to say. . . ."

Sitting apart from the others, McCrea removed a wrinkled sheet of V-letter paper from his combat pack and opened the cap of his fountain pen. He placed the point of the pen to the paper and tried to think. He raised his eyes and gazed into space. A few words' were not enough, could never be enough. If he were overly sparse in his letter, his wife would be certain to perceive the situation. She was positively psychic that way. All during the time he had been in the army, his moods at moments such as this had been somehow communicated to her.

He looked again at the blank sheet of paper, but his pen still did not move. Whatever he'd have to say would ring with the excitement of the few minutes just past and do more to alarm her than if he actually were to give her a detailed news report of the mad dash across the shelled field.

He carefully replaced the pen in his pocket and returned the V-letter paper to his pack. Later on, maybe that afternoon, or in the early evening if it were not too dark, he'd write a long letter. Then he'd have more time.

Kimmel, the replacement sergeant formerly of the Air Force, roused himself from his exhaustion-induced lethargy and began to work. First he stood erect and adjusted the straps of his combat pack; he experimented with and readjusted each strap until the pack finally rode high on his shoulders. He took a few steps up and down the road and found that it sat far more comfortably than before.

Then he loosened the fit of his cartridge belt. With the belt loosened he found that his insides were less constricted and that his breath came easier.

Lastly he readjusted his legging laces so that the stiffness of the new canvas was eliminated and air rushed in around his legs. He added a few final touches to each item of equipment, again removed his pack, and sat back on the road, feeling relief at being prepared.

He had found the source of his trouble and knew that things in the future would be simpler. It wouldn't be too hard for him to learn his job. A few days of activity and weight would sweat off. It might even do him some good to harden up. There were tricks to fighting, the same as in anything else, and he was determined to do as good a job as the others. He hadn't been made a sergeant for nothing, and he was more resolved than ever to keep his rank.

The two platoon scouts were lying close together, away from the others.

"It sure looks quiet to me," said Reilly, squinting down the road.

"I'd hate to know what's beyond the bend," said Greenberg.

"It won't be long before we see," said Reilly. "If this day ever ends, I'll be sure nothing can ever happen to me."

"Me too," said Greenberg. "If they haven't hit us by now, they never will." He crossed his fingers, cursing himself for squeezing his luck.

"If they put me back in a squad, I'll think I'm getting a rest," said Reilly.

"You'd get over it. Get back to a platoon and you'd want to be back with Battalion Headquarters; and get back to Battalion and you'd want to be with Regiment."

"Yeah, I guess every guy thinks the next place is the easiest until he gets there," Reilly reflected. "And when he gets there, he wants to go the next step back."

"Like the guys up in Army Headquarters who sleep in nice warm beds and get hot food three times a day," said Greenberg. "They write home and tell the folks how tough things are."

"And want to get back across the ocean out of danger. Me, I'd take a squad or Battalion Headquarters right now and be happy."

"You can say that again," said Greenberg. Anyplace would do where he wasn't up in front with his neck stuck out like a chicken waiting for the chopping block. He couldn't last another day. His eyes were going blind from endlessly searching the front and flanks, and his heart was tired from pumping like an overworked, rusty motor. There was a limit to how much a guy could take.

"When do you think we'll get relieved?" asked Reilly. "Beats me," said Greenberg. "Another few shellings and they won't have to relieve us."

"You mean there won't be an outfit left?" said Reilly. "Yeah. We'll get relief with Graves Registration."

"No kidding, though. You think they'll relieve us?"

"They're supposed to . . . any week now," said Greenberg. "I sure hope so. My feet are plumb wore out. Another day and I'll be walking on my stumps!"

"I'm on mine," said Greenberg.

Reilly bit on a piece of dried grass. Back home the old man had probably gotten some young guy to take over his work . . . some punk who didn't hardly know what it was all about . . . and rather should be up in his position, and he be back running the farm as it should be done. If only he had handled it smarter, he never would have been stuck like this. It never failed that he knew what to do when it was too late.

Greenberg wondered how he had managed to get so far. He had always been convinced that he wasn't cut out to be a soldier and would have laughed if anybody had ever told him that he would wind up as an infantryman. But it had happened and he was doing his job as good as the others . . . even better because he was a scout and did all the dirty, dangerous work. It was something to be proud of; to know that he was strong and had courage... a courage he never realized he had ... and that he stood with all the men as one of them. Still he wished it was over because the going was tough, and the next minute or second might mean his end.

At the head of his resting platoon, Paul Roth surveyed his men absently. He glanced for a moment at Verne Potter. The young man again seemed to be forcing the tears back. He looked as though he would let himself go completely if no one were around to watch. His lower lip quivered slightly and the whites of his eyes were lined with red streaks. He lay on his stomach, his chin resting on his crossed arms, morosely staring into space.

Roth awkwardly dropped his glance. He wanted to say something, but there wasn't much he could do. He had asked Dougall to have him relieved and sent to the rear, but the Company Commander objected too strongly. Potter had to go on with the others; he was no more exhausted and no sadder than anyone else. If his temperament took the form of tears, it was his way of manifesting the strain of the weeks gone by.

It was strange that he hadn't cracked; but it was possible that his strength lay in his weakness. Roth had heard somewhere that men with the ability to let off steam through escape valves were less apt to crack under strain than men who are thoroughly composed and integrated. In Potter's case it might hold true. When he cried, the tension sizzled off like steam through a radiator vent.

Roth swallowed and again glanced at Potter. "How're you doing?" he asked.

"All right," said Potter, a flicker of a sad smile crossing his face.

"You going to make it okay?" asked Roth.

"Yes, sir," said Potter, lowering his eyes.

"I mean... if you think you're..." Roth floundered.

"I can do what anybody else can!" said Potter, his voice rising almost aggressively.

Roth smiled. "Good boy!" One thing, the kid never complained much. In fact, he bitched less than the rest.

The sun burned hot and dry on the unshaded parts of the road. Roth had to shift his left leg to remove it from a blazing ray. If they didn't find trees to march under they'd certainly sweat. He couldn't remember one day of his army career that had been just right; it was either too hot or too cold, or it rained or snowed. Mild weather never blessed a soldier.

Lieutenant Dougall came lumbering down the road, cheerfully calling out to each man as he walked. He questioned their condition, their spirits, and offered words of encouragement; he seemed in better humor than he had for many days. He came up to Roth and grunting heavily squatted beside the platoon leader.

"What happened in that goddamned field?" asked Roth. "Someone in Battalion got the signals crossed," explained Dougall.

Roth shrugged his shoulders. "What the hell, it's nothing new . . . !" he muttered.

"Well, aside from that, I've got good news," said Dougall. "What?" asked Roth.

"They're definitely going to relieve us . . . late tonight or early tomorrow morning," said Dougall.

"Are you sure? We've heard it every day. . . I mean, this isn't like the other bullshit rumors . . . ?"

"This is positive," said Dougall. "Orders have come down from Corps Headquarters no less! The entire division is being pulled back!"

"Swell! Only I hope they don't change their minds!"

"They won't," said Dougall. "The deal is that we're going to be motorized. The whole division'll have to be reorganized."

"Good! I've often wondered how it would feel to fight from a half-track, instead of wearing off my legs up to my hips!"

"You'll do plenty of walking. You're still in the infantry. This is just to make us more mobile so that we can get places faster. We'll still fight on our feet."

"The important thing is that they're pulling us out! Boy, I can hardly believe it . . . hell, I won't believe it until it happens!"

"One more thing," said Dougall. "Don't tell the men about it, yet."

"Why not?" asked Roth.

"Well, just in case . . . official word will come down later."

"Oh, the same old story," said Roth, his spirits suddenly dropping.

"No, it isn't that," said Dougall. "But we don't want hopes to get all stirred up and then have something possibly go haywire."

"The same old crap!" said Roth.

"I'm sure *this* is it!" insisted Dougall. "It couldn't be otherwise. The division is shot to hell and we couldn't possibly make another attack without reorganizing."

"I just hope you're right," said Roth.

"I'm sure I am," said Dougall. "Get your men moving, now. We still have to get through before we get relieved . . . the same deal goes."

"And if we don't . . . ?"

"We will."

"You want us to move out right away?"

Dougall stood erect. "As quick as you can. Good luck, and watch your step!" He watched Roth for a moment as the platoon leader adjusted his equipment and then turned back toward the rear.

"On your feet!" Roth shouted. "We're moving out! On your feet!"

The order was taken up along the line and the men reluctantly secured their equipment and took their places in the column. They ceased talking and looked anxiously toward the front. Their rest was over, and thoughts again became exceedingly personal.

"Scouts out!" ordered Roth, and Reilly and Greenberg slowly moved down the road. They walked carefully and examined each leaf and blade of grass bordering the narrow cattle passage.

Roth waited until the scouts had sufficient distance between each other and were fifteen yards ahead of him. He raised his arm straight into the air, palm facing toward the front, and lowered it slowly to the ground. He moved off, and the First Platoon followed.

Chapter Twelve

THEY MOVED ON toward the next intermediate objective, the cluster of farm buildings that would be the jumping-off place for their final thrust to the high ground. The trees which had grown sporadically about the landscape disappeared, and they were again in familiar hedgerow country. The fields were narrow and overgrown. Each meadow was bounded on all sides by ponderous parapets of earth and brush and stinging-nettle vine growths. The terrain was rough and began to rise in elevation. The road ahead seemed to roll in gentle upward sweeps toward the sun.

In the distance on the right flank, they saw a series of steep hills, three of which were the approaches to the mysterious town of St. Lô, the always distant objective the armies had been trying to reach. Rumor had it that when St. Lô was taken the war from there on would be a waltz, an unimpeded march right through France and Germany and on to final victory.

The men gazed at the hills before St. Lô, dreaming beyond it to the region where quiet no longer would be filled with dread and where peace was tangible and could be embraced as firmly as one holds his lover. What they were undergoing now was a feverish nightmare of fear and pain ... forgotten portions of minds released and wallowing in the muck of primeval instincts. But the future was there, existing beyond St. Lô.

Paul Roth walked in the center of the road and tried to measure a steady pace. Ninety-to-the-minute he counted, glancing at his watch each few seconds as a check. The men were too bushed to go any faster, regardless of what Colonel Nielsen had set down as a normal rate of speed to be used when in approach-march formation.

The pleasure in the news of the impending relief had worn off, and he was as skeptical as ever. It wasn't Dougall's fault that he had received a message to transmit, but he did get a little overanxious whenever such rumors came down. Every day they had been informed of relief, and each new day still found them in the same position. This last rumor could be true but he hadn't much hope. They'd probably keep them in the lines until there wasn't one man left; then they'd move in another division and give them the same treatment. . . .

Roth felt the gravity pull of the rising earth, and he added effort to maintain the pace he had set. More hills. Whether in the comparatively peaceful maneuvers of training or during the wrack of combat, there was never any flat ground to march over. Always hills surging on into the distance where there would be other hills . . . and after the hills came the mountains. The hills never went down. It was a miracle they didn't eventually reach the heavens so that they could all shake hands with the gods. Up the hills and down the hills and over the hills, like Christ went to Golgotha. Christ went to Golgotha with a cross on his back, and he was going there with a pack and a rifle.

Christ went to Golgotha? Where did he get that from? Sure, Christ went to Golgotha, but he was not Christ and was not on his way to Golgotha. He was going up a hill with a pack on his back, and a weapon on his shoulder, and a steel helmet biting his brains from his head.

Where did he get that? This was war and he was only going up with thousands of other guys. Misery loves company and he had plenty of that. But maybe he was alone? He was a platoon leader stuck out in front of a group of men. His eyes burned from the sun and the dust, and his mind kept turning like a shaky wheel, on and off the track.

They moved on over a land that was a web of contour lines meeting in infinity. Dust from the shuffling of many feet became a brown circling blur. A vast, muted chorus of breathing rose and fell like an uneven breeze.

A sudden series of staccato bursts shattered the quiet, and the column hit the ground. The two scouts nervously scanned the front and flanks and fired a few wild shots in each direction. Roth surveyed the terrain but saw nothing; on all sides not a wisp of telltale smoke could be detected. There was a small hedgerow three hundred yards to the front, and a lone tree grew at the left of the road near the center of the column.

"Pick up the smoke if you can!" Roth shouted. He buried his head when a second series of bursts kicked up the dry earth.

The machine-pistol bursts began to spray the road with spaced shots every few seconds. Roth was worried and frightened; he was leading the point for the whole battalion, and there wasn't a thing he could do. He couldn't tell whether there was one or fifty burp guns. If they moved on they'd be slaughtered, and if they remained as they were they'd be killed. No matter how rotten the enemy's aim, it would have been impossible for them to continue firing without soon getting on the target.

There was a scuffling movement behind Roth and a hand shook his shoulder. Saunders had crawled up and was talking hurriedly: "I think I can git 'em ... there's only two! Keep the men firin' to the front, and I'll have us some fresh meat!"

Sergeant Saunders voluptuously spat some juice and crawled toward the rear, moving along the ditch that bordered the road.

Roth screamed some garbled orders about keeping up a steady stream of fire to the front and then held his breath and watched Saunders.

Still crawling on his belly, Saunders reached the center of the column. Behind him was the large lone tree with thick foliage growing almost to the ground. He swung around and faced the front. He lay still for a few seconds and seemed to be listening carefully. He slowly rose to his knees, jumped to his feet with a sudden snap, did a springing about-face, and fired into the tree. He fired a second shot. A shrill scream froze the air, and a limp figure toppled from the heights and fell with a thud on the pebbled road.

Saunders ran over to the figure, kicked it a few times, and commenced to rifle its pockets. Completing the process, he picked up the dead enemy's fallen weapon and, again crawling, returned to Roth's position near the head of the platoon. His face was flushed, and a demoniac grin was drawn back over his buck teeth.

"That's one of 'em, Lieutenant," he said. "Pretty good pickin's, too." He opened his fist and showed Roth a handful of crumpled franc notes. "Now I got me one of them burp guns! Watch it for me, sir, while I git the other bastard."

It was pure pleasure for Saunders. It was hunting with all the ammunition he could shoot up; and it was better hunting than back home in Arkansas because the bag was unlimited and no license was necessary.

Saunders crawled down the road toward the front. Suddenly, an enemy soldier rushed out of the hedgerow, his hands held high over his head, screaming, "Surrender! Surrender!"

Saunders placed his rifle to his shoulder and squinted through the sights. He hesitated; slowly and reluctantly he lowered the weapon.

The German approached the platoon. His lips quivered and sweat poured down his face. He stole fearful glances at Saunders, but when the sergeant stared back at him he quickly averted his eyes and nervously scuffled his feet in the dust.

Roth placed the sniper under a two-man guard and sent him back to the battalion interrogation team. Saunders looked depressed.

"How did you manage to spot them?" asked Roth.

"I jest had a hunch," said the Sergeant. "I figgered that if I was a sniper and out fer game like us . . . well, them are the two places I'd pick. Besides I heard the one in the tree, and I spotted the glare off en the weapon of the one hidin' in the hedgerow." He chewed thoughtfully and continued. "Dern if I ain't sorry I didn't kill the other son of a bitch when he come runnin' out with his hands up! Bet he had plenty of them francs in his pockets!"

The march resumed with the tension eased by the sight of the enemy. They were human and not at all mysterious; they were dirty and bearded and undersized, and their unwashed bodies richly stank. As the column passed the dead body, many of the men spat in disgust. A few cursed at the twisted form.

As the road grew steeper the pace began to slacken; Reilly and Greenberg, more by instinct than knowledge, sensed new dangers which they could not yet consciously perceive. They were more cautious as they scouted each hedgerow that came into sight and paused momentarily before rounding turns in the road. Their fingers tightened on the triggers of their rifles and they marched with their shoulders hunched over in readiness.

The mood was communicated along the line of the marching column and even the heavy breathing was curbed as the men grew more aware of all possibilities. The dominant sounds were the cadenced scufflings of thousands of feet and the constant bass rumble of the big guns miles away. The sky was a clear blue, brightened by the sun high in orbit and fringed with distant swirls of drifting smoke. Planes, too far away to be seen, hummed a lulling monotone. From the rear of the column, thousands of yards from the front, a voice from one of the headquarters units occasionally broke out with a word or a short, indiscernible sentence.

Roth held his eyelids open until the effort hurt; he watched his scouts and followed every movement. He scanned the heavy hanging quiet of the brush and the gentle swaying of the tall grass and read terror in each shadow. His hands sweated over the stock of his carbine. He heard the crunch of his feet as a thunderous roar warning the enemy that they were coming. He felt at his collar for the insignia of rank to make certain that it was hidden under the fold. The silence swelled until it became more horrible than a scream.

Reilly stopped, listened, and then moved on again. He felt with his feet, remembering what he had been taught about personnel mines; he wished he hadn't remembered.

Each step was a single venture. As a foot went down the sole elongated; the calf tightened; the knee slowly unlocked. The strain moved up to the expanding thigh, to the contracting buttocks muscles, and through to the tired back. The extremity straightened and the operation started over again, and over again, each one adding up to millions of planned ventures up the inclining road.

The sergeants conscientiously watched their men, signaling encouragement and caution with their arms. They shook their heads at examples of poor dispersion and clenched their fists at laggards. In each company a few men dropped to the ditch, victims of exhaustion and the sum total of weeks in the line. They stared blankly at their passing comrades and waited for ambulances which eventually would come down from the rear to transport them to havens of rest in places beyond the sounds of gunfire. There they would be doped with elongated capsules, and the days and nights would become an impenetrable curtain of unbroken sleep.

Roth withdrew his map from his pocket, opened it to the section he wanted, and hastily glanced over it. They were nearing the hedgerow, but he still hadn't seen anything of the group of farm buildings. He remained alert; they were in the vicinity, he was certain. Otherwise there wouldn't be that air of watchful waiting, that tightening of the entire line. It never failed; men's instincts were as definitive and sure as those of the forest beasts.

Verne Potter stumbled over with the 536 radio. "The Company Commander wants you!" he panted.

Dougall's hoarse voice came through the instrument. "We're approaching the farm buildings."

"I don't see them," said Roth, anxiety rising.

"They're right over the hill ... the last hedgerow you can see, and just beyond that!" said Dougall.

Roth raised his eyes; there was a hedgerow at the head of the incline. Beyond that he saw nothing. "I see the hedgerow ... nothing else...."

"It's off to the right," came Dougall's voice. "You'll see the houses when you get to the top. Get off the road now, and take the left side of the field.... Hartley'll be on your right!"

"What'll we do when we hit the hedgerow?" asked Roth. "Hold up for further orders... we may get some support!"

"Anything else?"

"That's all. Keep contact with Hartley," Dougall concluded. Roth handed the radio back to Potter, and shouted to Reilly and Greenberg. "Hit the field on your right, but guide on the road!"

The two scouts hurdled the ditch and began the ascent through the grass of the field on the right.

Roth raised his arm to the men behind, signaling both the change of direction and for a more extended formation to be taken up in the open field.

The First Platoon gradually flanked right, with dispersion between men lengthening; they marched in a staggered column of two lines, each man from ten to fifteen yards apart.

A perspiring, puffing runner dashed up to Roth; he was from Lieutenant Hartley's platoon. "Lieutenant Hartley wants you to slow down ... give him some time to catch up!" the runner panted.

"Slow it down until I give you further orders!" Roth shouted to the scouts and then turned his head back toward the rear. "Warner ... two men on the right flank to keep contact with the Second Platoon!"

"Abbruzio ... McCarthy ... get over on the right!" ordered Warner. "When the Second Platoon gets up, stay close to them! Don't lose contact!"

Abbruzio and McCarthy, the two replacements, moved over to the right of the first squad. They kept turning their heads to watch the progress of the Second Platoon marching rapidly across the field in the effort to arrive parallel with the First Platoon.

Lieutenant Hartley walked close to his first scout and gesticulated impatiently at his men for more speed. The gap slowly closed and soon the two platoons marched evenly across the field.

"Speed it up!" Roth called to the scouts. As the distance lessened, the hedgerow on top of the hill grew larger. It was a high parapet, many feet thick at the base. In some places it was heavily foliaged; in others it was barren of growth.

One shell landed in the field; then another exploded yards from the first one. The two scouts added speed. No approach route was ever left uncovered by the Germans; every important piece of ground was thoroughly plotted on their fire-control maps.

A series of shells fell. Explosions from enemy light mortars spotted the open field at the left of the road. Machine-gun fire came in, squeezed off from too great a distance to be of immediate danger. It was long-range harassing fire; the flattened rounds fell weak and spent to the ground.

The two leading platoons began to move faster; squad leaders bellowed for more speed and ranted and cursed at both men and circumstance. The scouts moved cautiously, but the hedgerow acquired increasing form.

Roth began to see the roofs and the upper-story windows of the farm buildings. He waved his carbine excitedly in the air, already sensing the protecting confines of the thorny landmark.

The German artillery added voice. Three trial detonations searched the ground in front of the embankment and hosed sprays of earth many feet into the air. There came a pause, and then more shells erupted, digging a narrow trenchline in front of the hedge.

Reilly and Greenberg reached the hedgerow and crouched with their heads below the top of the earthen parapet.

Roth was next; he beckoned hurriedly at his men. "Warner, place your men on the right. . . on the right! Motoya, take the center of the line! Olivet, on the left . . . from the road in!"

The squad leaders took up the cry and there was a hasty scramble for position along the hedgerow. Rodriguez and Saunders ran up and down the line and assisted the squad leaders.

More artillery began to fall and a section of machine guns from the buildings across the field fired a series of warning bursts.

Roth raised his head to the top of the hedge: A group of six well-dispersed buildings rambled over approximately four hundred yards of ground. In the center stood the main house, surrounded on both sides by various sheds, feed pens, and barns. One building on the far left was a high, round structure that looked like a silo. A tiny road zigzagged past each building and joined the larger road on the left. Behind the crooked line of farm buildings a low row of clipped bushes interrupted the view of the field beyond.

Roth could see no smoke from the guns and no movement in and about the area. As usual, the enemy was well hidden.

"Start digging!" Roth ordered. He moved up and down the hedgerow, his back bent to keep his silhouette below the line of fire. "Dig your holes! We may be here for some time!"

The first squad huddled wearily below the parapet. "Warner, get your men moving!" shouted Roth. Artillery and mortar fire exploded more fiercely, and a few shells landed in the field behind them.

"Stir your asses!" shouted Warner. He removed his shovel from his pack and began to dig.

Motoya and Olivet already had their men working. Motoya, his helmet cocked on the back of his head, peered interestedly at the farm.

"See anything?" asked Roth.

"Nothing. I can't tell where the bastards are!" said Motoya.

"Watch your head," warned Roth.

"They ain't gonna get me!" boasted Motoya.

Roth trotted over to the left. He gazed past the hedgerow down the road; he saw nothing. There was a lot of smoke on the horizon but the road was quiet. He ran back to the center of his platoon.

Verne Potter dug rapidly, and his shovel had already created the oblong shape of a foxhole in the side of the hedgerow. "Do you want me to dig one for you?" he asked Roth.

"Yeah... no, no," said Roth. "I'll do it myself." He removed his pack from his back and unstrapped the small entrenching tool from the canvas carrier. He applied the weight of his foot to the blade and began to dig. Sweat stained his back and poured down into his eyes. He dug a few inches and then dropped the tool. He picked up his carbine and walked over to the right side of his defense position.

Sparked by the taunts of their leader, the Second Platoon dug rapidly. Lieutenant Hartley spotted Roth and came running over. "This'll be a bastard!" he offered.

"What makes you think so?" asked Roth.

"Look at the position they got," said Hartley. "Observation and fields of fire in every direction, and I'll bet they're plenty dug in!"

"A battery of artillery'll drive them out," said Roth hopefully.

"I don't think they're in the houses," said Hartley. "I've got a hunch they're holed up behind those bushes...."

A series of loud flutters beat the air, and the two platoon leaders threw themselves down and against the hedgerow. The ground roared and opened up, and waves of clapping concussion smashed against their eardrums. They waited, counting to themselves, and finally regained their feet.

"Son of a bitch they sure know we're here!" Hartley said.

"It's that silo!" said Roth, his body trembling.

"I don't know what it is, but I wish to hell I was out of here!" said Hartley. He ran back toward the center of his platoon, shouting for more speed in the digging of the holes.

Roth's men needed no encouragement. They had removed their belts, packs, and gas masks and were digging rapidly. They had no thoughts for anything save a protecting depth to fit their bodies.

With the suddenness of summer thunder, a growing roar came down from the sky directly overhead. They heard the wind screaming in the churning engine, and they tried to bury themselves in the few inches of hole already dug. The single explosion tore excruciatingly against intestines, slammed under steel helmets, and made eyeballs swell painfully against reddened lids. The tidal wave of concussion raised bodies into the air, held them poised for an infinitesimal fraction of a second, then slammed them with sickening brutality back to the earth.

The men waited and then slowly raised their heads. The plane sped a few yards off the ground toward the front. Shouts started slowly, first in relief and then a rising chorus of anger: "The sons of bitches're tryin' to kill their own men!" "It's our own... a P-47... the no-good, motherless bastards!" "Ain't we got enough troubles without our own planes bombing us!" "The Air Force is winnin' the war... yeah, killin' their own troops!" "Why don't they just line us up against a wall... it'd be easier!" "If I ever get my hands on a pilot, I'll strangle the friggin' bastard!" "The son of a bitch'll get another cluster to his D.F.C. for this!" "Nah, this one's the Congressional Medal!" "Can't the pricks read maps?"...

Roth struggled to a sitting position and rubbed his head tenderly. In the center of the field was a perfect circle eight yards in diameter and three feet deep where the five hundred pounder had hit. From there on out he felt sure, if ever the opportunity were offered, he'd have his men fire on all planes, enemy or friendly.

The cries of anger subsided. They continued digging.

Chapter Thirteen

LIEUTENANT DOUGALL moved up to the center of the high hedgerow with the company command group. The runners, the mail orderly, the Communications-Sergeant, and the First Sergeant started to dig a control pit.

Roth shuffled over to the big lieutenant. "Why doesn't someone inform those bastards where we are?" he asked peevishly.

"What can we do?" said Dougall. "They're supposed to know the situation."

"I wonder if anybody knows what's going on! If they'd get a few line soldiers back there, maybe they'd learn to get their heads out of their asses!"

Dougall shook his head and smiled sympathetically. "It won't help to get aggravated. You pay admission and you see the show."

"We're overpaying," said Roth.

"Forget it," said Dougall. "We've got more important things to think about. Regiment is sending down four tanks to support the attack, and you're to move with them."

"How come me?" asked Roth.

"You're in the best spot. They're going to work in from the left, and you'll have to give them rifle protection. You'll outpost when the position is taken."

"It's always the First Platoon!" Roth said bitterly. "Why can't they come in from the right?"

"Orders. The road is the only approach, and being that you're nearest, you're stuck with the job."

"I'm being stuck so much I feel like a pincushion!"

"You're not the only one who's having it hard!" said Dougall in a sudden flurry of anger which subsided as quickly as it came. "Anyway, you'll have it a lot easier with the tanks than if you were out there alone."

Roth laughed cynically. "I hope so! When they start shooting eighty-eights at the tanks, we'll have to be broken-field runners to avoid the fragments!"

"This won't be so tough," said Dougall. "The tanks'll take care of anything that's in the way."

"How about artillery support?" asked Roth.

"All we get are tanks. The artillery is being concentrated someplace else. Now get your men working ... see if you can pick up something."

Roth walked back and signaled for his squad leaders, the platoon guide, and the platoon sergeant to assemble near him. The five men trotted over, and listened while he spoke.

"Start your men firing at those houses and anything else they can spot," Roth began. "Don't waste ammunition, and see how much you can pick up."

"We don't have too much left," offered Sergeant Olivet. "We'll get more," said Roth. "Saunders, take two men with you and get back to the Battalion Ammunition D.P. Get as much thirty caliber as possible, and don't let them argue you out of it. Also, get a few boxes of carbine ammo."

"I won't have any trouble," smiled Saunders.

"Make sure you cover everything, and space the fire well," Roth continued. "We're getting tank support to make the attack on the houses. Watch your men and keep them on both sides of the tanks; don't let them lag behind and don't get too far out in front."

"Do we get all the dirty jobs, Lieutenant?" Warner asked sullenly.

"I don't know if we get all of them. I haven't kept an exact count," said Roth.

"When do we get relieved?" asked Olivet.

Roth looked around cautiously. "I don't know whether I should tell you, but I don't think it makes too much difference ... only keep it to yourselves. I heard a while ago that we'll definitely be pulled out late tonight, or early tomorrow morning."

"It sounds like the same old crap we've always heard!" said Warner.

"No, this is supposed to have come down from a source higher than Division," said Roth. "I don't believe most of the rumors I hear, but this one sounds like the real goods. However, make sure you don't say anything to your men."

"I won't," said Olivet.

The others nodded their heads.

"Watch the new men. Don't let them get trigger-happy," Roth concluded. "You'll get the signal when we're to move out with the tanks."

The squad leaders scurried back along the firing-line to their respective units. Saunders went to find two men for the ammunition detail, and Sergeant Rodriguez took up a position fifteen yards from the platoon leader.

Artillery fire and mortar concentrations thrown by the enemy grew increasingly violent, and the activities of the platoons along the line became a spastic motion of alternate digging and ducking flat to the earth. The ground in front of the hedgerow was constantly excavated by the enemy bursts. More carefully directed rounds were beginning to explode behind the position. Waves of concussion surged over them, and small grass fires in and about the area added to the afternoon heat.

The First Platoon opened fire on the enemy position across the meadow. The squad leaders screamed and shouted fire orders and bellowed angrily as initial rounds inexpertly tore up the earth at varying distances away from the target.

As if in answer, the Germans roared back. Red-tailed tracers crisscrossed over the line, and a solid stream of rifle fire whanged and whizzed inches above the heads of the men along the hedgerow. Their knees went down instinctively, their steel-helmeted heads dropping below the grassy top of the parapet.

The squad leaders screamed louder: "Get up! Get up on that goddamned hedge! They're shootin' high! Get up and catch where the smoke is cornin' from!"

The men raised their heads until they again could see the houses, the silo, the assorted sheds, and the low line of bushes behind. They fired again, and again the Germans answered.

Roth lifted his binoculars to the hedgerow, camouflaging it a bit behind a bald bush. He saw smoke trickling out of one window in the main house, and then a shadowed figure running from a shed on the right into the house.

"There's some of them in the big house!" Roth shouted. "Watch the big house!"

Motoya's squad already had their fire aimed where the platoon leader wanted. They worked carefully, trying to find a target for every shot.

Roth unlocked the safety on his carbine, squinted through the simple sight, and began to fire. He watched sharply first, but seeing no movement he directed his aim towards the lower floor windows of the house in the center. The squeezing of the trigger and the power of the recoil prodding his shoulder had a leveling effect. He felt confidence in the strength of the light weapon held in his hands and forgot everything except the sport of seeking a proper target.

The Germans fired back. Tracer bullets arced, the trajectory path reaching the highest point near the center of the field and lowering gradually until they skimmed close to the top grass of the hedgerow. Rifle fire punctuated the continuous rattle of machine guns with well-ordered, rhythmic volleys.

Following the small-arms fire, the mortars searched in. Groups of ten, fifteen, twenty, reached across the field; fifty . . . ten . . . five yards in front of the hedge they tore up the ground. One landed on top of the parapet, a few yards from the company command post. Four . . . eight . . . ten rammed into the earth, directly in the middle of the First Platoon's position.

Heavy artillery came in a new wave. Flutters burned the air with the consistency of telegraph poles speeding by the window of a fast train. The earth gave up soil and roots and rock and grass, mushrooming them up and out and back to the ground. Concussion swelled and billowed, coil on coil smashing against each other in a head-shattering discordance.

Two broke near Roth. He was lifted from the earth, held suspended for a second of eternity, and flung back. Concussion surged in and poured down his throat to the depths of his intestines, twisted through his eardrums to his brain, and forced entrance into his nostrils in swelling knots. The second shell raised him again, but did not hold him poised in space. He felt himself hurled up and twisted back in a convulsive snap that whipped his spine like a piece of soggy rope. He was on the sea and the food did not hold; he leaned over the rail, the green bile gushing from his tortured belly. He heaved until there was nothing left but the dry rubberiness of his sour guts coming up in gaseous clouds. He puked and wanted to die, and if he had the strength, he would lift his legs over the rail and dive into the depths of the pounding water.

The water rose over him and he coughed hoarsely. Air rasped painfully over his sore lungs. Hands were squeezing his shoulders. His teeth bit into a hard, metal surface, and the cold became a delight.

The tossing slowly subsided. "Have some more water." The voice was soft, yet harsh with an embarrassed masculinity.

Roth blinked the film away from his eyes and looked up. Rodriguez gripped him by the shoulders, and Motoya held a canteen to his mouth.

"Concussion must have gotten you," said the Platoon Sergeant. "How do you feel?"

Roth tried to control his dizzy eyes. His denim shirt stank from vomit. He tried to struggle to his feet, and the two men assisted him. He coughed and spat, and a small bubble of blood spattered to the ground. He raised his hand to wipe his nose, and it came away with pale streaks of red.

"How about going to the aid station?" suggested Rodriguez. "You got in a bad blast...."

Roth gagged, but swallowed it back. "Ah . . . be all right," he mumbled, wanting to hold back a sob or to scream so that his voice would be torn from his throat. He'd be all right . . . he should go to the aid station . . . but what in the hell was a concussion? They'd all think he was gold-bricking or turned yellow. He was finished but hadn't turned yellow, or was he yellow? He tried to smile, and the taste of blood was metallic on his tongue. "I'll be all right," he said again.

"That was some blast!" marveled Motoya.

Roth gazed about. The First Platoon still fired from the top of the hedgerow. A quiet form lay face down a few yards away. "Who's that?" he pointed.

"Potter. He got it," said Rodriguez.

Roth felt a wet cloud film his eyes. "Dead?"

"Yes, sir," said Rodriguez.

"Shrapnel?"

"Not a wound on him!" stated Rodriguez admiringly. "The concussion did it! Maybe you *ought* to go back to the aid station?"

Roth shook his head and leaned against the hedgerow, his eyes turned toward the enemy position. His lower lip trembled, and a single tear rolled down his face.

Motoya and Rodriguez eyed the Lieutenant for another moment, shrugged their shoulders, and returned to their work.

"Fire at the motherless sons of bitches!" Roth screamed. "Make your shots count! Kill the filthy murdering rotten bastards! Kill the lousy stinking fuckers!" He raised his carbine and fired eight rounds, reloaded with a second clip and fired another eight rounds. He fired fast, without taking aim, and didn't know or care where the rounds landed as long as one, or two, or maybe three would reach out and tear into the foul heart of one of the scum across the field. His body sobbed, and more blood trickled from his nose. The nausea still existed, but he had nothing left to give to the earth; he choked back the heaves and continued to squeeze the trigger on his weapon.

The ground exploded and tore, rent apart by the steady concentration, but Roth hardly heard or cared. When the other men ducked, he kept his head silhouetted above the grassy fringe of the embankment and fired his shots. He screamed wild encouragement to himself and to his men. The daze existed, blood-red and dust-clouded, blotting out all feeling from his brain except that of hate and hopeless melancholy.

Saunders and the two men returned with the load of ammunition; the platoon guide addressed Roth: "All we could git was machine-gun ammo. It's still in the belts."

Roth turned his head. "What do you mean?"

"Even Battalion's runnin' short. They caint git the stuff down from the rear."

"Get a detail and take it out of the belts, then," said Roth. "Get it done quick... we haven't much time."

Saunders detailed one man from each squad, and they gathered in a circle near the CP to remove the spaced rounds from the canvas belts. Sergeant Olivet volunteered his help in the distribution.

Roth's head cleared slightly. He left the top of the hedgerow and began to walk left and right along the firing line.

The bombardment was constant. Shells broad-sided over the position, and machine-gun and rifle fire zipped over the hedgerow with the intensity of an arctic sleetstorm. Grass and twigs snapped off, and the men ducked and rose in jumping-jack cadence. Some of the new men huddled fearfully below the top, no longer rising to take careful aim. Their rifles were balanced on top of the embankment, and they reached up blindly with their hands to squeeze off wasted rounds.

"Get up on that hedgerow!" Roth screamed to Abadjian. The young soldier stared at Roth but did not stir from his crouched position.

"Get on that goddamned rifle, or I'll take it away from you!" Roth shouted angrily.

The man trembled and huddled in closer to the hedgerow.

Roth snatched the rifle from the parapet. "When you're ready to get up, you can get this from your squad leader!"

Roth handed the rifle to Motoya. "Watch your men!" he said. "Hold this rifle until that guy gets over his buck fever! And if you see anybody else doing it, take *their* pieces away!"

"Why the simple son of a bitch!" exclaimed Motoya. "If I see any of them doing that, I'll kick 'em so hard I'll drive their ass up through their heads!" He shouted to his squad. "Hey you guys! Any of you looking for trouble, just try keeping your heads down! This is a war, get it! We're fighting a friggin' war, and I don't want anyone to forget it!"

Roth ran over to Schonbrun. "Get up on that goddamned hedgerow!" he shouted. "Get up and don't let me see you down unless you're dead!"

The man sucked his lips nervously and raised himself to the correct position. He watched Roth through the corner of his eye as the platoon leader moved away.

"I'll be watching you!" Roth called back. "So stay where you are!" Schonbrun still looked familiar to him; there was something vaguely reminiscent....

A flat blast came from the center of the firing line, followed by cries of pain and fear. "Help! Help!" "Oh my good Jesus Christ!" "Oh, I'm hit ... I'm hit ... somebody do something quick!"

Roth spun about and ran back to where the detail had been stripping the machine-gun belts. One mortar shell had burst directly in their center, wounding all except Sergeant Saunders.

Sergeant Olivet held his left hand aloft and squeezed the wrist tightly with his right hand. The fingers of the wounded hand were a shapeless mass of pulverized meat.

Abbruzio lay on the ground clutching his leg grimly. The trousers covering his thigh had been ripped to shreds, and a thick red flow spread over his grasping hands. His olive skin had turned a pasty gray, and his lips were turned inwards and clenched between his teeth.

Hohmeyer sat on the ground, holding the upper part of his right arm. He moaned almost tunefully: "Holy good Jesus Christ.... Holy good Jesus Christ!" He swayed back and forth on his haunches and stared at his reddened sleeve.

Stepkowicz lay sprawled on his side, both hands pressing against his stomach. He groaned convulsively, his eyes tightly closed. The wound bled little and his torn jumper was practically dry.

"Where're the medics?" shouted Roth.

Saunders pointed to the open field behind them. The concentration of mortar and artillery fire, and the steady stream of tracers burning to the ground, was so thick that a rabbit could scarcely get through alive.

"Where's Cawley... our aid man?" asked Roth.

Saunders held out his hands. "Didn't come back from the aid station last night. Said he had an achin' back, or somethin'."

"Send a man back," ordered Roth. "There should be some way for them to get through."

"I'll try," said Saunders. "Hey, you, come over here!" he called to one of the men on the hedgerow. Kimmel, who had been watching the scene, jogged over to the platoon guide.

"Do you think you can find a way back?" said Saunders.

The former Air Force man cast a worried glance at the shelled field. "I don't know," he said.

"Try the road. It's not so heavy there," said Saunders. "The medics should be about five hundred yards back. Tell them they gotta get up here... and with a couple of stretchers."

Sergeant Kimmel licked at his lips and nodded. He walked back along the hedgerow, his head bent low, toward the country road on the left.

"Saunders, give me a hand here," said Roth, and began to detach the first-aid packet from the rear of Olivet's belt.

"Sit down," Roth said.

"I'll be okay," said Olivet in a husky whisper.

"I can do it better if you're sitting," said Roth. He and Saunders assisted the wounded squad leader to the ground. Saunders held up the torn hand, while Roth opened the first-aid kit. He ripped apart the paper envelope containing sulfa powder and poured it over each shattered finger. He then unrolled a bandage pad, wrapped it around the hand, and fastened it securely to Olivet's wrist.

"Hurt much?" said Roth.

"No," said Olivet. "Thanks a lot, Lieutenant."

Roth spoke to Saunders. "Who's next?"

"This kid looks worse," said Saunders, pointing to the muscular Stepkowicz. "Gut wound."

They bent over the wounded man who now lay quietly, half-conscious. Roth reached around to the man's back and removed the first-aid kit from his belt. He slowly raised his shirt, and loosened the layers of uniform and heavy underwear covering the wound. There was a deep hole near the navel, and the small amount of blood which had flowed was starting to coagulate. Roth saturated the tear with sulfa powder and placed the bandage pad over it. He covered the pad with the layers of clothing to hold it in place.

Abbruzio had a painful fracture of the thigh bone, plus a slight hemorrhage. A tourniquet was applied, but they decided to wait for the aid men to handle the fracture.

Roth patted Abbruzio on the shoulder. "Take it easy, fellow, you're going to be fine." The olive-skinned man was silent, but he thanked the platoon guide and the Lieutenant with his eyes.

Hohmeyer merely had a deep flesh wound. He continued to moan while Saunders and Roth bandaged his arm and, when the operation was over, pleaded with them to be taken to the rear. Roth remained silent, but Saunders, as they left the man, muttered: "Shut up! You only got a scratch! If I hear any more bellerin' out of you, I'll put you back in the line!"

Roth made a final round of the wounded men, inquired of their condition, and attempted some comforting words. He then returned to the firing line.

He adjusted his binoculars on the enemy position and reconnoitered the area. Occasional puffs of smoke were now visible; they trickled from the windows of the houses and sheds and from the line of bushes beyond. Machine-gun fire rattled in all directions, crisscrossing in uniform final-protective lines from excellently camouflaged emplacements over a three hundred yard front. There was little visible movement, but from the fire power being demonstrated Roth guessed there was slightly over one heavily reinforced infantry company, well dug-in.

Roth lowered his glasses, replaced them in the leather carrier, and trotted over to Sergeant Rodriguez. "The third squad is without a leader," he spoke hurriedly. "I'll have to put Reubens in charge."

"How about that new sergeant we got . . . Kimmel?" suggested Rodriguez.

"I don't think so," said Roth. "He hasn't had enough experience."

"I guess so. . . we don't have a decent man left to take over," said Rodriguez.

"Reubens will do all right," said Roth. "He's been around a long time and he knows the ropes."

"He's not a leader, though."

"We'll give him a chance."

"Who'll take the bazooka?"

Roth mused over this for an instant. "We could use Schmidt, he's the assistant. . . . Yeah, use Schmidt. And give him that big fellow, the new guy . . . what's his name? . . . as assistant."

"You mean Wysocki?"

"That's the fellow."

"Reubens! Reubens! Get your ass over here!" shouted Rodriguez. Reubens turned his head and pointed his finger at his chest.

"Yeah, you! On the double!" said the Platoon Sergeant. Reubens lowered his rifle and joined Roth and Rodriguez. "You're taking over the third squad," said Roth.

"Me?" Reubens asked.

"That's right," said Roth. "We're making you a squad leader . . . think you can handle it?"

Reubens' face lit up with a delighted smile. "Yes, sir . . . sure. . . I mean sure I can!"

"Okay. Get your stuff and get over to the third squad quick," Roth said. "Turn the bazooka over to Schmidt."

"Oh boy!" exclaimed Reubens. "I finally got rid of the son of a bitch!" He ran back to his equipment and with fumbling hands began to array himself for the short move to the other squad.

Suddenly the men on the line began shouting cries of admiration and welcome: "Here they come!" "Look at the big bastards!"

Four huge gray tanks lumbered and clanked down the road, directed by crash-helmeted tank commanders standing astride the clumsy mounts. Shellfire began to shift to the road, and the tanks maneuvered into the field to take advantage of dispersion offered by the open spaces. They veered and swerved and clattered into the grass behind the First Platoon. The tank commanders jumped down from their lofty turrets, ran over to the company command post, and entered into a hasty discussion with Lieutenant Dougall. Dougall displayed his map and pointed out the situation on both the paper and the ground.

The helmeted men sprang back to their tanks, and Dougall shouted orders. "Roth, get your men ready! You're moving out!"

Roth blew some sharp blasts on his whistle. "Saddle up!" he shouted. "We're moving out!"

Shellfire began to spray up the earth around the tanks. The tank commanders dropped to lower levels and pulled the hatches over their heads.

"Remember, keep to the sides of the tanks!" shouted Dougall. "When you get past the houses, hold up for further orders!"

The tanks advanced their throttles and moved back on the road. Eighty-eight millimeter, flat-trajectory fire began to tear up the pebbled earth of the road, and flying shrapnel clanged against the steel sides of the mechanized monsters. They maneuvered quickly, rolled past the line where the hedgerow joined the road, turned right, and dispersed into the field in front of the First Platoon. They swerved and twisted in zig-zag fashion, dodging the bursting shells, and awaited the protection of the infantrymen.

Roth went to the dead body of Potter, picked up the 536 radio, and strapped it over his shoulder and under his armpit.

The tanks maneuvered back and forth and opened up in unison with their fifty caliber machine guns. They crossed their fire, lowering and elevating the firing mechanisms to form a wild phantasmagoria of blazing streaks against the sheds and farm buildings.

The tanks began to move forward. Roth blasted furiously on his whistle and shouted commands which were lost under the din of the firing.

Sergeant Rodriguez, his pipe clenched between his teeth, shouted at the men to jump the hedgerow.

Reilly and Greenberg were first. They leaped over the hedgerow, fell flat on the other side, and huddled in frozen fear of the awful storm of tracers and screaming shrapnel overhead.

Roth followed, landing a few yards from the scouts. He wildly waved his hands at the men who hesitated on the hedgerow, and a few more climbed over and fell to their stomachs in the field.

"Let's go!" shrieked Roth.

The scouts heard, but remained immobile.

Roth stumbled to his feet and took the lead. He moved up to the tanks and trotted beside the one on the right flank.

Reilly and Greenberg rose from the ground and followed; they ran close to their platoon leader.

The other men behind the hedgerow gradually vaulted into the open field and moved in behind the platoon leader and the scouts.

The squad leaders howled orders and pushed and shoved their men to disperse them properly around the tanks.

The tanks began to blast at the buildings with thirty-seven millimeter canister fire, its devastating grapeshot sounding like empty cans being thrown from the top of a tall building and flattening accordion-like on a concrete paving.

The ponderous vehicles dodged and maneuvered in un wieldy lumbering gyrations, backing in and out and twisting like some gargantuan ballet team.

Eighty-eight blasts, mortar explosions, and endless machine-gun cackles scorched the field in a molten steel-saturated oven. The men of the First Platoon moved with the tanks, running and falling to the ground and rising to run again, their chests heaving convulsively, eyes wide with dread, and hands sweating soggily on the wooden stocks of their weapons.

They reached the center of the field. The tanks stopped, as if undecided about further movement, and began to hurl charges of canister fire and fifty-caliber ammunition into every section of the farm. The silo caught fire and erupted in a brilliant blaze, ringed with heavy clouds of sooty smoke. Shells banged off the sealed armor of the tanks, exploding in a blasting, whining, ricocheting nightmare.

The men lay huddled on the ground, awaiting the next forward movement; but the tanks remained immobile, continuing to pour their firepower across the field.

Roth circled his tongue around his dry mouth. The defense seemed to be just as strong as it had been; they were probably well-emplaced and protected.

The tanks suddenly rolled on again, and the platoon followed. They moved a few yards, again indecisively, and stopped for the second time. The men hit the ground.

The tanks opened up in a crazy crescendo of machine-gun fire and blasting canisters, then suddenly turned to the rear. They wavered and veered, paused for an instant, and started to speed back across the field toward the hedgerow.

Roth screamed after them. "Come back . . . come back here, you sons of bitches!"

The tanks quickly added distance between themselves, and the men left in the open.

Roth jumped to his feet and waved his arms at the men. "Let's go . . . let's go . . . we're moving in!"

Stunned, the platoon followed. Roth dodged toward the cluster of buildings. It seemed as if the enemy firing had slackened a bit, but still the ground shook with mortar and artillery explosions.

The buildings grew larger. The silo threw out heat waves which burned against their tired eyes and dried the sweat on their faces. Bodies lay grotesquely in the side courtyard of the main house, broken over fallen weapons and sprawled in final deformities.

The machine-gun fire continued, but the rounds were mostly wasted, harassing bursts with the lead falling flat and spent to the earth. The mortar fire was lighter, scattered bursts hitting wide of the target. Artillery fire continued to fall with the same cadence in the open field.

Roth reached the bushes beyond the houses and slid to the earth. The scouts followed, and the rest of the platoon moved in close behind. They spread out in a thin skirmish line along the row of bushes.

Roth peered through the brush, but he saw nothing of tactical importance. There was tall grass beyond, and rising ground that demonstrated very little. He saw no foxholes or pillboxes from which the Germans could have operated while the attack had been going on.

"Can you see anything, Saunders?" he shouted to the platoon guide. Saunders was up close to a sparse bush, carefully surveying beyond.

"Not much," answered Saunders. "They ain't a thing out here."

"They must've been fighting from behind this hill," shouted Rodriguez.

Roth edged in closer to the low bush and warily thrust his head through the thin foliage. The terrain rose up in a gentle slope, with a few scattered trees growing near the top. There were few signs of enemy occupancy. The most likely possibility was Rodriguez's guess about a defense on the other side of the slope.

The Second Platoon began to line up on the right. Lieutenant Hartley ran up and down the line shouting orders and hurrying the remainder of his men who were still scurrying across the field.

"Keep your eyes open!" warned Roth. "They may be just over the hill!"

Sergeant Saunders stood erect and shielded his eyes with his hand. "They ain't much up there, 'cept a few bodies!" he called to Roth.

A sharp crack caused the sergeant to flatten himself on the ground. "Son of a bitch, they still got their goddamned snipers!" he exclaimed.

Roth saw the battalion moving up in the rear. The area behind the hedgerow which they had evacuated was becoming alive with men and vehicles. The four tanks were there, and the crews were seated on the ground sucking at their canteens. One of the tank crew seemed to be talking to the Battalion Commander.

The rear echelon trotted across the open field. Messengers, communications men, the First Sergeant, and the Company Commander hurried towards the thin line of bushes where the First Platoon stood.

A whistle on the left suddenly began to vibrate shrilly, and a number of men with panic in their voices cried: "Tanks!"

A tinny clatter of a motor was transmitted along the line, and the next second the fiat snout of a vehicle poked around the corner of the farthest shed on the left. It fired a hasty machine-gun burst and quickly backed away behind the shack.

"It's an armored car!" shouted Motoya, who had charge of the squad on the left flank. He fumbled around to a canvas bag at his side and hastily screwed a grenade-launcher to the muzzle end of his rifle. He fitted a rifle grenade to the firing mechanism and began to crawl toward the shed which hid the armored vehicle.

The First Platoon wildly fired rifles at the wooden structure.

"Watch those rifles!" shouted Roth. "You can't do any good with them! Squad leaders, get your grenade-launchers working!" He jumped up and cautiously moved after Motoya.

Holding the rifle with the grenade-launcher in readiness, the tall Mexican moved in close to the wall of the shed. The armored car thrust out again, fired another burst, and pulled back.

Motoya changed direction. He sidled along the wall in the opposite direction of the armored car and moved toward the rear of the shed.

There was a short wait of freezing seconds. The armored car again moved out into the clear, and this time Motoya moved to its blind side. He expertly shoved the grenade-launcher into a firing slit cut in the armor plate and fired the grenade. He dived away from the vehicle and slid on his side towards the shed.

The armored car thundered in a series of chained blasts as the grenade and thousands of rounds of ammunition within the closed car exploded simultaneously. The vehicle rose up like a wounded animal on its haunches, the front wheels hovering freely in mid-air, and then rolled over with a crash on one side.

Motoya rushed over to the smoking wreck, yanked a hand grenade from his pocket, pulled the pin, and dropped the explosive into another firing slit. There was another blast as the grenade detonated. Flames shot from the motor and black billows of smoke poured from the slits.

Motoya rushed away from the vehicle, threw himself to the ground near his men, and watched the demise of the armored car. Small-arms ammunition inside crackled with the consistency of half-inch firecrackers, and red flames, black-fringed with oil and gasoline smoke, rushed noisily towards the sky.

"Jesus Christ!" exclaimed Roth. He rose to his feet and ran over to Motoya.

The men shrieked with delight and shouted large words of praise at Motoya. One triumph such as his was enough to blanket every fear and doubt and add hope for the future. Nothing was invincible; when one man alone could destroy an armored vehicle, his victory could be absorbed by everyone in a mass transfusion.

Motoya lovingly patted the stock of his rifle. He spoke gruffly as he gathered his squad together.

Chapter Fourteen

LIEUTENANT DOUGALL arrived at the head of the command group. "Good work!" he said to Roth. "I always claimed you had a good platoon!"

"It's the men in it!" said Roth. "Did you see what Motoya did?"

"Yeah, I watched him as I came across the field. Don't forget to recommend him."

"Silver Star?" asked Roth.

"Just make the recommendation. Let them decide at headquarters," said Dougall. "Now, what's the situation here?"

"I don't know," said Roth. "They may have pulled back, or they might be holed up behind that hill."

"We'll have to move ahead and take the chance," said Dougall.

"How about getting some artillery down first?"

Dougall shook his head. "We won't be able to get it."

"If they're waiting for us, it'll be slaughter," said Roth. "What was the matter with those damned tanks? Things get too rough for them?"

"They got orders on their radio to return to Division."

"Right in the middle of an attack!" said Roth. "Christ, we could have been murdered! I'd like to turn in a report on them!"

"Don't worry, I'm going to," Dougall said.

He thoughtfully surveyed the area. "Well, one of the units coming up will have to search those houses," he said finally. "We don't have enough time. Get your men started, Paul. Move out."

"Saddle up!" ordered Roth. "We're moving out! Straight ahead ... and watch the reverse slope of this hill!"

Sergeant Rodriguez came over. "We moving right up the hill without any preparation?" he asked.

"It looks that way," said Roth.

"They've thrown out all the books!" Rodriguez said disgustedly. He walked away and began to hustle the men for speed.

"Let's go!" shouted Roth. "Scouts out!"

The movement up the hill was painfully slow. They walked carefully, feeling for mined ground and hesitating every few paces to listen. They held their rifles stiffly at port, hands squeezed close to the bayonet studs. The distance to the crest shortened; the pace became slower. Each step was measured against the beating of a heart.

Three rifle shots carved into the silence and the platoon dropped to the earth. More silence. Greenberg and Reilly sweated over their weapons as they tried to peer beyond the crest.

"Move in!" ordered Roth in a hoarse whisper.

Reilly kept his head to the front, but Greenberg turned around for a moment with a questioning look in his eyes.

"Get going!" shouted Roth. "We can't stay here!" He got to his knees and crawled up to the first scout. "Come on . . . follow me!" he whispered. He moved forward, and the two scouts followed close behind.

The Lieutenant crept a few yards and stopped to listen, went ahead some more yards and again stopped. Two additional shots cracked. He felt gritty earth fly up and spray his face.

Roth listened; again fear was heavily astride him, prodding him, weighing him down. Scarcely conscious of where or why, he moved slowly toward the top of the hill. He bore the stigma of leadership; he had to move ahead even though his heart was expiring with fright.

Reilly drew up parallel to Roth, with Greenberg slightly behind. The three men stopped where the hill began to slope in reverse, felt in their pockets, and removed cone-shaped hand grenades. They pulled the safety pins, cradled the explosives in their hands, and hurled them in unison. There was a series of detonations followed by silence.

Roth sprang to his feet and sprinted over the crest of the hill. He took out another grenade and hurled it. Reilly and Greenberg followed in, firing their rifles with machine-gun rapidity.

A chain of deep foxholes and sandbagged emplacements, staggered in depth toward the bottom, were dug in along the reverse slope of the hill. Roth had dropped his grenade into one of the holes near the top, and a wounded German lay inside, unconscious and bleeding from numerous wounds on his back and chest.

The other foxholes and emplacements were empty but showed signs of recent occupancy. The wounded soldier had evidently been left behind to effect a minor delaying action by his sniping.

"That's one bastard who won't give us any more trouble!" Greenberg stated cheerfully.

"We better get going," said Roth. He stood near the top of the hill and waved his arms at the rest of the platoon. "All clear up here!" he shouted.

"Get back on the road!" Lieutenant Dougall shouted from the bottom. "Take the road and keep going!"

"On the road!" Roth relayed to the scouts, and they veered off to the left.

Roth's legs were stiff from climbing, crawling, and running, but he felt relieved at having acquitted himself in front of his men. He knew that he had some more borrowed time in which to travel. Few realized just how tired he was, and whatever happened . . . unless the errors became too obvious. . . he would remain known as a leader of men. He was playing his role to the hilt, overplaying it probably.

"Turn on your radio!" the call transmitted down the line from man to man shocked Roth back to the presence of the road under his feet. He switched on the 536.

"Come in! Come in! Roth, come in!" Dougall's voice crackled.

"This is Roth. . . . Roth speaking. . . ."

"When you get to the intersection, take the right fork," said Dougall. "Look carefully, because it's not much more than a cow-trail."

"Are we near it?" asked Roth.

"Not many more minutes," said Dougall. "When you get to it, keep going. The objective'll be right across the valley."

"Are we going to get artillery?" asked Roth.

"You'll get plenty," said Dougall.

"Who's going to lift it?" asked Roth.

"It'll all be taken care of," said Dougall. "Keep going and don't stop until we take the high ground." There was a slight click as the radio switched off.

Roth opened his map and scanned the printed symbols. The road they were on was clearly defined, but the crossroads were blurred by many intersecting lines, any one of which could have been the road they were to take. One branched to the left and three to the right. Beyond the crossings the contours widened to symbolize a valley; and beyond the valley was the high ground, the final objective of the day.

Roth replaced the map in his pocket. When he got to the crossroads he'd be better able to determine from the ground the direction to take.

They marched on. The road began to narrow and the foliage became thicker. The ground, which had been dusty and dry under the hot afternoon sun, showed signs of dampness. A low hedge, thick at the base and thin near the top, bordered the passage toward the final objective. At a few points they had to open heavy cattle gates, and once they had to climb over a gate that had rotted into the ground. Tiny gnats buzzed through the damp air, and the sound of constant slapping rose above the tired shuffle of feet.

The road still sloped upward. Only a few patches of sun seeped through the heavy foliage and the heat was wet and oppressive. Sweat rolled down their backs and faces and burned the irritated spots on their bodies. A low murmur of voices hummed down from the units in the rear, but the men up front were silent. Their eyes flicked from side to side, searching behind and between the hedges, the tall grass, and the gathering trees. Their fingers rested on the triggers of their rifles.

Squinting until his eyes throbbed, Roth tried to spot the first evidence of the turn to the final objective. One more fight, a few more hours of blasting, shrieking shells, and the whole thing might be over. One more objective and they'd move to the rear, to the rest area where this present and future would be forgotten. Anything could happen there. He could be transferred to an administrative job; the outfit could be redesignated as M.P.'s; the war could end; the Russians could move down in one sweep and take Berlin . . . relief possessed a thousand possibilities. One thing, they'd be out of it for endless hours of sleep and rest, away from the fluttering of a million shells. Death is exalted, they say, but they had never thoroughly indoctrinated him.

The platoon heard shellfire in the distance. At first they thought it came from the German side, but when they heard constant flutters over their heads and blasts in the hills to the south they realized it was their own. Their legs swung out with renewed vitality. They had had little artillery support until now. Miles away in the hills, through the matted tree tops, they saw columns of smoke spiraling on the skyline and heard the blasts of the seventy-fives, ninety millimeter, and long range one-fifty-fives. As the shells sighed overhead men raised their heads in an attempt to see the friendly projectiles going past.

A mass of civilians suddenly appeared on the road. They walked quickly, shoving and stumbling over each other in a closely compressed, frightened group. The two scouts hesitated and then stopped. They raised their rifles and turned to their platoon leader in bewilderment.

Roth held up his hand to stop the column, and walked toward the civilian group. They were all elderly people, men and women over fifty. Their leader, or the one who seemed to exercise what little control there was, stepped forward to meet Roth. He was a tiny, stoop-shouldered man with black hair and a thick mustache that covered his lips.

The little Frenchman smiled at Roth and started to chatter in a high-pitched, nasal jargon. He gesticulated excitedly at Roth, pointed at the people clustered behind him, and then, with great sweeping motions of his arms, pantomimed toward the rear.

"I don't know what you mean," said Roth.

The man shook his head and made larger gestures.

Roth held out his palms perplexedly. The old fellow obviously was excited, but there was no knowing what he wanted to say. His group all chattered loudly and constantly turned to look back up the road they had traveled. When they stared at the American soldiers, their faces mirrored excitement, happiness, welcome, and fear. A few laughed nervously and some openly cried.

Lieutenant Dougall came running down the road, his face angry under the red flush of heat and exertion. "What the hell's going on?" he asked.

"I don't know," said Roth. "These people just appeared out of nowhere, and they're all excited about something...."

Dougall hastily surveyed the group, and then started to speak in French to the one with the thick mustache. Dougall spoke fluently, even to the frantic gestures, and declaimed with rapidly rising inflections to the Frenchman. When the discussion ended, he patted the old man on the shoulder and turned to Roth.

"He says there're five hundred, maybe a thousand Jerries holed up on top of the hill."

"How does he know?" asked Roth.

"He claims they just came from there," said Dougall. "I don't know whether to believe the story or not."

"Why should they lie?" said Roth. "They're Frenchmen, not Germans."

"I don't know... it could be a trick," said Dougall. "The Jerries've sold plenty to their way of thinking. Remember how it was back on the beach?"

"That was different," said Roth. "They had to have collaborators there."

"They certainly look as though they've been chased from the area. I'd better get in touch with Nielsen," Dougall decided. "You keep going, and if you don't hear from me you'll know it means you're to continue on to the objective."

"What about the five hundred . . . the thousand? If it's true, you don't expect us to dance right through them?" asked Roth.

Dougall shrugged. "It's whatever the Battalion Commander orders."

Dougall spoke a few more words to the leader of the refugees and beckoned for them to start moving.

The people hurried by. There were tears in the eyes of many.

"If you don't hear from me, keep going," Dougall said. Walking behind the refugees, he returned to the rear.

Roth signaled the platoon, and the march resumed. They moved on toward the hills across the valley.

New worries began to plague the platoon leader. Five hundred or a thousand Germans ahead, and probably well entrenched. Whenever they received pertinent information it was never correctly evaluated; lives and limbs would be wasted because someone up above wouldn't believe the information supplied by the French peasants. And Nielsen would send them on even if he were told that there were a million Jerries in front.

The artillery continued to fling an endless chain of shellfire overhead and the explosions, as they burst in the hills, became louder as the column came closer to the enemy. The smoke seen through the trees was thicker, and they now could detect the flash of brush fires in different spots along the horizon. The road narrowed until it would only permit the passage of one man, and the ground began to slope downward. Damp moss grew at the base of the trees, and the fallow, shaded earth had a musty smell.

Reilly was the first to see the narrow trails crossing the road. He waved to Roth and pointed out a break in the forest. The Lieutenant moved up quickly, passed Greenberg, and overtook the first scout. The crossroads were directly ahead.

Roth held up his hand and stopped the column. He opened his map on the ground and compared it with the terrain around him. One road went to the left at a forty-five degree angle, and three roads, or paths, fingered out to the right. The latter consisted of a center path and two others forking off at sharp angles.

Roth raised and lowered his head from the map as he tried to compare each separate terrain feature. A maze of contour lines and an intersecting grid-zone line made the map difficult to read. The important features, the three paths, showed as a streaked blur of fine lines crossing one on top of the other.

He opened his compass, placed it on the map, and moved both around until each was oriented for direction. The road to the left of the center one seemed to be the route. It crossed over to the valley and, except for some more confusing terrain markings near the middle, led directly to the objective.

He refolded his map, closed his compass, and signaled the scouts to move down the next narrow trail.

The new trail narrowed every few yards until after about eight hundred yards it was little more than a blazed path through a heavily wooded forest. Ahead it faded almost entirely in the thick trees.

"Reilly, hold it up!" Roth called, a worried huskiness in his throat. He opened the small radio and signaled the Company Commander.

After an impatient wait of elastic seconds, Dougall's voice came angrily over the radio. "What's the trouble? What the hell's going on up there?"

"Am I on the right road?" queried Roth. "It doesn't seem to be leading anyplace . . . ?"

"Turn back . . . you're on the wrong goddamned path!" Dougall seemed to be shouting. "You should have taken the center one!"

"I can't tell a thing from my fucking map! It's all loused up!"

"Pass through the column with your men . . . quickly! And take the center path!" ordered Dougall, and clicked off.

Roth felt a nauseating frustration crawl in his stomach. It wasn't the first time he had done it. He might have led the men anywhere;

anything could have happened . . . ambush, slaughter, the loss of a company or even a battalion of men. . . .

The First Platoon moved back through the company column. They were looked at by the others with contempt and anger, but no words were exchanged.

As he went by Roth saw Hartley smile sympathetically; but when he passed the Company Commander standing cross-armed at the road junction, Roth averted his eyes. He had been known as a good soldier; he couldn't face Dougall now.

Chapter Fifteen

THEY PICKED UP SPEED on the new road. It was as wide as the one they had been on before the detour, and the surrounding terrain was more open. A three-foot hedgerow bordered each side, and close-cropped grass carpeted the earth. On their left the ground sloped gradually down into the valley. They could see the high ground on the far side and the rising smoke from the shells of their own artillery support. The blasts were stronger, and there were vague rumblings underfoot.

As the road grew steeper, the valley on the left became more clearly defined. Roth estimated the objective to be another five hundred yards ahead and then across the valley.

The scouts had just reached a sharp bend in the road when a newer, more ominous sound shrilled above the distant rumble of guns. A solid sheet of flaming tracers broke across the road bend, fired from machine-guns on the high ground directly opposite them. The scouts fell to the earth, and the men behind huddled low against the bordering hedgerow. One shell with the flat bam of an eighty-eight tore up the turf to the right of the road.

The machine guns paused, and Roth shouted to the scouts. "Can you make it? They've stopped! See if you can get through!"

Reilly and Greenberg got up and sprinted around the road bend. A split second after Greenberg's figure disappeared from sight, the machine guns again opened up in long, spaced bursts. They sprayed the road at the bend and chewed at the meadows on each side.

"We're going through!" shouted Roth. "Keep your asses below the hedge, and crawl! Watch me!" On hands and knees he snaked along the pebbled strip, shuddering with fright each time he felt that his back might be displayed an inch or so above the hedgerow. When he reached the road bend he heard the flat splat of rounds soaring above him. He crouched still lower and scuttled faster. Sweat ran cold down his spine, and his knees and palms tore on the graveled roadway. When he flattened himself behind the scouts, he no longer heard rounds passing overhead.

"Move up!" Roth ordered the two scouts. "Give the others a chance to move in!"

The three started moving forward, still creeping on hands and knees, and the rest of the men followed. More shells fell in the field below, but the bursting range placed the First Platoon in no immediate danger.

Roth clambered to his feet, signaling for the men to rise, and the advance continued on up the road. They breathed heavily and constantly watched the high ground across the valley. A few more hundred yards up the road; and then six hundred yards across the fields approaching the objective.

The slope heaved and thundered, and geysers of earth and grass were hurled into the air. The entire valley suddenly erupted in one convulsive, volcanic upheaval. A huge trench was blasted a few hundred feet from the road, showering the men with earth and stones, and an expanding tidal wave of concussion brutally smashed against their ears. They slammed themselves to the ground, buried their heads between their arms, and spasmodically kicked at the gravel with their toes.

There was a moment of silence, and then another concentration split the valley with smoke and bowel-emptying crashes. Storms of concussion surged in upon the men who lay choking and waiting. Another well-directed preparation came down; the field on the right began to rock. The First Platoon was sandwiched in the tiny safety zone of the graveled cut between the two hedges.

One man shouted in falsetto-voiced fear: "They got us zeroed in! They got the whole goddamned place spotted! Christ, let's get out of here!"

Another voice roared: "Shut up, you stupid, fuckin' bastard! Wanta start a panic!"

Another quavered: "They're lookin' down our throats! What're we gonna do?"

The men shouted their fears or screamed and cursed madly at their fate.

Fifteen more avalanches of exploding steel roared on each side of the road. Roth counted them; a compulsion too powerful for him to resist forced him to count each cadenced group of blasts as they abominated the earth. He counted them and felt them search in closer, and for a while he hoped for one to land on him and end the nightmare; then he prayed for some unnamable God to save him; but each paced second carried the knowledge of the release to come, and the horror that with the release there would be no more... no more? His face scraped in the gravel; blood was on his tongue, and dust scorched his throat.

Silence. Each second held shimmering in the air and counted as the shell bursts had been counted; a skull-pounding, deafening stillness that spoke more menacingly than all the shufflings overhead.

Roth peered over the top of the low hedgerow. Circular, black-rimmed excavations pocked the ground in every direction. The hill across the valley appeared as quiet as before, as though the step of man and the terror of his inventions had never once disturbed its pastoral tranquillity.

Sergeant Rodriguez crawled up to Roth and spoke hastily. "We better get out of here, Lieutenant! They'll saturate us in another couple of minutes!"

"We can't go down in that valley!" said Roth, his voice trembling. "They'll be looking right down our throats!"

"We ought to go back then and join the others!" said the Platoon Sergeant.

"What do you mean, join them?"

"Wherever they are," said the Sergeant. "I just came from the back, and they ain't nowhere near us."

"I don't get you ... what're you talking about?"

"I can't even see the Second Platoon. Either we've gone too quick, or they've pulled back. I tried calling them, but got no answer. Our whole rear is exposed."

Roth sucked his dry lips. They were out there alone, a handful of men smeared on the horizon like a red signal flag. "What the hell are they trying to do to us!" he suddenly shouted. "They don't expect us to take the objective alone!"

Roth switched on his radio and hysterically began to repeat the company call letters, but there was no decipherable sound except for some dim sputterings. He shook the radio and cursed vehemently. "What the hell's going on? They don't even know we're up here! Jesus Christ Almighty, what do they think we're made of? Sons of bitches stuck us out here like bait!"

"Maybe we ought to try and make the hill?" suggested Rodriguez.

"Are you crazy? We'll be murdered!"

They heard a sudden snapping of machine gun fire, followed by the scraping noises of a man sliding on his chest and stomach along the road. There was a rush of running feet, some more sliding, and an excited figure landed beside the Sergeant and the platoon leader. A second figure, slower than the first, arrived carrying a large field radio strapped to his back. He lowered himself to the ground a few yards behind the three men.

The new arrival, with his radio operator, was Major Adams, the battalion's executive officer. Adams was a tall, bespectacled officer of commanding appearance who constantly carried a forty-five caliber automatic in his right hand and was seldom many yards behind the point of every attack. "What's holding you up here?" he asked Roth crisply.

Roth felt comforted by the Major's presence. "Christ, they've got this whole place zeroed in, sir! We can't move another inch!" he stated.

The Major looked over the hedgerow and surveyed the valley. "You can make it!" he stated confidently. "You see that hedgerow, and the line of trees growing next to it?"

Roth raised his head and looked. "Yes?"

"Move down that hedge, and when you come to the junction of the bushes angling to the right, move down them. It'll take you halfway to your objective."

Roth gritted his teeth. "We won't be able to make it, Major!" he argued. "There isn't an inch of ground not under artillery observation!"

The Major's voice lost its businesslike tone. "There's no such thing as can't! You're going to have to take your platoon up that hill! This is the last attack, then we'll be relieved!"

"How about the others? Where's the others? We can't make this attack alone!" Roth's voice rose in half-controlled hysteria.

"Don't worry about the others. You have your job to do," stated the Major.

"There are at least a thousand Germans up there! I can tell... I *know* by the fire power they've got! And I don't even have a full platoon!"

The Major again peered over the hedgerow, but ducked quickly when the splat of a bullet sped near him. "I'm going with you!" he said. "We'll move down the road, jump the hedgerow, and take the approach down to the line of bushes... then we'll flank right! Another hour and it'll be over!"

Roth glanced back at his men. They lay huddled on the road, fearfully awaiting new sounds to break the strange silence. Many of them were replacements experiencing their first battle. He was under strength in noncoms and low on ammunition. He knew the outcome if they attempted to move across the valley.

Roth looked at the Major, and his lips quivered as he spoke. "I can't take this platoon down there... it's murder! The whole place is zeroed in! The Jerries have the entire area prepared; artillery, mortars, machine guns! Christ, we won't be able to go fifty yards...! I've seen traps like this before...!"

The Major hardly seemed to listen. There was a reflective smile on his lips as he scanned the valley.

Roth struggled for control. "All right, sir, it's your responsibility! I won't lead them into slaughter! If you want to take the responsibility, I'll follow... but I'll go as a rifleman, not as a platoon leader! I'm through leading men into traps for someone else's mistakes! I'm through taking them into God knows what-in-the-hell they're going to get! I'll fight, but I won't lead them down there!"

The Major turned. "You know what this means?" he said quietly.

Roth shrugged. He knew what it meant. He knew murder when he saw it.

The Major turned to the men who were lined prone along the narrow road. "Men, we're moving out!" he shouted. "We're going up to the objective, and by God, we're going to take it! Hit hard, and keep on hitting! This is the last attack, and then we'll be relieved! We've got to get through!"

Roth wanted to offer more objections, to say something that might stop the slaughter, but the words stuck in his throat; if they did come out they'd come with sobs. He rubbed his grimy fists in his eyes to force back the tears.

Rodriguez shouted: "This is it, fellows! Goddamit, we're going through, and we're going to take that fucking hill! Sanchez, get up here with your BAR . . . stick close to me! You other guys keep together! We're going down, and then to the right! This is the last one, then we'll be relieved!" He turned to Major Adams. "Are you ready, sir?"

The Major nodded his head in assent.

Rodriguez jumped to his feet. "All right, goddamit, let's move out. . . on the double!" He sprinted down the road, followed in turn by the scouts, Roth, the Major, the Major's radioman, and the personnel of the platoon.

Machine guns from every section of the hill across the valley blazed open and streamed flaming tracer fire inches above the heads of the running men. Artillery and mortar fire again began to concentrate, and shells pounded the fields on each side of the road. Ahead, the slope was a web of gushing flame and thundering detonations.

Rodriguez leaped over the hedgerow and started down the side of the intersecting parapet. A blast opened the ground directly in front of him, and he was momentarily lost to sight by the eruption of smoke and earth, but when it cleared he was still running.

The platoon followed, panting and frightened, no longer propelled by conscious messages from brains to legs. They ran blindly, each man stumbling close on the heels of the other, newly released instincts driving them wildly.

Tears streamed from Roth's eyes, and sobs weakened his churning knees, but he stayed close behind Rodriguez. He tripped in the soft spoil of a shallow excavation, fell to the ground, and rolled head over heels; without losing speed he regained his balance and continued running.

Heavy artillery, medium artillery, and mortar fire roared all about the running men. They stumbled and tripped; a few fell, but immediately rolled to their feet and continued on. Machine-gun and rifle fire hummed past their ears, spattered into the earth, and flattened with dull thuds in the hedgerow on their left.

Rodriguez reached the line of bushes that formed the juncture with the hedgerow and flanked to the right. He ran about fifty yards along the bush line and hurled himself to the ground. Roth landed beside him.

The Sergeant raised his head and peered through the sparse bush. "There's another hedge near the bottom... we can make a run for it and go on from there!" he said to Roth.

Roth glanced through the leaves. On the right and approximately fifty yards down from where they lay, he saw a small hedgerow about forty yards long. "They'll have more observation on you!" he shouted. "The ground's too low!"

Rodriguez hardly appeared to have heard. "It'll get us right up close...." he muttered.

Most of the men were already flattened behind the bush, but a few still dashed down along the other hedgerow. The Major and his radioman were no longer behind Roth and did not seem to be anywhere in the platoon group. There were two dim figures back on the road, but the distance was too great for anything to be distinguished.

"Let's get back to the road," Roth said. "We'll never make it!"

The Sergeant raised himself to his knees and pointed to the bottom of the valley. "Let's,go! Over to that hedgerow!" he cried loudly to the men.

"Stay where you are!" shouted Roth. "Stay where you are . . . we're going back!"

Shells landed in every direction, their explosions punctuated by the sounds of machine guns and rifles. The smoke was heavy.

"Goddamit, let's go!" shrieked Rodriguez. He hurdled the bush and started down the slope toward the hedgerow at the bottom.

Some men followed, and others remained behind with Roth. The men behind Rodriguez wildly zig-zagged down the open incline, dancing madly between the earth-spraying of the bullets and the explosive spasms of the shellfire. They reached the hedgerow and dived to the ground. Before they had time to settle into position, a new rain of destruction poured down upon them. Clouds of dust and smoke obliterated the forty-yard area, the blastings growing in violence and then holding a climax of explosive fury. The small group no longer could be seen under the gray fog.

"We're going back!" Roth screamed to the men who had remained with him. "Back the way we came! Last man move out first! Back to the road!"

The frantic withdrawal to the road began. The rearmost man sprang to his feet and sped across the field; when he reached the juncture of the hedgerow and the bushes, he turned left and dug his feet into the rising ground. The others followed. They whirled and danced and clumsily spun, hoping that such maneuvers would decrease their vulnerability to the shell and small-arms fire blanketing the draw.

When he reached the top the first man clapped his hand to his shoulder, hesitated momentarily, and then continued onward to stumble drunkenly over the hedgerow bordering the road. He fell over on his side on the pebbled surface.

They ran and zig-zagged, gagging from exertion and fright, and clawed up the incline to reach the road. They struggled over the hedgerow and went down on their faces in the gravel, choking new breath back into their lungs.

Lieutenant Roth was the last. As he ran he could feel the jagged-edged razors of shrapnel and the steel-tipped noses of machine-gun and rifle bullets pacing him up the lung-bursting climb to the road. His back was wet, sweat blinded his eyes, and his heart was a voracious monster lacerating the tender nerves in his chest. His intestines crawled, and large chunks of granite ground together in his stomach. He reached the top of the slope, threw himself over the hedge, and fell to the road. He twisted his body until it came up against the hedgerow and then lay still as he moaned in fresh blocks of air. His legs and arms shook spastically.

Major Adams was on the road with his radio operator. His glasses were gone, and slender red valleys streaked his face, ran down over his torso, and dripped to the dry earth below him.

His clothing was ripped, and one legging hung loosely from the torn laces. He was calling fire orders to the radioman who huddled with his equipment beside the hedgerow.

The Major completed his orders to the radioman and then turned to Roth. "Til get some artillery on those bastards!" he ranted. "I got 'em spotted ... we'll blast out the bastards, and then take the hill!"

"Why don't you go back?" said Roth. "You better go to the medics . . . you're all cut up...."

"Not until this job is finished ... never ...!" shouted the Major.

"You'd better get out of here ... you're losing a lot of blood," said Roth. The son of a bitch was looking for another medal, but he'd be damned if he'd recommend him.

Adams raised his hand to his cheek, drew it away, and laughed hysterically. "Hell, it's only a scratch... only a scratch...!"

A few minutes after the radio operator had repeated the orders, the flutters of the artillery arrived. Roth buried his head between his arms. One... two... three... four... five... six... seven... eight rounds landed on both sides of the road... another dropped on the road, near where the last men of the platoon were huddled.

The Major was on the ground next to Roth. "Raise it... raise it... five hundred yards!" he shrieked in panic to the radio operator.

Eight more chained impacts rocked the road.

Roth crawled to the radioman, grabbed him by his shoulders, and cruelly flung him to one side. "Cease fire! Cease fire!" he screamed into the radio. "You're coming in on your own troops! Cease fire! Stop this fucking firing... goddamned dumb stupid sons of bitches!"

The radio operator lay on his side, staring bewilderedly at Roth.

"Get the hell out of here, you murdering son of a bitch!" Roth screamed at the Battalion Executive Officer. "Go back to the medics, but don't bleed to death around here! Goddamned fucking bastard, I hope you do bleed to death!"

Like a child who has been beaten for an act which he cannot comprehend, the Major rolled his head from side to side, his hands upraised questioningly. "I... I'm sorry. I didn't know... down there, the artillery. Up here... I..." he floundered.

"It's too late! It's too late, you son of a bitch!" Roth shouted.

"Sorry... sorry... sorry..." the Major muttered, almost whimpering.

Roth turned away, vomit clogging his throat.

Their own artillery stopped, but the concentration from the enemy still continued. Roth looked down the incline to the hedgerow where Sergeant Rodriguez had led the men. Prone figures were sprawled in various aspects of deformity, with each body lying close to the other. Slight movement could be detected from one or two, but the others lay slack and immobile. Perfect observation from the high ground to the low ground was an accomplished fact, and the enemy's fire mission on that section of the field had been complete.

The Major beckoned his radio operator to climb over the hedgerow at the far side of the road. When the operator had dragged himself and the heavy radio to the top of the parapet, new tracer streaks fingered out from the hills. The radioman quickly rolled, fell with a heavy thud into the adjoining field, and began the tortuous crawl to the rear.

Major Adams followed his man over the hedgerow. Disregarding the bullets which sprayed the wall and the ground, he moved as though he were drugged. Slowly he climbed over and, when he was silhouetted on the skyline, glanced back at Roth. He eased himself to the grassy field and crawled after the radio operator.

Chapter Sixteen

Roth crawled back along the dirt road and checked on his men. Wong, Reubens, McCrea, Northrup, Motoya, Schonbrun, Groggins, and Sergeant Saunders were all who had remained with him. The others were in the twisted group at the bottom of the valley.

Motoya was working over Northrup at the rear of the group. "Give me a hand, Lieutenant," he said when Roth neared him.

Roth crawled over to the two men. Northrup leaned against the Mexican, his left arm dangling limply at his side. Blood pumped out, and a knife of white, slivered bone, sheared near the shoulder, shone through the pouring crimson. The wounded man's face was a sickly gray color, and black lines of pain were wrinkled on his forehead and at the corners of his mouth.

"Hold it steady," muttered Motoya.

Gripping the torn arm, Roth felt the warmth of the blood spraying over his hands.

Motoya ripped open a first-aid kit and dusted Northrup's torn arm with sulfa powder. Then he searched in the dust until he found a twig of proper length. He knotted a bandage above the painful wound, thrust the twig inside the loop, and twisted it until it grew taut over the artery. Finally he removed a dirty handkerchief from his pocket, placed it over the tourniquet, and secured it.

Northrup's face became pastier under the excruciating pressure of the tourniquet, but he ground his teeth in silence. When the process was completed, his eyes closed and he slumped limply against Roth. Easing him to the ground, Roth placed the man's pack under his head for support.

Motoya's usually tanned face was pale under a coating of dust and grime. "How about a splint?" he asked.

Roth shook his head. "We'd better leave it this way until the medics get him. Anyway, there's no wood large or straight enough for that around here."

"What'll we do with him?" asked Motoya.

"We'll just have to let him stay there until we can get some help," said Roth. He began to crawl back down the road.

McCrea had his head up over the hedgerow and was squinting intensely towards the figures lying in the dust at the bottom of the valley.

"What's up?" asked Roth, when he came parallel to the soldier.

"There's a couple of them still alive down there," said McCrea. "They shouldn't be left like that...."

"There's nothing we can do now," said Roth. "If we don't get them, the enemy will. It won't be so bad in a prison hospital."

McCrea continued to squint his eyes at the bodies in the valley.

"What're we gonna do, Lieutenant?" asked Sergeant Saunders, his Adam's apple dancing nervously as he revolved his teeth over his tobacco cud.

"That's what I'm going to find out," said Roth, placing the 536 on the ground in front of him. He turned over on his side and held the radio close to his ears in order to be able to hear under the incessant shelling.

"Man, listen to 'em shells a kickin' and a pissin' and a moanin'," marveled the platoon guide. "A few of 'em was jest to hit this road..." He spat.

Roth droned out the call signal over and over again, his voice gradually rising until it reached a tremulous falsetto. Minutes passed with only staccato cracklings coming back in answer. He was about to close the circuit when a low voice came in. "What is it?" The voice was a strange one that he couldn't place. "Give me the Company Commander," said Roth quickly. "What company commander ... which... if you want Dougall, he's dead. This is Carter.... I've got the company for the time being."

Lieutenant Carter, the Weapons Platoon leader, was at the other end.

"This is Roth... what happened... did you say Dougall is *dead?*" His flesh suddenly felt empty, a hollow cask.

"That's right... about half an hour ago," said Carter. "Colonel Nielsen had me take over."

Roth remained silent for an instant. Then he shouted: "Where the hell is the rest of the fucking company? We're out here alone fighting the whole goddamned German army!"

"We had to pull back up the road... back past the intersections," returned Carter's voice. "The Jerries are starting a big counterattack and we're going to have to hole up."

"I'm pulling back, too!" said Roth. "We're almost wiped out... another few minutes and there'll be none of us left!"

"Hold what you've got, until I get further orders," stated the new Company Commander.

"Are you crazy? How can I hold what I've got with eight men? I couldn't hold this ground with eighty!"

There was a slight pause before Carter's voice again came in. "I'll call you back in five minutes. I'll have to see what Colonel Nielsen has to say." The circuit clicked shut.

"Crazy sons of bitches!" screamed Roth. "They won't be satisfied until we're all dead!" He glanced at his wristwatch: Five-thirty in the afternoon, still many hours before the long French twilight would fade behind the hills.

"Of all the goddam... look at him go!" exclaimed Saunders, who was crouched beside the platoon leader.

Roth raised his head. McCrea was sprinting down the incline toward the bodies at the bottom of the valley. Shells blasted every inch of the way, and machine-gun and rifle bullets reached out to spatter gravel split inches from his feet. He spiraled like a frightened rabbit, his arms and legs revolving like unleashed pistons. Every other moment he was hidden from sight by the smoke of the bursting shells, but when the haze lifted he was still in the clear.

McCrea reached the forty yard long hedgerow at the bottom of the draw and slid in a side-swiping hook to the edge of the prostrate figures. He moved among them, his hands pawing over their bodies. He stopped at one and then another, until he had examined each body separately. He moved back toward the center and began to raise one of the figures to his shoulders. He lurched and swayed and finally struggled erect with the limp form hanging partly over his back and partly over his chest. He glanced back at the enemy terrain and began the ascent to the road.

Roth held his breath. The men held their breaths. Saunders swore softly; it sounded like a reverent prayer. Shells blasted the field, and rifle and machine-gun fire trailed the figures of McCrea and his burden; but he moved miraculously through the hail of steel. Every other second it appeared to the men watching from the road that it was the end, but not a fragment nor a bullet touched either McCrea or the figure on his back. The movement was slow, and he stopped each few yards to regain his breath and showers of earth and gravel fell upon him; but during those throbbing moments the field seemed to have been blessed by some ineffable being who had changed the course of death. Slowly, gradually, agonizingly the distance to safety narrowed until McCrea reached the hedgerow. Hands reached over and grasped the body; others pulled McCrea to the road. He sprawled where he landed, his lungs wheezing in hoarse, grating gasps.

"Good boy!" said Roth, as he crawled over to McCrea. "What the hell ever made you do it?"

"I . . . I couldn't see them lie out there!" panted McCrea, his lips curled slightly in a sad smile. "Too . . . too much death . . . maybe I could do something. . . ."

"Who is it?" Roth shouted to Saunders.

"Warner," said Saunders. "Shrapnel got him in the back . . . he can't move . . . think he's paralyzed."

"Any other wounded down there?" asked Roth.

"They're all dead," said McCrea. "All except one man, and he doesn't want to be moved. Got shot in the ass . . . the whole thing's torn off. Says it's too painful . . . rather stay there and let the Jerries get him. . . ." He pillowed his face on his arms and sucked in strong gulps of fresh air. He closed his eyes; his body still twitched from the exertion of the rescue.

Roth felt a sudden momentary exhilaration. Men could still fight and sacrifice when it came to a showdown. McCrea, a man with a wife and children to think of, had deliberately exposed himself to almost certain death and gone out under a hail of fire to bring in a wounded man. Why? There must have been something more than the few words of sympathy uttered in between gasps of exhaustion.

Shellfire continued to isolate the fields. The handful of men were trapped, as though they lay on a small reef awaiting a tidal wave they could see inexorably rolling in on them from a stormy horizon. The road behind, at the bend, received a devastating concentration, and the road ahead smoked and blazed under the fury of the barrage. Their small sector was the only immune area; it seemed as though they were in a vacuum and that no shells could land there until some divine signal were given.

Machine gun rounds, however, continued to penetrate their haven, coming in so low that they clipped the top foliage of the hedge. Visual reconnaissance became impossible without risking a bullet through the brain, so they lay there close up against the hedgerow and were silent. A few ate their rations: a can of chopped egg, a piece of cheese, or a concentrated chocolate bar. Some lacked appetite.

Roth chewed on a brittle piece of chocolate, devouring it greedily. His stomach burned with a hunger for solid food. He was out there and he had to eat to live, even if the living were only for the next few seconds. He gulped down the last sticky mixture of saliva and bitter chocolate and drained the remainder of the rancid water from his canteen. He lay against the hedgerow and listened to the whining of shrapnel, humming and buzzing like giant bees in flight, and half hoped for a fragment to land on him. Over the hedgerow: a painful crawl to the rear, medical aid, a stretcher, and the long journey back to the hospital to sleep. . . a sleep undisturbed by the moans of dying men and the cries of wounded men; sleep, wrapped in the warm blessedness of blankets; a canvas cot; cool crisp sheets . . . and nothingness.

He reached out his hand and slowly pulled a large jagged-edged piece of steel towards him. He turned his head surreptitiously to the rear, but the men had their heads pillowed in their arms, each one blind to the actions of the other. The heavy piece of shell fragment came closer until it lay under his hand at his side. He grasped it and held it, feeling the razor sharpness of its edges. It was about a foot long and weighed approximately ten pounds; in full flight it could shear a man's head from his body or tear his torso completely apart. He raised it from the ground, rolled over on his side, and brushed the sharp edges across his knee. He held it a few inches above the joint, and let it drop. It fell against his knee, and he felt a sharp pain. He lifted it again and brought it down a little harder, but still no skin was torn and the knee remained flexible. He raised and lowered the shrapnel ten more times, each blow on his knee heavier than the last. His knee throbbed, but the force with which the shrapnel struck was not enough. Finally he dropped the fragment to the ground and shoved it away. He knew that if he had given himself a smashing blow the damage would have been done, but each time the hand holding the steel had come down his muscles had tightened, and its force had been controlled.

He glanced at his watch again: Five-forty-five; Carter's five minutes had stretched to fifteen. He clicked on the radio, and started the repetitive calling of the Company Commander.

"Hello, Roth," finally came Carter's voice.

"What the hell is going on?" said Roth. "I thought you were supposed to call me back in five minutes?"

"Yeah, I know, I know . . . but we've been as busy as a one-armed paper hanger with the crabs back here."

"What in hell do you think we've been doing up here?" Roth's voice grew louder. "This isn't a joke! What the hell're we supposed to do?"

"Hold what you've got until we give you further orders," said Carter evenly.

A film splashed in front of Roth's eyes. "Hold what we've got? Why, you crazy son of a bitch, I'll give the Jerries another five minutes before they'll be in on us . . . !"

The voice at the other end attempted pacification. "Yeah, I know how it is, Roth. But you'll have to use your head . . . see if you can hold out for a while."

"Hold out? Hold out! I've only got eight men left! Eight! Do you hear that, you crazy bastard!"

There was a pause at the other end, before Carter again spoke. "I'm sorry, Roth, but you'll have to hold what you've got . . . regardless! Outpost that road until we can get dug in back here!" he said.

"It's impossible, Carter! It's impossible . . . impossible!" shouted Roth.

"You'll have to stay where you are! The safety of the entire battalion depends on your holding down that approach route!"

The film again splashed before Roth's eyes. "Why don't you come down here and show me? If you're so goddamned fucking smart enough to be a company commander, why don't you get your ass down here and *show* me how to hold out with eight men! Why don't you get your ass down here and show us how to save our own asses?"

"That's an order, Roth! Stay where you are!" The radio abruptly snapped off.

"Goddamned dirty stinking rat son of a bitch!" Roth screamed in a wild sob. He blew his nose on his sleeve and scraped the back of his hand into his running eyes.

"Some bastards back there ain't gonna like you nohow," said Sergeant Saunders.

"What the hell do they expect from us?" said Roth. "Now it turns out that we're outposting for the whole goddamned battalion!"

Saunders laughed dryly. "You know a lot of guys've swore if they ever saw Nielsen on the line, he wouldn't last a minute."

"They can save themselves the trouble," said Roth. "I'll do it myself! I'd like to meet the bastard some dark night... I'd tear out his guts with my hands and stuff them in his mouth!"

Saunders raised his head to the brim of the hedge, but rapidly flattened himself as a spray of bullets burned the air above his head. "Son of a bitch, they sure know we're here! What're we gonna do, Lieutenant?"

Roth shook his head defeatedly. "I'm going to get myself court-martialed...."

"What's that?"

"Yeah. If they don't give me orders in another few minutes to pull back, we're going to pull back anyway."

"We're doin' about as much good up here as a flea'll do crawlin' up an elephant's ass," said the sergeant. "Lord, it sure beats me!"

"Hey there! Hey, Lieutenant, look what's goin' on down there!" shouted Motoya excitedly. "Lieutenant... down in the draw!"

Roth took a hasty glance over the hedgerow and quickly flattened as bullets spattered. A line of German troops were slowly advancing across the bottom of the valley. Approximately fifty of them were spread out in a skirmish line. They were approaching the small hedgerow where the rest of the platoon had been trapped.

"Keep 'em down!" shouted Roth to his men. "Fire... anyway, as long as you keep 'em down!"

Saunders already was on top of the hedgerow, firing his rifle in short bursts and diving for the earth each time bullets sprayed over his head.

Motoya fired and shouted orders at the men. A few warily raised their heads, fired a shot or two, and then ducked. They fired again and dropped, and repeated the procedure.

Roth fired an entire clip of carbine ammunition before he slipped to the ground. He reloaded, fired three more shots, and again lowered his head when the return seemed too thick. The Germans moved in slowly and surely toward the road; they ran a few yards, hit the ground and fired in unison at the hedgerow, and sprang up to run again. Roth tried for the figure who appeared to be their leader, but missed each time. The distance was still too great for the short range of a carbine, and the zig-zagging running of the leader was difficult to follow in the simple sights of his small weapon.

"They're gonna get up here surer'n hell!" shouted Saunders.

"We'll try to hold them off!" shouted Roth. "If not . . . !" If not, he had a white handkerchief in his pocket. He wouldn't risk the lives of any more of his men, nor did he care to continue risking his own. If the enemy got much closer, he was going to raise the handkerchief and surrender. Surrender was the only alternative. A prison camp couldn't be any worse than the hell they had been through, and most likely lots better, regardless of the stories they heard.

"How about me goin' back for help?" shouted Saunders.

"I don't know. . . I don't think it'll do any good!" said Roth. "They'll only send you back and tell you we have to hold what we've got! They're looking out for their own asses back there!"

"Maybe they'll give us a couple of extra men?" said Saunders.

"Well . . . you can try . . . it won't hurt. But be careful . . . they've got us zeroed in!" warned Roth.

"I'm goin' back!" said the Sergeant. "Just this one!" He aimed carefully and for a moment seemed impervious to the rain of metal spraying the hedgerow and the air around him. He squeezed slowly. "Aaah, look at the son of a bitch!" he exclaimed, as one of the advancing Germans spun around in a half-circle and twisted to the ground.

Saunders removed his pack and his gas mask and laid them on the ground beside his rifle. "I ain't gonna need these," he said.

"What about your rifle?" said Roth.

"I'll move faster without it!" shouted Saunders, already crawling across the narrow road to the other hedgerow. He hesitated for a moment, and then quickly yanked himself up and, with a cloud of bullets spraying all about him, went over the top and fell on the other side. "Okay, I'll be back soon!" he shouted.

Roth looked over his shoulder, and saw the Sergeant's helmet intermittently appearing an inch or so above the hedgerow as he sped back to the rear. He ran and hit the ground, crawling when the concentration of fire became too thick. Roth watched until the Sergeant disappeared from sight beyond the curve in the road, where the shellfire was heaviest.

He shifted his glance back to the imminent. The platoon's sporadic fire had slowed down the Germans a little, but they still maintained a steady advance up the hill. They had reached the small hedgerow at the bottom, had gone over and around it, and were making the steeper ascent.

Machine-gun and mortar fire grew heavier, but still none had fallen directly on the platoon's position. Blasts broke to the left and right of the hedges and along the road both front and rear.

Roth could see the dim outline of the German faces. He felt for the handkerchief in his pocket and waited. Another hundred yards, and it had to be one way or the other; either fight and die, or give in and hope for the best as a prisoner. Again he opened his radio. This time there was a raucous spluttering, a windlike whining noise, and then the voice of the new Company Commander came in.

"Hello... hello, Roth! Come in Roth...!"

"Roth speaking...!"

"Hello Roth! I've been trying to get hold of you!" said Carter. "I want you to get back to the CP right away!"

"With my men?" asked Roth.

"No. Come back alone. Leave your men where they are for the time being."

"I've got wounded who need help, and my men can't hold out a minute longer!" shouted Roth. "I'll have to bring them in!"

"They'll have to hold out!" said Carter. "That's orders!"

"Fuck your orders! I'm bringing them in, and you and the whole goddam army won't stop me!"

"If you disobey orders, you'll have to take the consequences!" said Carter.

"All right... if you want eight prisoners to be taken, it's up to you! *I'll* be back! But send some stretcher bearers down, and send them down in a hurry... I've got wounded here!"

"Make it snappy!" ordered Carter.

"I'll make it when I good and goddam please!" shouted Roth. "What the hell do you think this is—maneuvers?" He placed the radio on the ground and switched it off.

"Motoya! Motoya!" Roth called. "Come down here! I've got something to tell you!"

Motoya lowered his rifle and crawled down the line to the platoon leader.

"I just got a message from the Company Commander. He wants me back at the CP for a minute," said Roth. "I want you to take over and try your best to keep the Jerries down."

"What if we can't?" asked Motoya.

"That's what I want to tell you. The stupid bastards back there want us to hold out at any cost, but they don't know what the hell the score is! If the Jerries get another hundred yards, I want you to take off for the rear with the men... and to hell with orders! Try to take the wounded with you, and if you can't, get them over to some comparatively safe place!"

"I get you," said Motoya. "Another hundred yards, and then we'll move."

"Here, take my radio and if anything new turns up, I'll contact you," said Roth. He picked up the 536 and handed it to Motoya.

Roth removed his gas mask and his pack, slung the carbine over his shoulder, and crawled to the hedgerow at the opposite side of the road. He quickly struggled over the embankment, and fell to the grass on the other side, his knees skinned, the breath smacked out of his chest. He lay still for an instant, readjusted his bearings, and then began the passage to the rear. Artillery and mortar fire fell in his field, the closest ones landing about thirty yards from him. With his hands and knees tearing into the earth, he crab-moved back.

Every few minutes he was forced to stop, either to catch his breath or to bury his head in his arms when shells crashed too close. His brain jangled from the tearing concussions, and thought was a jumbled confusion of hopeless anger, fear, and the omnipresent knowledge of exhausted defeat. He was moving to the rear, to a safety so much more secure than the position he had left, but the way back was worse;

alone, quivering, frightened under the constant pounding by the enemy; one close one would mean the end. But if he did get back he knew he could never return to the road, regardless of what the insubordination would cost. The day had accomplished the final draining; the last drop had dribbled from the sponge.

He was through. The end had come in the orders of a battalion commander who was blind, and in the crazy grandstanding of a glory-hungry major, and with men lying unnecessarily dead at the bottom of a valley. Eight men to hold a road under the concentrated fire of God knows how many German battalions. They could courtmartial him, reduce him to a private, hang him, shoot him, make him a gravedigger.
. . .

The earth was a blinding, heaving regurgitation of explosive violence. The road got it heavy, and he felt the telegraphed force as they thundered on the solid surface. His field sprayed up fountains of earth and growth and hosed gravel down his neck and back. He sweated, and the running salt liquid burned his eyes.

He passed the road bend on the right . . . the turn that was receiving the heaviest concentration of fire . . . and sprang to his feet. He ran for a short distance, then again had to take to the ground when two shells opened up the earth directly in front of him. He continued to crawl, his eyes twitching from fright, his sides heaving with exertion. If the Germans were counterattacking, as Carter had said, they were using that part of the terrain as an aiming point and searching in from there.

Roth continued on toward the rear, alternately running, creeping, and crawling with the ebb and flow of the explosions. When the blasts were heaviest, he snaked along on his belly; and when there seemed to be some respite, he tore along on his legs with his torso bent over double. His throat was clogged with dust and powdered gravel, and his tongue felt as though it had been grooved by fire. He saw nothing but a mad nightmare of blasting; his head whirled in the shattering noise. Nothing existed save the goal of the company command post . . . the rear, an oasis of quiet. He knew he had to get back because it was a new beginning, a start of something completely different from anything he had ever known. He would never return to the road.

He ran and fell and crawled and crept, and picked himself up again to run like a drunken hunchback. His world was blanketed with smoke. Shells trailed a web of whispering sound overhead, traveling toward the rear. Between the crashes of the closer ones, he heard them explode in other areas.

He hit the ground again and started to crawl more cautiously. Through the smoke he finally saw the outlines of the road crossings and heard the spitting of his own battalion's machine guns searching toward the enemy. One clumsy move on his part and his own troops could fail to recognize him as a friendly soldier. He moved closer to the crossroads and spotted figures dispersed in position at both sides of the junction.

A fifty-seven millimeter antitank gun was dug in on the right side of the road, firing spaced bursts across the valley. On the left side were two heavy machine guns, manned by gunners, assistant gunners, and ammunition-bearers, and surrounded by a handful of riflemen for local security. Shellfire tore up the ground and small-arms rounds spattered the positions. The crews of the weapons and the protecting riflemen fought quietly; sweat poured down their faces, and their eyes squinted intensely.

Panting and gasping for breath, Roth moved slowly toward the friendly troops. When he was about fifteen yards from the first group, he shouted out rapidly and clearly so that there would be no chance of error. "Hey! Hey, fellows, where's B Company? Where can I find B Company?"

The men threw startled glances in his direction. "Where're you from?" one asked, lowering his rifle from his shoulder.

"Same outfit's you!" shouted Roth. "Which way is the B Company Command Post?"

The soldier beckoned with his hand to Roth, and then back toward the rear on the far side of the road. "Get across here, and then go up this field . . . they're about four hundred yards back! Watch your step, and make it fast . . . this whole fucking place is zeroed in!"

Roth dashed across the narrow road. A shell blasted somewhere near the front, and a thin trickle of bullets kicked into the gravel as he ran. He reached the other side and hurled himself breathlessly beside the informative soldier.

"You make it all right?" smiled the soldier.

"I. . . I guess so!" panted Roth. He surveyed the field he had to traverse; holes magically appeared while he watched. "You say they're back there?" he asked.

"Yup, but watch your step," said the soldier, returning to the business of his rifle.

Roth sprinted toward the rear. Through the smoke he saw a hedgerow cutting horizontally across the field. His breath seared his lungs, and his knees stiffened each time he threw himself to the ground. His intestines knotted and twisted, and blood-tasting bile clung stickily to his tongue. The hedgerow,
broad protection from the blasting and the spattering, was the goal.

Men were dispersed along the embankment, their rifles resting on the sandy spoil. Roth reached the hedgerow. Up and over, and down into the dust he fell. He lay there trembling, his body vibrating like a snapped steel cable; with the tension over, physical control was gone. He raised his head; he jerked with each blast.

"What the hell's going on up there?" Carter, the new company commander, stood over Roth.

"Didn't Saunders... didn't you see Saunders?" panted Roth.

"Yeah, but you still had orders to hold that ground," said Carter.

Roth sucked in air. He fought to a sitting position against the hedgerow and tried to stop his head from lolling back and forth like that of a broken-necked doll's. "Can't hold it any longer... eight men ... maybe less...."

Carter had his helmet cocked over one eye and a brace of German pistols stuck under his belt. He seemed cool and confident. "You had orders..."

Roth's lower lip quivered. "Orders be fucked!" he muttered. "Always orders... no one gives goddam about slaughter ...!"

Several close blasts reverberated, and Roth rolled over on the ground. He shivered and counted, and struggled back to a sitting position.

Carter still remained erect, his hands resting comfortably on his hips. "They're not that close," he said disdainfully.

Roth's lips continued to quiver, but he kept silent. Another series of explosions sounded, but he restrained himself from hitting the dust. He shivered.

'I'm pulling your men in," said Carter. "You can go and bring them back."

Roth's arms and shoulders began to twitch. "What'd you call me back for?"

"I had something else in mind, but the situation's changed," Carter said.

"Why in the hell don't you go up and bring them back?" Roth's voice raised to falsetto. "You're all so goddamned brave when you're back here!"

"Take it easy, old man," said Carter, as though it were the proper thing to say at such a time. "You're getting away from yourself."

Another stick of shells landed, and Roth hit the ground. He stretched his body flat along the base of the hedgerow and remained there.

"Who did you leave in charge?" asked Carter.

"Motoya."

"Does he have a 536?"

"I left it with him," said Roth.

Carter started toward the right, where the communications sergeant was bent over the field radio.

"Stretcher-bearers... they need stretchers... wounded men!" Roth shouted to Carter.

Carter turned his head slightly. "I'll see what I can do."

Roth continued to tremble spastically. His head oscillated from side to side. He wanted to lose his mind, to run screaming toward the front or rear, to become lost in a wild frenzy. He wanted to tear his hair and froth at the mouth, to blind his eyes and soul with madness; but it wouldn't come, and he lay there quivering and sterile under the power of his fright and sense of loss. He couldn't move except to press against the hedge whenever a shell landed; and his eyes remained open to the sight of the earth erupting, the tracers flaming, and the serious men lined up along the parapet.

Sergeant Saunders was going back. He had another man with him, and between them they carried a stretcher. Saunders chewed nervously and cursed at the man with him for added speed.

Roth felt a slight surge of relieved conscience. He watched the two men go over the hedgerow and prayed that they would make it with the stretcher, and that the eight left on the road would have a safe return. He was through; his job was done, and all that was left was the safety of the remaining men. Whatever they did with him would be anticlimax, a flat joke uttered after the audience had left the theater.

Chapter Seventeen

THE COUNTERATTACK grew in intensity. The Germans used more and bigger guns and concentrated their main fire effort on the three battalions comprising the regiment. The sky was filled with the weird cries of screaming-meemies, and the earth roared with the thunder of large-caliber railroad guns, flatter eighty-eights, and canister charges. Machine-gun fire increased, reaching a greater number of targets with each succeeding minute. Echoes of calls for stretcher-bearers and aid men resounded throughout the area. Reserves from hospitals far in the rear had come down, most of them volunteers, but they were being used faster than they could arrive. The regiment received a number of the medical volunteers, but they were far too few to take care of the mounting numbers of wounded.

Men along the hedgerow were being hit, and the battalion aid men worked against time. They poured sulfa powder, slapped on bandages, applied tourniquets and splints, and even when it was too late offered a comforting pat on the shoulder.

No enemy riflemen appeared; it was a counterattack of artillery fire, mortar fire, and machine-gun fire. The Germans were thorough; they had patience. When the big guns' work was done their infantrymen could move in for the relatively simple job of mopping up.

Roth's men came over the hedgerow. Warner was carried in on the stretcher and in a spray of bullets and shrapnel was hurriedly eased into the waiting hands of Company B men on the other side. Northrup, his arm hanging limply at his side, was helped by Motoya.

Followed by Northrup they carried the paralyzed little Sergeant back to the aid station. Motoya patted Northrup on the back and sent him off to take the rest of the route alone.

Except for Saunders, who returned to the aid station with Warner, the survivors of the First Platoon distributed themselves along the hedgerow. They squatted or sprawled on the ground and allowed themselves the luxury of breathing again.

Motoya came over to Roth and sat beside him. He lit a cigarette and spat angrily. "I can't blame you, Lieutenant!" he said.

"What for?" asked Roth.

Motoya gestured vaguely with his hands. "You know what I mean ... the whole fuckin' thing! The way they left us holding the bag, and everything..."

Roth shook his head slowly. He had no more words left, and Motoya's avowal only made things worse. He wanted to be left alone, his shaking and trembling hidden from all eyes. If only there was a hole in the ground that he could crawl into, and remain until he died. If he could get to the rear he'd do it; dig a hole and crawl in like a wounded animal... to die and forget. Backwards or forwards, it was all the same. It was shells blasting in his heart, and dying men clawing at his mind, and machine-gun bullets ripping into his soul. If death was blind and unfeeling and senseless, he wanted it... and wanted it soon. He had no more time to wait. From dawn to dusk and throughout the lonely nights life was a pandemonium of sight and sound, of blasting pressures integrated into a meshed mosaic of screams and moans, and red blood staining the earth a bitter black. It was the smell of putrefaction borne on a foul wind; it was the nauseating anticipation under a hissing shell; it was the stink of function in the foxhole when one had no place to go under the hell of a barrage. Death had a place, but there was no room for life.

The sun dropped below the smoking hills, and a murky red appeared on the horizon. Shadows began to grow, and in a short while the late-arriving night would appear to blanket the fields. The men along the hedgerows dug indecisively, wondering whether or not they would remain in their present position.

Lieutenant Carter sent a runner down the line carrying orders for his platoon leaders to assemble.

Lieutenants McNamara, Kalman, and Garvey gathered around Carter. They were dusty, covered with sweat, and red-faced with excitement and worry. Roth joined the group.

"Where's Hartley?" asked Roth.

"He got it," said Lieutenant McNamara, a tall rangy Ohioan. "I took over his platoon."

"Bad?" asked Roth, knowing what the answer would be.

"Dead."

Carter scribbled some notes on a message pad. He cleared his dry throat and began to issue orders for the coming night. "Second and Third Platoons stay where you are along this line ... get your men well dug-in. Roth, take the rest of your men and get back along that other hedgerow." He pointed to the rear, about four hundred yards back, where another high hedgerow segmented the terrain. "Kalman, put your mortars near Roth ... space them about a hundred yards to the left of his last man, and over. We're going to have to hold this ground until the other outfit moves in."

"You mean we're getting relieved?" asked Lieutenant Garvey.

"The reserve outfit moves in sometime tonight, or early tomorrow morning. They'll come in squad by squad and take over each position separately. I'll send orders around later about where we'll assemble for the move back."

"Where do you think it'll be?" asked Lieutenant Kalman. "We don't know yet," said Carter. "The Battalion Commander is going to have a meeting later to tell us. Remember, hole in deep ... because Jerry'll throw everything tonight! If your men can get some rest, all well and good. If not ... well, we're sure to be out of it by morning at the latest." Glows of relief became visible on the faces of the assembled officers. Their shoulders straightened and the lines seemed to clear from the corners of their mouths.

Roth stared at the ground. It was a long time until tomorrow. Besides, he was finished; he saw it in Carter's eyes, and it was present in the glances of everyone who saw him. The future held other things for him, but not relief.

He had Motoya gather together the few remaining men of the platoon and lead them back to the hedgerow in the rear. He followed their slow scuffling and chose a position for himself near the center of his men.

Roth sat against the hedgerow and watched the men digging their holes. His shovel was gone, left with his pack and other equipment back on the road; he waited patiently until somebody would be finished with a tool that he could use.

They dug slowly and were quiet, and were forced to rest after each series of difficult strokes into the hard earth. When shells landed too close, their labors were interrupted. Expressions were hidden under the matting of beard and dust and dried sweat, but their eyes peered dull and exhausted through the gray masks.

The spreading night gathered in from the horizon and slowly began to sweep the fields in from the front. A faint glow hung in the west and outlined the surrounding hills in a dusty halo. Swirls of smoke wisped upward to disappear into the darkening sky, and streaking tracer bullets created a spidery suspension-bridge effect. In the hazy twilight, Roth saw that one of the men seemed to be finished with his shovel. It was Schonbrun.

Roth walked over to the stoop-shouldered man and asked to borrow the entrenching tool. As the little man nodded his head in assent, Roth suddenly remembered something.

"Where're you from?" whispered Roth.

Schonbrun looked up puzzled. "New York . . . ?"

Roth stared at the man through the haze. There was a memory. "You're from mid-town, aren't you?"

The soldier nodded his head.

"I thought I saw you someplace," muttered Roth, and walked back to his position with the shovel. He didn't want to get involved in any conversation, but now he remembered the man. He had been a clerk in Siegal's stationery store on East Sixtieth Street. Siegal's store, a million miles away. He used to play the pin ball games there an eon ago when he was still in high school. And Schonbrun had been a permanent fixture in the place.

Night finally came down and took possession of the smoky, stench-drenched area, smothering the thorny fields under an impenetrable blanket of black. The big guns, as though controlled by some giant hand, blasted away more fiercely than during the hours of dusk, scattering screaming missiles over the sad, beaten fields. Flashes of fire from the gun muzzles periodically opened wedges in the dark void, bursting into tired eyes like splashes of molten lead.

Intermittently the staccato cackle of spitting machine guns, followed by white-hot tails of tracers, added mournful overtones to the deep bass of the big guns. During lulls, moans could be heard, moans which were sometimes punctuated by chilling screams that reached in and sucked at intestines with freezing lips.

Carefully, cautiously protecting all approach routes, other units within the regiment disengaged from the enemy to hole up for the night. Each company exhaustedly single-filed into an assigned field of perimeter defense, and platoon after platoon within the companies dispersed into smaller sectors of responsibility.

Men removed clawing packs from their throbbing, sweat-sogged shoulders and began the nightly horror of digging holes. They dug to live another day and fight, or die, or live to dig again another night.

Within larger sounds the crunching of hundreds of shovels could be heard. Some men cursed, or bitterly wept as their shovels either struck an unyielding rock or smashed against a steel-hard root hidden under the spiny hedgerow.

Paul Roth made one last gesture at checking on his men and then slouched back to his section of the hedgerow. He surveyed the mound of earth, brush, and thorns and wearily, sadly, shook his head from side to side. He bent over, picked up the borrowed shovel, and straightened up with the tool dangling limply from his hand. Once again he sorrowfully shook his head, slowly lowered himself and squatted on the ground, and took deep draughts of fresh air into his lungs. A short rest was necessary before starting the tortuous procedure of digging a hole to fit his body.

Melancholy lumps of despair, the physical awareness of exhausted defeat, brushed against the lining of his stomach. For days it had grown until it pounded against his burning eyes, almost in cadence with the shuffling of his heavy feet. While on the march, in preparation for the attack, during the attack, holing up for the night, supervising the distribution of rations, the complete knowledge of defeat had grown until it finally became a malignancy consuming every pulsating fiber of his being.

Roth was through; he was exhausted and knew it. The finish had come during the blasting of the road and the last dash toward the final objective; he had shown his colors, colors as bright as the flaming rays of the noonday sun. But did the others realize? No indignity could be more debasing than to be known as a finished leader among the men of one's own command. And they did know; it blazed from their eyes and twisted almost verbally from the corners of their lips. It spoke from half-averted, sidelong glances. They whispered it when his back was turned and laughed when they thought he had gone out of sight. It was as evident as the thorn-torn lines decorating his palms. He was a finished leader, and there was no possible way out; no way except to be killed or wounded. God, how many times had he hoped and prayed for the blessed relief of a sniper's bullet, or for a fragment of razored steel to tear some meat from his body, or for the frenzied succor of insanity to rip the roots from his brain?

To be wounded. To bleed some, and then to rest. To sleep a dreamless sleep secure in the knowledge of unfeeling nothingness... a nothingness undisturbed by the moans of dying men, the cries of torn men, the stink of putrefaction, the nauseating anticipation before the final bursting of a fluttering shell... the naked glow of defeat. To sleep and not to dream; possibly to die, if death is what is wanted. But death had not yet been made fashionable.

Shirring, whishing, whispering whirr! Roth hit the dust and smashed down his body with all remaining strength. He folded his arms, buried his face between them in the dirt, and shook spasmodically. He held his breath in hushed, fearful expectancy and awaited the explosion. Fear clutched his anus in an icy vise, and all hopeful thoughts of wounds were forgotten. Heaven and earth and the last depths of hell split and smashed within the dreadful embrace of the exploding cacophony. His body left the ground as though it had been lifted by some gargantuan monstrosity, and when he hit again all breath was torn from his aching lungs. He spat a slippery, brassy tasting fluid from his mouth.

Silence. An ear-splitting, impatient silence. To wait? To wait for the other shells? No more? No more.... Through quivering lips he sucked in gasps of air and felt with his hands over his body. Relieved... and disappointed... he saw his hands return with only some clammy, muddy sweat. No wound; no sleep for endless hours. No anesthesia...

He rose to his feet and, with shaking hands, grabbed the shovel and started to dig. After every few strokes he had to pause and struggle for breath; his body was drained and sterile, senile and old.

Finished.... Through.... Impotent and dry. The texture of leadership had been burned out in the white-hot ovens of a speed-paced war. In the beginning he had had it, or had thought he did. The early days of combat found him like a young stallion during his first season turned out to service.

Actual fear had been almost unknown, although it was vaguely present as a warning light of sensible caution. After many days in the line without relief, the fire burned as brightly as always. There had been weary days, and days of the pain of exhaustion, but knowledge remained: the knowledge of his own strength and of the strength of the men with whom he fought. But had he really had the strength? Had he hypnotized himself with the uniform, the dreams of glory and the return, scarred and bemedalled?

Now he was alone, trembling in his misery. Hartley was gone, vanished as if he had been less real than a puff of smoke. Dougall was dead; big, solid, dependable Andy who was always there, booming, angry, pleasant, commanding... a friendly voice. Gone with the others. Dead in the black dust of fading day. Alone.

The pace grew faster as each heated hour went by. Move and fight, and fight and move, to dig for hours to fight again. Patrolling through the dark with fear a voice, a partner, a fiend, a ghoul tearing at your soul with spiked hooks of horror. Where did the fear come from? How did it start? It never really had appeared until a day... a week... two weeks ago....

Lie down one hour or two, and a hand clutches at your shoulder... "They want you out tonight, Lieutenant... yeah, a patrol I think... the rations are in... you'll have to make this reconnaissance, you're one of the few experienced platoon leaders left... fifteen bodies just outside St. Mère du Prée and we got orders to bring them in, the old man's going crazy with the stink... take the point... take the point... goddamittohell I've had the goddampoint every day the last three weeks!... watch the water if you don't want the cramps... you're going on patrol, yeah I know, but you're the only man...."

Stones grow between toes, embedded in blistered soles, and walk on knives, on spikes, on fire, and hit the ground on torn-up, nauseous guts. "Follow me, we're moving out! Keep dispersed... keep dispersed, you goddamned fool you'll kill us all! Hit the dust, they're coming in! Hit it! When I wave my hand, open up... and don't get trigger-happy! Get some more ammunition! I don't give a fuck whether they've got it or not... get it from the heavies... the sons of bitches aren't doing any good in this stinking underbrush! Christ, where'd the bastards ever get the idea that three months trains a man for combat?"

On on on on, up the hill, and Christ went to Golgotha . . . we're going up, up, over, down, below, between, on top of the hills, and they never end. Christ, where'd he ever get the idea about Christ going to Golgotha?

A charmed life. Not a wound . . . maybe a scratch and a Purple Heart to make a guy a hero when he gets back. What is the limit? Leading forty men over the length and width of France. Mother, father, sister, and brother to them. Thinking for the forty, feeding for the forty, checking for the forty, reconnoitering for the forty . . . leading forty men to life or death. What is the limit . . . where is the slip? Where does responsibility begin and end for the lives of forty men? If one is beaten, does the guilt for forty lives rest eternally upon the one?

The release of death would solve all problems. Yet, death wasn't fashionable. Alone. Finished in the night, alone in the presence of defeat.

With a groan Roth straightened his knotted back, wiped the pouring sweat from his face, and stared at his handiwork. Two inches of hole. Two feet and ten inches to go. To dig for what seemed like hours, days, years, an eternity, and then discover only two miserable inches!

The other shovels were already silent. Realization of his impotency welled up like a cauldron boiling over, and a tear trickled down his cheek. Two inches. The leader of conditioned strength, of courage, only had two inches. Other men slept, but he had no room in those meager two inches.

He sank to the ground, stretched out against the hedgerow, and pillowed his head in his arms. If the fates ordained that there was to be no hole, there would be no hole. If death was to come this night, death would be welcome. If the Jerries' aim was good enough to hit this beaten form this night, the lid is doffed in admiration to their marksmanship. If a limb was to be torn off this night of despair, it will come as a welcome gift: the end of all the pain, the horror, the exhaustion, the madness of move and fight and fight and move, of holes two inches deep in the granite soil of Europe. He slept. He twitched.

On on on on up the hill to the top to see what lies beyond . . . another hill? Another hill rising from the plain, one more annoying lump on the sprawling landscape which has no end but continues on and on into the distance, with no horizon to break the monotonous outline. Only hills, and the road winding into nowhere, and the spiked, thorny hedgerows rising pyramidically, growing larger with each second until the sky is dark and the sun has died forever. Hedges and horses and cows on broken limbs chewing drowning mountains of foaming cud bubbling into my throat and I am choked.

Your throat between my hands; I squeeze until the crimson flows from your ears and your nostrils and all your pores and casts a dark stain on the dry earth; and greedily the earth sucks up your blood in revenge, in retribution, for the crimes you committed. You will never return, enemy, for we are brave and strong, except for a few who lose their strength ... but we regain it with your blood, enemy!

Use a ten minute fuse when you set the charge, and get back quick. ... I'll cover you! If they start coming out let 'em have it ... but hold your fire until you have a target, and for Christ's sake don't hit me! If anything happens tell Rodriguez to take over ... no, I lost my watch; the strap broke so what's the difference?

Let's go, this is the last one and maybe we'll get relieved to get some rest, to drink some cognac, to find a broad, to see a movie, Paris! If we ever get there the Place Vendome, Montmartre, The Left Bank, champagne, naked women ... nightclubs. ... Wowie! Picasso in slippers ... watch that charge!

Lovely warm breasts rising up over his face, the lush red nipples swelling under the pressure of his tongue. Scent of love, the all-embracing flux of passionate movement, and death in the womb. ... Please dear don't you think it best that we wait until all this is over so many things can happen when two people are away from each other. ...

Silver Star in the closet behind the old clothes, in a hatbox with the Purple Heart and you found it. It's so much crap ... goddamit I'm no hero and I hide my shame from the others, the world, the stinkers who fatten on glory, adoring death and afraid to die because it isn't fashionable. But you are life and I am death because I died before I was even born. ...

Your throat between my hands; I squeeze until the crimson flows. I love you I may be killed wounded ... you won't have any fun. ... Watch that charge! And take off like a ruptured duck. Lost under a mountain of crawling blood-hungry maggots is all we'll ever get like that kid we found in the woods . . . and a Requiem Mass or whatever they get when they die . . . but it's salvation—something we'll never get—lucky kid. First squad on the right, second on the left, the third in support. We move out at 0600. Battalion aid station in that wooded gully four hundred yards to the rear . . . any questions? What a broad! Paris is filled with them for a pack of butts . . . sure just like London. . . . . Watch that charge!

Blasts in series of three shook the universe, and geysers of earth and rock and scorched grass erupted into the flare-brightened sky. Roth's eyes stared transfixed at the high fires, and screams gurgled and vibrated from the ground beneath him. A hand filed at the roots of his brain with a sliver of sandpaper, and knives were at his eardrums. His mouth was open and he could not close it. Bubbles of froth mixed with vomit oozed out to make a sticky porridge on his quivering chin. His hands opened and closed clutchingly, and his body shook with gigantic frenzied spasms. Silence and the vacuous night closed in.

They had his arms, his throat, they pressed his head, they fought him, tried to kill him. . . .

"Let me go! Let me go! Lemme go you no good lousy bastards lemme go I want to get out of here!" someone screamed, and it was him, but it didn't seem to come from himself, but from someone else, someone in the darkness.

"Grab him! Grab him! Grab the Lieutenant! He's blowin' his top. . . his top. . . his top . . . his top. . . ." Someone had shouted, somewhere.

"The poor bastard . . . poor bastard . . . bastard. . ."

There was movement, then darkness, then moments of terrible light gouging at his eyes. Always movement. More movement. The vehicle chugged, rocked, bounced, stopped, started, stopped again, then roared away into the distance, towards oceans, waves, clear skies, black skies. . . .

"Let me out of here! Let me go! Lemme out of here you lousy bastards. They're coming in! They're coming in!" the voice shouted, the voice from under the bed, or over the bed, or from the dark field where the shells were falling.

"No more hypos, no more hypos unless . . . unless . . . unless . . ." a voice, some voice said.

Laughter. Someone laughed.

"He'll pull out of it soon... pull... soon... soon..." the voice said, and then it was night, horrible night, and they marched through Normandy, over the hills, under the hills, always hills... hills....

"Blew his top... bastard blew top...."

"Lemme go! Lemme go! Lemme go!" the voice, the voice....

Laughing, they were laughing, laughing, laughing....

They had his arms, and he couldn't get loose, to the beach, the water, anywhere but there, the shells, the stink, the death, the loss....

"One pill every four hours," the voice....

One screaming-meemie. All it'd take's one screamer....

Oh, Ellen, I don't love you any longer, I can't love you, I can't, they've taken it all away, everything, nothing's left but the decorations in the closet....

"He'll come around. He'll come around soon... soon... soon..." the voice....

"Just let him sleep."

Sleep, but there was no more sleep....

I can't get out of here!

No more sleep....

Only white, all white, a lovely white. There was space, soft sounds, voices, the white again, then silence. Silence, a clean linen sheet, a perfect crisp silence, better than pleasure, more than music. The white whispered and came closer, so close that a hand could touch it, hold it, be friends with it.

The whisper became louder, disturbing....

Roth opened his eyes, and gradually the elements of a face, a man's face, appeared.

"I'm glad to see you awake," the face said.

Roth closed his eyes, touched the white, then opened them again.

"How do you feel?" the man's face said, teeth white behind a mustache.

There was a flapping above, like the roof of a tent blowing in a wind. And it was a tent, because it was brown and blew in the wind.

"What...?"

Figures passed, in khaki uniforms, soldiers.

He was on a bed, soft, a bed, a good bed....

"What...?"

"You're in the hospital... the exhaustion center," said the face.

A good bed, with white sheets, crisp.

Roth giggled, and he felt a painful laugh wrack his body, but it was good to laugh and get it over with, to feel it come out of him as though it were from someone else.

"Who . . . ?" the word moved past his lips.

"I'm Major Lampman . . . your doctor," the face said.

It was a tent, a very big tent, and someone, somewhere, was softly sobbing.

"Why . . . why . . . why?" Roth heard himself say, his

eyes watching the flapping of the tent, the tiny rufflings above.

"You're going to be fine, Lieutenant. You've been very tired, so we thought we'd let you sleep for a few days."

An arm reached out from near the face and patted Roth's arm.

Roth giggled convulsively. "They didn't get me . . . I'm not hit . . . dead . . . ?" he said.

It was a friendly face, and it smiled. "No, you're in perfect shape . . . except that you were completely bushed, went out of your head for a while," it said.

"Out of my head . . . out of my head?" he had heard that somewhere, and it sounded good, decisive.

"You just rest, boy. Get some sleep. In a few days you'll be as good as ever," the face said.

"Thank you . . . thank you," Roth said.

"Now, hold still a moment . . . just a moment," the face said, and something in the hand reached out and pricked Roth's arm.

Roth closed his eyes.

"Let me out of here! Out of here . . . out of here!" the voice started, then stopped.

The white came in again, and the whisper, the voice, receded into the distance. It was okay, everything was fine, even with the thing whining and crying and moaning and laughing under the bed, screaming:

"Lemme out! Lemme out! Lemme out you lousy bastards . . . bastards . . . bastards . . . !"

A hill appeared. Bent figures, with humps on their backs, struggled up the hill. But he no longer cared.

Printed in the USA
CPSIA information can be obtained
at www.ICGtesting.com
CBHW071229070324
5067CB00013B/1077